Wolf Mountain

Wolf Mountain

Peter Lars Sandberg

P❦P A Playboy Press Book

All of the characters in this book are fictitious, and
any resemblance to actual persons, living or dead, is
purely coincidental.

Published simultaneously in the United States and Canada by Playboy Press,
Chicago, Illinois. Printed in the United States of America. Library of Congress
Catalog Card Number: 74-33551. ISBN 87223-423-1. First edition.

PLAYBOY and Rabbit Head design are trademarks of Playboy, 919 North Michi-
gan Avenue, Chicago, Illinois 60611 (U.S.A.), Reg. U.S. Pat. Off., marca
registrada, marque déposée.

THIRD PRINTING 1975

This book is for my wife Nancy,
and my brother Dave,
who gave me slack when I needed it
and caught my falls.

To me it is a sin to kill a man. Even Fascists whom we must kill.
To me there is a great difference between the bear and the man and
I do not believe the wizardry of the gypsies about the brotherhood with
animals. No. I am against all killing of men.

Hemingway, For Whom the Bell Tolls

Contents

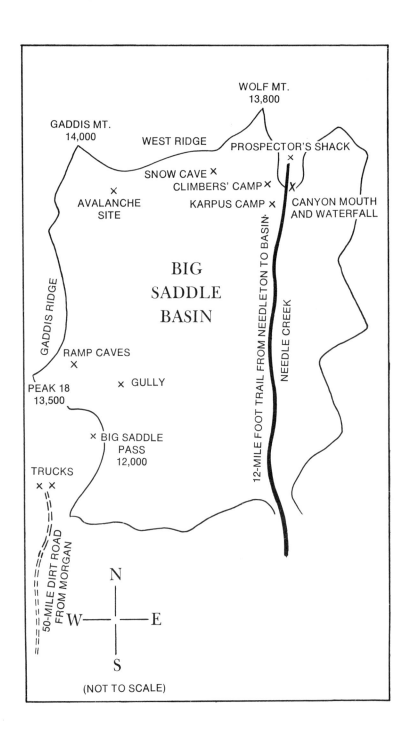

PART ONE

JUNE 4

ASCENDING

1

Matt Whittaker, U.S. Air Force retired, was a mountaineer, a tall, blond, bearded man. He found the crippled
deer late in the morning of his second day on the abandoned logging road that ran from Morgan, Colorado, up
into the Big Saddle and the high mountains of the San
Juan Range. The road had become soggy and unpredict-
able from the early June thaw, and Whittaker, who drove
a green Ford pickup, had had to keep both axles engaged
for miles now and winch the truck out of many bogs and
soft sand gullies.

The deer was lying on its side just off the road in a
shadowed place which also held a crusty patch of snow.
Tire tracks, half filled with water, swerved violently toward the animal, then backed away, going on up the road
to the place where it curved out of sight in the still thick
forest of second-growth conifers. Even before Whittaker
got out of the pickup and studied the tracks he saw that
the deer, its rear legs crushed, had been struck deliberately and left here to die a long, unnatural death.

The air was crisp, even chilly in the shade of the
trees, and he hunched his shoulders against a need to
shiver. Six weeks ago he had been in Southeast Asia, had
been there for the better part of three years. He thought
his blood had thinned, guessed he could not take the

cold as easily as he had once, wondered how long it would be before his blood would thicken again. Maybe it wouldn't. Maybe in the twenty years he had left, if he had that many left, he would go around wearing a white knit shawl on summer evenings, like the nuns in Mitchell, like Sister what-was-her-name? Sister Agnes. I'm all right, he thought, as if to persuade himself it was true. He had spent the last thirty days climbing rock in Boulder and Eldorado Springs, had pushed himself as hard as he could, first up the easy routes he remembered from the days when he and Ike had done them, then up the more difficult ones, trying to get back what had been his finesse, trying to get tired enough to sleep. His dreams had been terrifying.

He had hoped that by now the prospect of doing some high climbing might have generated in him a sense of excitement or anticipation, but so far it had not. So far it had only been familiar, and tedious, and now there was this.

In the glove box of the truck he kept a .45-caliber revolver, a long-barreled English Webley he had found in a London pawnshop just before his first combat tour. In Viet Nam he had carried this revolver, tucked into a holster strapped to his leg over his G-suit, in the cockpit of the F-4. During his second tour, just before his retirement after twenty years in—this time in Laos—the Webley had saved his life. It was for this reason that he kept it in the truck when he went into the mountains to climb.

He took the gun with him now as he went to the shadowed place where the deer lay. It was a winter-thin doe and as he approached she lifted her head and rolled her eyes back in a kind of half-terror as if she had suffered too much already to fully apprehend anything more. Whittaker made no sudden moves and talked quietly to the animal. He could see where she had chewed out a crescent in the snow, how she had dragged herself to it before the trauma of her injuries had stopped her.

He sat down then and gently stroked her head which, after a moment of tension, she finally lowered again to the wet earth.

"You didn't know they were going to do this, did you?" he said absently, listening to the sough of the breeze in the high branches of the firs. "You were probably in the road early this morning and heard them coming and stepped off into this place. . . ."

He believed in the inevitability of combat, of men against men, and, although he was not a hunter, he believed in the dignity of the hunt. But incidents such as this, of which he had witnessed some few in his life, he had never been able to understand. From where he sat he could see the tracks the two men had left when, after they had struck the deer, they had gotten out of whatever vehicle it was they drove and had walked over to the animal. The ribbed boot soles of one of the men were longer and leaner and more worn than the similarly ribbed boot soles of the other. They had stood for a while, long enough to smoke a cigarette, perhaps, for here was a stub in the heel of one of the long, lean prints. Then, it appeared, they had walked back to their vehicle, had backed it off and driven away.

Whittaker brought the muzzle of the revolver to a place just behind the doe's left ear. "I wonder what kind of fun that was," he said abruptly, surprising himself with the sound of his voice. "I wonder if they could tell me."

"If you go back to Viet Nam, we're finished," she had told him when he had returned from the first of his two tours. *"I mean it, Matt. I won't go through this again. I won't let the children go through it."*

The sound of the gun was flat, neither as precise nor as impressively loud as he had remembered it.

2

The abandoned road was fifty miles long and evidently little known for it was not indicated on the maps that measured this region. It gained 4000 feet in elevation before it ended in a small clearing at the foot of a high mountain pass. When Whittaker reached this place, in the early afternoon of the same day, he saw what the men had driven: a red and cream-white Dodge pickup with a crew cab and Utah plates. The front left headlamp was broken, the grill and left fender dented. Beer cans, crumpled, grease-stained paper bags and empty cigarette packs were strewn about the seats and floors as if, oddly, the same men who had purposely run down a deer had not wished to litter the roadside as they went. A gun rack bolted across the rear window was empty. Two sets of tracks led away from the truck, east-northeast up into the pass. Whittaker guessed the men were hunters, or thought of themselves as hunters, probably ginned up and on a tear.

He shouldered his red Kelty pack and 150-foot coil of Perlon rope. He had replaced the spent shell in the revolver and for a moment it occurred to him that he might do well to take it along, but it was heavy and, he decided, might go further in provoking than preventing an incident between himself and the two men should he meet them on the uptrail or in the basin that lay on the other side of the pass. And so he returned the Webley to the glove box, locked both doors of his pickup and, ice ax in hand, he followed the tracks across the moist soil of the clearing.

The longer, leaner tracks of the man with the worn soles had been made first. He had a stride that matched Whittaker's own. The tracks of the other man followed. He had a shorter stride and Whittaker saw that even before the far edge of the clearing he had had to run once to catch up. Here then, the pilot decided, were the outlines of a relationship, etched briefly into the earth: of a man who went first and one who went second; of leader and led.

As the ground began to rise steeply a half-mile to the pass, he lowered his head and moved with a dogged, irritated deliberation, as much against the burden of his depression as against the sharp angle of climb and the weight of the pack he carried. For a long while his career had gone well, for almost twenty years it had. He had earned his promotions one by one; he had not sucked ass. He had a box full of medals which he kept in a trunk in a warehouse in Denver on the off-chance his son might want to see them someday. The Air Force had been good to him, fair with him, had told him he had an excellent chance of making lieutenant colonel: It was, they had said, in light of his combat record, all but assured. Understandably, his days in fighters were behind him. There was a desk in Los Angeles, aerospace contracts to look after. Everyone had been very goddamn polite. As for himself, he had wanted to scream.

Something had happened to him during his second tour, after his divorce from Marie had become final. He had become morose, half suicidal on a mission once, had developed a sense of rage that the war in which he had risked his life and a lot of good men had died was going to end up being what Marie had started calling it as early as '67: an ill-conceived, futile, botched-up mess. Even her starchy old man had agreed—off the record, of course.

Whittaker had gone to see her and the children in Denver as soon as he could after he was out, as soon as he thought he could handle it, had hoped in some vague way he might be able to persuade her to try again. He timed his arrival to the cocktail hour. She met him at the door, her brown hair swept back the way he liked it, her cheeks windburned from skiing he guessed, her brown eyes thoughtful as she greeted him.

"Hello, Matt."

"Hi," he said. "You look outstanding, you haven't changed a bit."

"You've lost some weight."

"A little. I'll get it back, I'll start tonight. Where are the kids?"

"Next door. I thought it might be better if you and I . . ."

"Sure," he said. "Things were pretty rough the last time I was here."

She nodded. "I thought the two of us could have supper, then go get them."

"Fine."

"You can stay a while, can't you? A few days at least?"

"Sure," he said, wondering if she was trying to limit him to that. He had thought he might stay longer, several weeks even, assuming things went well. Already he had had to suppress his anger that the children had been sent away, though her reasons for doing that were understandable enough. There had been some ugly fights before he had left the last time.

They ate by candlelight a several-course meal she had obviously gone to considerable length to prepare, and for a little while they got along by remembering other times. Then the curtain fell again, the old arguments sprang into place (incredibly, he found himself defending the war as if he had never become disillusioned with it). Little Ben and Amy seemed curious about him at first, then indifferent and finally fearful as, in spite of his efforts to be pleasant, his temper grew increasingly short.

He left after a week, throwing his gear into his truck, heading for Boulder, for Morgan, for the high mountains, not because he wanted to but because it was all he could think of to do. He shook his head now as he climbed toward the pass. The sun was bright, the sky blue. A mountain raven glided overhead. When the children were older they would go camping with him. He would earn back their trust and love. He should never have alienated them in the first place. Marie had been right about the war. He had been wrong. He had never been quite that wrong in his life. It made him feel dumb, as if he had been had, as if he had bought a dry well.

"Be honest, you liked it," she said when he came back the first time. *"You enjoyed it. That's why you want to go back, that's why you insist on going back even though they don't insist on sending you. It's what you've been practicing for ever since you enlisted at eighteen. The killing, I mean. It justifies who you are, all those years flying fighters over Arizona and Nevada. Be honest, Matt. It props you up, doesn't it? It's the way you account for yourself."*

He leaned stubbornly against the straps of his pack, saw a drilled wet place on the slight trail where one of the two men had relieved himself. He had once during his first tour been credited with 112 enemy dead by verified body count in a single mission. The story had been in the Saigon papers; he had saved one of the clippings. On his way back from a sortie, he had answered a request from a forward air controller to help out a platoon of South Vietnamese Rangers trapped by the Viet Cong in a crossfire not twenty kilometers from the capital city itself. Two .51-caliber rounds had come up through the floor of his F-4, two more had ripped through the canopy. He had gotten some Plexiglas splinters in his jaw, had gotten Ike to pull them out for him with a pair of tweezers, had turned down the recommendation for a Purple Heart. The Air Force had been passing out decorations as if they were merit badges. Some of the good jocks he knew who had earned theirs would not wear them anymore. The infantry grunts had started blowing up their NCOs and officers. Civilians were being slaughtered in trenches. That's what it had come to and it made him want to puke.

"I hope whoever these guys are they hunt this place and get out today," he said aloud. "They've already got their deer."

3

The shorter of the two men, whose name was Johns, had wanted to follow the game trail that led from the tents, across the top of the talus and on into the canyon because it was close and looked easy; but Karpus, the other, had said no they would drop down by the stream and follow that trail. So Johns had gone along as he always did go along, hurrying to keep up with the taller man who carried the rifle they had taken and who moved as if he knew exactly where he was going and what he would find when he got there.

The stream divided the floor of the canyon in a busy meander, coming at them as they went in. The talus went up 300 feet on either side at forty-five-degree angles to the steep thousand-foot canyon walls. Johns felt small here; he had never liked the outdoors. It was mid-afternoon and it seemed to him they had been walking for five days since they had left the truck. His head throbbed, beating out the message of a stunning hangover. His boots were new and much too tight, he was developing blisters on both heels, his pack felt as if Karpus had secretly filled it with stones. Karpus had insisted on bringing everything: not only the bedrolls and blankets, the tinned food and whiskey; but also two lanterns, a bucksaw, even a folding aluminum cot. Karpus wore a blue and black checked mackinaw, fatigue pants and a pair of Redwing boots he had worn ever since Johns had first met him, a couple of years ago now. Johns wore a new navy pea jacket, gray twill pants and these new boots that were killing his feet.

"My ass is dragging," he said as good-naturedly as he could. He had been afraid to admit it until now, but now he was seriously beginning to wonder if he could walk any further.

"We're going to rest soon as I see where they are," Karpus told him, his familiar whispery voice a comfort here as it always was.

"I don't care if I see them," Johns allowed. "I don't need to see anybody."

"Maybe they'll see us. Maybe they already have. It's that kind of thing I mean," Karpus said, continuing an earlier conversation. "It's that kind of thing you should think about."

Johns, who admittedly had not thought about it,

tried to think about it now. Somehow it did not seem
important. Nothing seemed important right now except
sitting down as soon as possible out of the breeze that
had come up fresh, sitting down against a rock and taking
off his boots and putting his aching feet into the running
water of this stream. He had grown up in places like
Albuquerque and Phoenix, a fat, blubbery kid who was
usually the butt of other people's jokes ("Hey, Johns,
why don't you go flush yourself! Ha, Ha!" That sort of
thing), first in the neighborhoods of the crummy foster
homes that passed him around like a leaky soccer ball,
and then in reform school, and later in prison. Once, a
gang of kids in Phoenix had taken his pants down and
stuck a garden hose up his ass, stuck it up there and
turned it on. He remembered screaming, and filling up
like a balloon, and the sound of girls laughing. He had
a quick mean temper, had always gotten into fights which
he always lost. He had had his teeth knocked out and his
nose broken, his ribs cracked and his balls kicked so
many times they ached whenever the weather got cold,
as it was starting to get cold now. Then Karpus had come
along, had celled with him in State Prison, and overnight
everything had changed. It wasn't that Karpus was so
good in a brawl—Johns assumed that he was, but had
never actually seen him in one—it was simply that people
left Karpus alone. There was something about him, some
kind of message he sent out, and ever since Johns had
been with him, which was almost two years now, people
had left Johns alone too.

"My feet are killing me," he admitted.

"All right," Karpus said quietly. "I've got them
spotted." He had stopped on the path by the stream, and
Johns, who had been looking down at his own sore feet,
nearly ran into the back of his friend.

"Chrissake," he complained, lurching off balance.

"Keep it quiet now," Karpus advised as if he were talking to an awkward son. "Get your tail down."

Johns had not seen anything, but Karpus was already on his elbows and knees, moving like an infantryman, with his rifle cradled in the crooks of his arms. When Johns tried to do likewise he was pulled off balance by the weight of his pack and wound up on his back, kicking like an upturned turtle; then he got right side up again and bellied along. Karpus had rested the rifle on a boulder and was looking through the scope at a point both higher and further into the canyon. Johns sighed and began to pull off a boot.

"I've got a fucking *blister*," he whined.

"There's six of them," Karpus said, still looking through the scope. "Bunch of girls looks like. Maybe four girls. I'd say four girls and two guys. One of the guys is a kid looks like maybe fourteen, the other one's your age, maybe twenty-nine, thirty."

"I've got *two* blisters," Johns said. "One on each goddamned foot."

"The older guy is going up on the cliff."

"We got any Band-Aids?"

"They're in my pack. Outside pocket. All that stuff's in a yellow sandwich bag. That guy's going right up the cliff. . . ."

"Where's the whiskey?" Johns asked.

"That's in my pack too. Where you left it. I could pick that guy off from here. It might take me two shots, but I could nail him all right. Hey, Johns, that would be some sight: Let him go on up a ways and then pick him right off of there. He'd come down in the middle of the rest of them. I'd say there's four girls. One of them's about his age; the one that's going up the cliff, I mean.

She's holding the rope for him. Big tits. Then there's a couple look like sisters or something, and there's a fat one."

Johns, who had never liked hearing about people who were fat, found the whiskey, uncorked it and had a pull, then gave the bottle to Karpus, and while Karpus was pulling on it Johns took the rifle and tried to see something through the scope.

"Not there," Karpus said softly. "Higher. Follow along where the rock slide meets the cliff." He bellied closer to his friend and tried to help him line the scope up right. "See him?"

"*No,*" Johns said impatiently, but then he did see something. "Yeah. Chrissake. What's he doing?"

"He's going up that cliff, up the side of that mountain."

"What for?"

"I could pick him off," Karpus said, as if he did not care to speculate about the motivation of the climber.

"Sure," Johns muttered.

"You don't think so?"

"Sure I do. You're a good shot."

"How do you know I'm a good shot?"

"You said you were, for Chrissake. You told me." Karpus laughed.

"What's the matter?" Johns wanted to know. It would have been all right with him if no one ever laughed in his presence again.

"That's got to be four, five hundred yards," Karpus told him.

"I've got blisters on both feet," Johns said. "And my back is killing me."

"You did great."

The fat man shook his head as if no one could be

more disgusted with his performance than he was himself, as if in twenty-nine years on the planet Earth he had never done a single thing that could even remotely be described as great. But he was also pleased.

"You did, Johns. You did great. We're almost there, mile, mile and a half maybe. That shack is a beauty. I spent a month in it once by myself. You'll like it if some sonofabitch hasn't pulled it down."

"We better wait until they clear out," Johns replied. He was glad to have a reason for waiting, was glad too that Karpus seemed to be in a good mood. "Let me have some more whiskey," he said.

"Sure. Too bad we ran out of pills."

"Yeah. I know it."

"We really flew, didn't we?"

"Yeah," Johns agreed. He laughed shrilly, and Karpus advised him to please keep his voice down. Johns nodded. "You think that deer died yet?" he asked finally.

"How the fuck should I know?"

The fat man shrugged. If it had been up to him, if he had been the one driving, he did not think he would have tried to hit the deer. There hadn't been much kick in that, at least for him there hadn't. But he had not been driving, Karpus had. Utah had finally put in a furlough program, and Karpus, who was about as smooth a mover as there was, had managed to con an overnight for both of them, and once they were out they were out. During the twelve hours when no one had been looking for them, because they were by virtue of the new system legitimately out, they had grabbed some pills from a pharmacy, some whiskey from a liquor store, the rifle and a pistol and a bowie knife and outdoor gear from a discount sporting-goods store, had stolen the pickup, knocked off a gas station and driven out of Salt Lake toward Morgan. They had picked up a couple of hitch-hikers outside of Castle Gate, a couple of hippy-type kids, and Karpus had bought them all some Big Boy hamburgers and milkshakes in Price and had struck up a friendly conversation with them and then somewhere between Green River and Moab he had pulled over to the side of the road and asked them to please step out and they had and he had shot them both with the pistol, first one and then the other. Johns had gotten a kick out of that because right up until they had seen the pistol come out the two hippy kids and Karpus had been having a nice easy conversation and were laughing about how dumb the police were and how only a shit-for-brains would waste his time in school; then Karpus had brought out the pistol and had shot them.

Karpus said he had killed some other people too, but that so far nobody knew about it except him and the people involved, and of course they were dead. Johns had taken it as a tribute to be let in on this and had said he also had killed a couple of people although in fact he had not. When Karpus had asked for some details, Johns had invented some from the running stream of his fantasies. Karpus had seemed pleased. Johns was not sure that Karpus really believed him, but he had seemed pleased. He liked the story about how Johns had stuck a knife between the ribs of a big nigger in Truth or Conse-quences, New Mexico, and had then cut his nuts off and mailed them to Senator Montoya. Unfortunately, noth-ing about this had appeared in the papers, at least not in the ones Johns had read, and so he had no proof.

"What kind of rifle is that anyway?" he asked. He had found a place of concealment near enough to the creek to put in his throbbing feet. The water was clear and ice-cold. A school of minnows came up and began to nibble his toes. "Cut it *out,*" he said. He lashed at them with his foot, but they were too quick for him; they were like everything else.

"It's a Weatherby," Karpus told him. "It's one of the best they make. It's a three hundred Magnum, hundred-and-eighty-grain bullet. It's sighted to hold dead on up to three hundred yards."

Johns nodded, remembering the guy in the sporting-goods store had said that, or something like it. "Let's just lie low here, all right?" he said. He wanted no more hiking for a while, or excitement either. "Let's just cool it here until they take off."

"Okay," Karpus said. "We haven't got much further to go. I'd say a mile and a half."

"I've got to take a crap," Johns admitted.

"Okay," Karpus said. "Just stay low, and keep it downwind and out of the stream."

"It'll harden up tomorrow in the sun," Johns said. "Then we can mail it to Montoya."

Karpus laughed at that. He laughed for quite a while, but he did not make any particular sound, and when he had finished laughing he got on his belly again and looked through his rifle up to the higher place where the climbers were.

4

It was past four in the afternoon when Matt Whittaker reached the top of the pass. He had maintained a slow, steady pace, resting infrequently, hoping the wind that had begun to rise would not bring on a spell of foul weather. That, he knew, would do nothing to improve his mood. The elevation of the pass was 12,000 feet. Across its cover of consolidated snow he could see the tracks the two men had left. Less pronounced than they had been in the mud of the clearing, they dropped a thousand gradual feet to timberline where the snow ran out and the area of rock-slab surfaces and stunted firs began.

Surrounded on all sides by 13 and 14,000 foot summits, the floor of the basin itself was a hundred-and-fifty-acre green grass meadow crossed in its eastern sections by a quick stream. The stream, Needle Creek as it was called, had its origins deep in a blind canyon at the northeast corner of the basin. It was near the mouth of this canyon at a point just above timberline on the south slope of Wolf Mountain that Whittaker, from his position three miles distant atop the pass, thought he saw an unnatural swatch of color.

He kept a lightweight ten-power scope in one of the pockets of his pack and, curious now, not only about what he had seen but also as to the whereabouts of the men who had gone before him, he got the scope out, adjusted it to infinity and at once was able to identify the swatches of color as three bright orange tents: the base camp, he assumed, of a party of mountaineers who had come into the basin by the standard Needle Creek trail.

Although he scanned the basin floor for several long minutes, he could find no trace of the two men and guessed they were quite well ahead of him, as much as three or four hours perhaps. The sky over the basin was still clear, but the wind was brisk and he thought it had shifted somewhat from the southwest into the southeast.

"We're going to get something," he said. "Rain or sleet or even snow if the temperature keeps going down."

Ordinarily he might have dropped down into the timber, set up a snug camp, waited out the weather, and when it permitted might have made his first ascent the east face of Peak 18 which was the closest high summit to the north of the pass. He had climbed that peak years ago during his first trip to this basin, had spent the night in the caves situated low on the face, and he remembered it now as a pleasant and not very strenuous route. But instead he decided to go on at this point, to go down from the pass and through the trees and across the green grass meadow toward the distant southern slopes of Wolf Mountain. Although he had observed that above the climbers' camp even at this late hour of a chill afternoon there was no rising of smoke, he hoped he might find somebody home. A little conversation, the mere presence of people, might go a considerable way, he decided, in lifting his spirits.

5

Kate O'Rourke's spirits had risen steadily all that day. At first she had been annoyed that Neil and the others had insisted on sleeping so late—she was a stickler for schedules, especially those of her own design—but now, sitting comfortably astride a large boulder atop the already shadowed talus slope at the start of the standard east-face route, paying out rope to Neil Markham as he climbed, listening to the others call to him (*"Gee, Neil, are we there yet?"*), hearing him call amiably back (*"It's just over the next hill!"*), she knew he had been right, knew they had all been exhausted by the long two-day hike into the basin, by the mud and mire on the lower creek trail, by what had seemed an endless succession of minor yet time-consuming incidents (broken pack straps, lost wallets and lipsticks, skinned knees), knew finally it had been best to put off the actual ascent of the east face by one day, to come here instead at their leisure, establish a fixed rope, practice the rappel, relax, relax.

Why, she thought, is that always so mercilessly hard for me to do? Because, she assured herself, you are a driving perfectionist whose inflexibility as you've said before is only outweighed by your ambition and insufferable pride.

She laughed. The chunky girl Myke who was sitting next to her and who had been intently looking up at Neil Markham as he moved easily on the steep rock face now looked at Kate. The rest of the group had rushed away on some spur-of-the-moment mission of their own. Kate tried not to worry about them.

"I can't believe the way he climbs," the chunky girl said. "He makes it look easy!"

"That first pitch is steep," Kate replied, paying out rope. "But there are lots of good holds. You'll see."

"That's what I'm worried about."

"Well you don't have to try it today, but you probably should. Neil's going to put in a couple of pitons and set the rope at a hundred feet or so. Then he can give you an overhead belay. You can climb on up and rappel down. That's good practice, Myke. The twins will probably want to go first. Once you see how easily they do it, you'll change your mind."

Myke appeared to remain skeptical. She cupped her hands around her eyes as if to improve her vision, craned her neck until she could look up the thousand-foot shadowy face to the place where it met the sky, where the movement of a few scattered clouds gave the towering granite wall the appearance it was toppling forward.

"*Wow,*" she breathed.

Again Kate laughed. Myke was new to the club, and Kate had found her annoying at first. She seemed needlessly unattractive and the older woman itched to put her on a strict diet, buy her a new wardrobe, create in her an aggressive rather than self-effacing attitude. ("Don't just sit there and be useless and plain," she wanted to say. "You've got assets; for God's sake, use them.") But during these last few days, with all the annoyance and discomfort they had brought, she had begun to accept Myke more on the girl's own terms. After all, she had made it this far in spite of herself, had remained generally cheerful, had done more than her fair share of the chores. But her hair was a mess, and that awful sweatshirt . . .

"Neil!" Kate called. "That's far enough! Set things up, all right? We need to get going or there won't be time!"

"Will do!" he called back. She heard the echo of his voice mingle with the dying echoes of her own.

"Where are Dianne and the others?" she wanted to know.

"I'll get them," Myke offered. "They went to see if they could get a better look at that old shack down by the creek."

"I want them back here," Kate said. "If they practice on this pitch today, there'll be nothing to it tomorrow."

"Sure, and while they're doing that," the chunky girl offered, "I could go back to the tents and like get supper going!"

"*Myke.*"

"Okay," Myke said. She stood up and stretched, heaving her ample bosom toward the granite wall, pulling her sweatshirt down. She turned finally to pick her way along the slender trail atop the talus, following along the base of the cliff, deeper into the canyon toward the place where the others were just visible, the bright colors of their parkas reduced by distance, the soprano song of their voices muffled under the more persistent sound of the stream that snaked along the canyon floor 300 slanting feet below the place where Kate O'Rourke sat on belay.

Neil was pleasant, Kate thought. At least he had asked her if she wanted to set up the upper belay. Most of the men she climbed with would not have done that, would have assumed she preferred climbing second, or would not have bothered to think about her at all. His asking had made it easy for her to decline. She actually preferred to remain here where she could keep an eye on her group. She would keep them moving efficiently, would get them all back to camp in time for an early supper, would somehow persuade them to turn in early in order to guarantee the success of the next day's climb. Although she was recognized as one of the better climbers in the club, this was the first time she had actually been in charge of a trip. Neil was referred to as a co-leader but was in fact second in command, not that it mattered a great deal.

Why were most men so absurdly arrogant? She did not think of herself as a Women's Lib type, though she guessed she understood why some people did think of her that way. She wished her students at the university would call her Dr. O'Rourke or Katherine or Kate. She could not abide being referred to as Miss O'Rourke, which was the form of address most of them—and indeed most of her colleagues—seemed to prefer. *Miss* O'Rourke! It set her teeth on edge, called to her mind the image of a thin, waspish, undersexed Victorian-Irish child who was rude, unintelligent and finally obedient in spite of herself.

She shivered. The canyon was narrow. She had looked at the topo sheets but could not remember exactly how narrow it was: maybe 100 yards, maybe 150. The sun had left it; a cool breeze had begun to blow. She had on her shorts and a jersey and that was about all. She decided she would get her parka and wind pants out of her pack and put them on as soon as Neil went off belay. Neil, who had been taking his time, had finally reached a suitable ledge and was driving his pitons now; the sound they made going in, the rising metallic pitch, always reminded her of the sound a blacksmith made straightening a horseshoe on an anvil. She was willing to bet there were already some pitons driven above the ledge, because during the months of July and August a lot of people came in here to do the east-face route. But Neil would not want to trust old pitons, and while she approved of that kind of caution she could not help feeling restless.

"How does it look?" she called, and heard her voice echo from the canyon walls.

"No problem! Either one of the twins can lead this pitch. I'm going to rope down, okay?"

"Okay!" she called back. It was a change in plan, but not an important one. Dianne could climb to the ledge and then belay the others. Squinting up, she watched him untie the rope at his waist, saw him secure his end of it to the pitons he had driven. The rope was a 150-foot-long, 7/16-inch-diameter Goldline, and judging by what was left of it in the coil by her side she guessed he had climbed about 120 feet up the steep wall to the ledge where he now stood, his back to her, clipping the fixed rope through his seat sling. Apparently he had felt the chill too, for he had gotten into his parka, until now knotted around his waist.

"Myke!" she called. "Dianne! Dietz! Come on!" And as she stood, letting go her end of the rope, she saw they were coming, heard their spirited cries advancing, echoing across the talus. She shook her head. They were good kids, her kids, at least for now they were. Perhaps someday, if she decided to get married again . . . Relax, she reminded herself. Take four deep breaths. Don't say another word. She glanced up at Neil who, feet planted against the wall, had leaned back against the fixed rope and was beginning his descent. He was good. Not flashy, but solid, dependable, and though she had not known him well until now she was pleased he had been the one chosen to help her with the trip. Not one of the club's macho males. She wanted no part of them.

She yawned, stretching the way Myke had. Her muscles felt stiff. She was lean, full-breasted; her straight dark hair fell halfway down her back. She turned her head, appreciating the beauty of the canyon. She had been here before and each time it had seemed more perfect than the last, a remote, inviolate place that so far had escaped the depredations of the outdoor mob. She heard the pinwheel rush of a swallow, turned to catch its swooping flight above the surfaces of the stream that wound out of sight toward the mouth of the canyon, toward the solid comforts of their high camp. The warmth of a fire would feel good, she thought. And now what in the world was that?

In the distance, near the spot where the stream wound out of sight and close by the stream itself, she had seen a quick bright flash as if a lingering ray of sunlight had fallen upon the polished surface of a small mirror. It was gone now. Nothing important. Neil had already come half the distance to the ground; he was descending steadily against the rope, knees bent slightly, feet on the wall. . . . After all, she thought as the others approached breathless to tell her of whatever adventure they had had, I'm only twenty-six. Paul hounded me as if there was scarcely a moment to lose. I'd want to have two boys, I think, or maybe a boy and a girl. And plenty of money to hire someone to look after them well.

Dianne, one of the twins, arrived first, saying they all were in favor of skipping the practice climb because after all they had done it before, at least some of them had, and were going to do it again first thing in the morning, and couldn't they go now and explore the shack at the blind end of the canyon? It looked like a terrific place to poke around.

Kate sighed. This was the sort of thing she always had trouble with. Do it my way, she wanted to tell this bright young miss who was, she had learned, every bit as fiercely independent as she herself.

"Let's see what Neil has to say," she said, glancing up at the sky. "I'm afraid we may be in for some bad weather."

6

Whittaker reached the tents at twilight, approaching cautiously in what had become a raw, gusting northeast wind. There were no lights visible. The camp had been neatly and competently laid out, and because it had he was puzzled to find the tent flies open and a line with towels hanging from it, some of which had already been blown down and were scattered along the ground like lost sheets of paper. He picked them up, folding them and anchoring them with one of a circle of stones that had been used to contain a fire. The ash was cold and damp, as if many hours ago someone had poured water on it. He was determining this when he found the stub of a cigarette.

The stub was less than an inch long; there was no way he could be sure it was the same brand as the one he had found by the crippled deer. Here, the ground was too hard, too rocky to reveal tracks. It was possible that the men had come this way, attracted by the tents; but it was just as possible they had not.

For a while he hunkered by the cold fire with his back to the wind watching the sun drop behind Peak 18 and the western range, listening to the sough of the pines and distant roar of the water where it fell hundreds of feet from the mouth of the blind canyon to the dusky basin floor. Then he got up and zipped down each of the tent flies, glancing in first to see fine down sleeping bags and air mattresses, six in all, and several rucksacks but no climbing gear visible except for the handful of pitons that had been used to secure the tent guys.

Apparently whoever had set up this camp had left it sometime earlier today to do a climb: almost certainly the east face of Wolf Mountain, the standard route. The first 900 feet were not difficult, though the face rose steeply above the canyon floor. The final hundred feet were rugged, but he knew any experienced party should have been able to complete the face in half a day—less, if they were good—descending to this camp by way of the gentle south slope.

The open tent flies and towels on the line seemed to indicate that such might have been the plan of these people. If they had gotten into some kind of trouble on the steep rise of the east face, he might be able to help them, at least let them know they were not alone. And so he set out once more, carrying his pack and rope and ice ax, following the thread of a game trail that wound into the canyon across the top of the talus, 300 feet above the narrow canyon floor where the stream rushed and burbled toward the fall.

Bats whisked in the dusk around him and the wind came against him fitfully and in gusts strong enough at times to stop him in his tracks. He kept his flashlight in hand, but was somehow reluctant to use it and he had to stop frequently and squint into the gloom ahead before he could be sure of his way. In the absence of light, an apprehension he had managed to ignore during most of the day began to rise. He felt it as an added weight pulling against the cramped muscles of his legs and shoulders. He was hungry. He had taken small snacks throughout the afternoon but had not had anything substantial since breakfast early this morning on the long road from Morgan.

"If there were six of them," he murmured, for it helped to hear the sound of his own voice, "and they were climbing in three ropes of two, they should have been back long before this. Even two ropes of three couldn't have spent a whole day on that face unless they were awfully damn poor. . . ."

It seemed he had gone much further than a mile when he saw something ahead of him, close to the steep rise of the wall, at a place he recognized as the start of the standard route: the silhouette of a figure half crouched against the cliff, and above that figure, lashing whiplike in the wind, the long thread of a climber's rope that had, apparently, been anchored to the wall.

Ordinarily he might have called hello, but there were too many things about the situation he did not understand. He paused for a moment, settling quietly between two boulders. He watched the motionless figure and the whiplike rope above it, and tried to put things together.

The figure appeared to be on its hands and knees. It was facing away from Whittaker, gazing perhaps toward the blind end of the canyon. There was something furtive in its crouch as if whoever this was did not wish to be seen. If a party of six mountaineers had come this way, there was no sign of them now, and if it had not been for the rope lashing against the wall above, Whittaker would have assumed that the figure he was watching was one of the two men who had crippled the deer; but the rope complicated that theory, for he could not imagine why the climbers, however inexperienced they might be, would have left it behind.

It was conceivable, he guessed, that five of the party had dropped down to the canyon floor and followed the stream to its beginnings at the far end of the canyon, to explore that place and the abandoned prospector's shack that squatted there; but it did not seem very likely that by this hour they would not have returned.

Then it occurred to him that all six of the climbers might have gone on into the canyon and that the person crouched by the cliff was indeed one of the two men who had driven the Dodge truck with Utah plates; but if that was the case, where was the second man, and why had the climbers left a fixed rope on the wall?

He felt impatient now and strained his ears to try and catch some hint of an explanation, but all he heard was the windrush and when that would die briefly the more distant sound of the stream that wound along the canyon floor.

All right, he thought. *Let's find out what this is about.*

He stood up and began to walk toward the man, calling a greeting as he went, but the man neither rose from his crouched position nor called any greeting in return.

"Hey, buddy," Whittaker said when he reached the place. Then he saw that the man was not crouched at all but bent over an outcropping of rock as if he had fallen that way, and when Whittaker switched on the light he saw a dark stain the size of a dinner plate that covered the back of the green parka, and in the center of that plate an asymmetrical hole where the bullet had gone in. The man wore the clothes of a mountaineer. He was young, not more than thirty. The pilot turned him over gently and saw stitched above the front pocket of his parka the words NEIL/DENVER SCRAMBLERS and the leader's emblem of that club, two white summits against a blue field. There was not a lot left of the parka below its pocket. The bullet had flattened as it tumbled through the chest and had come out the size of a fist. Bits of down blew away on the wind.

Whittaker switched off his light and sat down wearily next to the body.

"Oh, Christ," he said softly.

A mile distant, at the farthest end of the canyon, he could see now the lighted windows of the prospector's shack. They looked almost friendly, beckoning to him.

Here, in the familiar presence of violent death, he knew he would have to decide what to do, whether to go on or go back. It would have been nice if things had worked out with Marie. He would not be sitting here now. He closed his eyes. His luck had not been very good of late. Neither had this man Neil's.

7

Johns, whose luck had never been good, was at the edge of losing his temper. His chest had locked up tight and there was a whirring in his brain that felt as if a carpenter had gone through the top of his skull with a high-speed quarter-inch drill. There was a cast-iron stove in the shack and Karpus had told him to keep it going; but for nearly an hour the miserable fires he had kindled had sputtered out one after another and he had exhausted himself hauling kindling in from the pile Karpus had showed him along the east wall of the shack, and then had blown his guts out against the draft that came down the rusty stove pipe, a draft that hummed like the wind in the rigging of a sail and farted smoke into his face, causing his ears to ring and his eyes to water and putting his poor fires out as if to say Fuck you, Johns, I'm nothing but wind in a rusty pipe and even I can make you look like an asshole.

"What's the matter?" Karpus wanted to know. His voice always sounded the same, a whispery monotone like Rod McKuen's. Johns liked to hear McKuen read his poetry because it was easy to figure out and usually had something to do with being lonely and because McKuen sounded like Karpus who was the only person apart from himself that Johns gave a damn about. He had never heard Karpus shout or even raise his voice in a crowd, but people always seemed to hear whatever it was he was saying. "What's the matter?" he said now. "You need help with that?"

"It keeps going out," Johns blurted. He was crouched on his hands and knees, facing the stove as if it were an opposing lineman on a team that was guaranteed to beat his team by at least forty points. The whirring in his head had become so pronounced he was afraid he was going to faint and he pressed his forearms against his temples. Then his nose started to leak and he had to blow it on his T-shirt. He wanted to take the stove and drag it outside, kick it off the porch and into the creek and spend the next week watching it rust. If Karpus wanted a fire, he could set fire to the whole fucking shack as far as Johns was concerned. He could burn it to the ground and those goddamned girls along with it; he had not heard them laughing at him yet, but he knew they were going to, knew they had been watching from the corners of their eyes his pathetic efforts to do something as easy as kindle a goddamn fire in a stove with dry wood and plenty of matches and "It's the fucking *wind*," he said. "It keeps blowing the *flames* out."

Whenever he got upset, and sometimes even when he was not upset, he tended to whine; and as far back as he had memory, people had listened to him whine and then had told him not to. For Christ's sake don't whine, Johns, will you? But he had never been able to control it. If he got even a little bit upset, he was liable to hear himself whining and would try to stop and would have no luck. He had gritted his teeth so hard one time when he was a kid he had split two of his molars. It was the same thing when he laughed. There was something shrill about his laugh, something almost girlish and giggly. For Christ's sake don't *giggle*, Johns, will you? He thought if he added up all the people who had pleaded with him not to giggle and not to whine the final list would include just about everybody who had ever known him at all, every-

body that is except Karpus who had never mentioned
either of these things.

"Use some kerosine," Karpus advised. He crouched
down and put a hand on the fat man's shoulder. Johns
snuffed up the mess that had developed in his nose and
spat it onto the grate of the stove which was, as yet, not
even warm. "No problem," Karpus said. "We'll use a
little kerosine. She'll go up fine."

"Okay," Johns said. Under his friend's touch he had
begun to relax a little. "I don't think *any* sonofabitch
could get it going with that much wind in the chimney."

"Naw," Karpus agreed. They had brought two quart
bottles of kerosine plus what was in the wells of the two
lanterns, and he got one of the quart bottles out of his
pack and brought it over and poured about half of it on
the charred stack of kindling that Johns had piled like an
offering on the grate. Then he drew a matchstick out of
the breast pocket of his mackinaw, snapped it to life
under his thumbnail and tossed it on. The flames exploded clear up into the pipe, and Johns, who had to
back away from the heat, knew this was a fire that was
going to burn for a while. It had been so simple: Pour on
some kerosine, toss on a match. Jesus. Karpus had
figured it out and gotten it done in the time it had taken
Johns to blow his nose on his shirt. And there he Johns
had been, dicking around for almost an hour with all
those young cunts watching him and he knew what they
were thinking and it browned him off.

Why the hell should it be this way? He didn't hold
it against Karpus that he was so good at everything he
did and looked like a fucking movie star except for his
teeth maybe, but why for Chrissakes couldn't he Johns be
good at something too? At least Karpus was willing to
give him a chance—at least he didn't say Jesus Christ,

Johns, you're such a numb-nuts you better let me do that. But what good did having a chance do when you screwed it up every time the way he always did, always had?

They had leaned their packs against the wall of the shack just beyond the stove and Johns found the whiskey in Karpus's pack and sat down next to the stove with his back against the cold wall, uncorked the whiskey and took a long pull. Across the room from where he was he could see the others, four of them, all seated around the small square table as if they were about to start eating their supper only of course they couldn't do that because he had tied their hands behind them. He looked at them quickly, then looked away toward the rear of the shack where the young kid was sitting tied up on the floor and Karpus was busy hanging an olive-green blanket from a rafter as if to screen off the cot he had set up there.

Johns knew Karpus had some sort of plan worked out, but he could not begin to figure out what it might be. If it had been up to him he never would have gotten involved with these climbing people at all. It irritated him because he had been looking forward all day to spending the night in this place with his old cellmate, chewing up some beef jerky and beans, passing the whiskey back and forth, sharing a cigarette, telling some lies, letting the fire melt some of the ache out of his bones. It just didn't seem smart, shooting that sonofabitch off that cliff out there for no good reason, and then rounding up this bunch and dragging them all in here, tying them up as if you had kidnapped them on purpose and were just waiting around for word the money had been dropped so you could finish them off and get out.

But he did not like criticizing Karpus, even in the secrecy of his mind. Karpus had done too much for him.

And Karpus had never been wrong. He had said they would get the furlough, and they had. He had also said they were going to get a good truck and plenty of outdoor gear, and they had gotten that too, and the whiskey and guns. Even though they had both been flying toward the end of it, Karpus had run everything through just the way he had said he would.

Where were these girls going to sleep? Probably on the floor if Karpus decided to keep them around. By now those two hippy kids had probably been found by somebody, but so what? They were just a couple of kids who had gotten their faces shot off. It happened all the time these days; you saw it on the tube, read about it in the papers. There were plenty of roads leading out of Salt Lake and no reason to think anybody would figure they had taken the one to Morgan. "They'll figure Phoenix," Karpus had told him. "Because they know you and me have both been there. That's how their minds work. I told the therapy guy as soon as I got paroled I was going to Phoenix and work for the Salt River Project. He'll tell them that. They're dumb," Karpus had said. "Believe me."

The therapy guy must have been dumb, because when Johns had made the mistake of telling him about that time those kids had reamed him with that garden hose, the therapy guy had said, "Pretend I was one of those people, Johns. What do you want to say to me? What do you want to do to me? Don't hold back. Go ahead. I'd guess you were pretty mad."

Jesus Christ. According to Karpus the guy got paid for his time. Somebody paid him, took care of him. Johns shivered. He had taken his pea jacket off while working on the fire. Now he thought he should probably put it back on, but he didn't feel much like getting back up. He could not help thinking about those tents, the three orange ones staked out above the trees on the side of the mountain just before the start of the canyon. Karpus had spotted them from clear across the meadow. They had stood out like flags. Anybody who came snooping around would see them right off, would probably check them out and decide something smelled, and then the hassle would begin.

He had wanted to go all the way back there in spite of his blisters and take the tents down, but Karpus had said no. Instead, Karpus had teased him a lot about those girls, had told him to pick one out, but he did not want any part of that. The only real experience he had ever had was in Mexico once, in a whorehouse there, where he had paid the bartender four bucks and tried to plug an old lady but his unit hadn't worked and he'd gotten mad and told her he'd pull her tits off if she didn't go down on him which, as soon as she understood what he was driving at, she did; and after a long and painful time he had managed to get it off. It had not been a very big deal, it had not changed his life.

He had told Karpus about this in prison once, trying to put it all in such a way he would come out sounding like a pretty mean stud, but it hadn't worked and Karpus had said he understood, had never mentioned it again. "You may be partially impotent," the therapy guy had said. Well fuck him.

He took another tug on the whiskey, looked at the table across the room. The fat one in the sweatshirt had her back to him and he was grateful for that because she looked exactly like the kind of pus-gutted sister he knew he would have had if he had had one. The two young girls who looked alike sat across from each other. They didn't do a thing for him either, except irritate him when the one would start to whimper and the other would say, "It's okay, Dee-Dee, everything's going to be all right." She would have to be a real dummy to believe that. In fact, of the whole bunch, there was only one who even remotely did anything for him at all. She was the big-titted, dark-haired one in the shorts who every time she caught him looking her way would look back as if she blamed him for just about everything that had ever gone wrong in her life, as if all this had been his idea instead of Karpus's.

"Hey, Johns," Karpus said from the rear of the room where he had apparently finished hanging his blanket.

"Yeah, what?"

"You check that notice over the table?"

Johns had seen it but had not checked it. "No," he said. "What's it say?"

"It says the Sierra Club keeps this place up. That's an outfit in California. It tells about the old fuck that used to prospect around here."

"By himself?"

"Yeah. Okay," Karpus said. "I'm going to have me a drink and a smoke. How's that fire doing?"

"Not too bad," said Johns, who had not bothered to look. "It will probably need some more wood."

"We'll get some. I'll get it. You've already gotten your share."

He sat down next to Johns, fixed himself a smoke, and then they passed that and the bottle back and forth between them. The wind was blowing hard enough to rattle the metal roof of the shack. Johns could not see anything beyond the windows, and he figured it had gotten pretty dark out there. He could not imagine being in a place like this alone. He could feel the rough warm wool of Karpus's mackinaw along his own right arm,

could feel the tough bunch of the taller man's muscle as
he reached for the bottle.

"You going to use that cot or what?" Johns wanted
to know, jerking his finger toward the blanket his friend
had hung.

"Might as well."

"I keep thinking about those tents. . . ."

"Just forget them."

"Yeah but . . ."

"Just forget them, Johns. I'll take care of them. Just
take it easy, all right?"

"Yeah but I . . ."

"You worry too much."

"I know but . . . Jesus, I don't know," Johns said.

"We're on a furlough, right?"

"Yeah, right."

"We're having a little party here. We're taking it
easy." Karpus laughed. "We're just taking it easy," he
said, as if it was a pretty funny thing to do.

Johns nodded. He felt the wool of the mackinaw
move across his shoulders, felt the weight of his friend's
arm, raised his knees instinctively against what he feared
might be the beginning of an erection, closed his eyes
against the unthinkable, against the vivid image he carried of what Karpus had done in Salt Lake. . . .

"Maybe I'll use it first," Karpus said.

"*What?*" Johns said. He had been startled.

"The cot."

"Oh. Yeah. Are you going to take a nap or what?"
Karpus laughed.

"What's wrong?" Johns wanted to know. "What, did
I say something, or what?"

Karpus gave him a hug, then he pointed to the kid
who was tied up on the floor. Johns smiled, but he did

not exactly feel lighthearted. The whirring sensation was gone from his head, but his chest still felt tight and he wondered if he had hurt himself blowing into the stove.

"I don't care," he said.

Karpus looked at him, gave him a hug.

8

Tucked into the area between the top of the talus and the start of the wall, Whittaker found two large rucksacks, several ropes, ice axes and a half-dozen short loops of webbing from which hung an assortment of pitons, carabiners, chocks and other climbing gear. He put his own pack here, removing from it first a four-by-six light-weight tarp with which he covered the body of the man who had been shot.

He was not sure what he would find when he set out again, unburdened now, descending the rocky slope to the canyon floor where he picked up a footpath that followed the stream, moving against its flow and into the wind, toward the pinprick lights that showed from the shack; but he knew that some people were in trouble, most likely at the hands of the two men who had crippled the deer, and that except for himself there was no one within two days of this place who could be called upon to help.

He had gone into the war in just this way, at least in the beginning he had; had gone to help some people who his country said were worth helping. Marie had thought otherwise. He wondered what she would think now if she could see him going on into this canyon.

"Maybe I'm trying to prove something," he said. Maybe he was.

But he was afraid, and this fear made him angry and at the same time even more cautious than he had been until now. He wished he had trusted his instincts and brought the revolver with him instead of leaving it in the glove box, miles behind. He would not hesitate to use a gun. As far as Marie was concerned, this made him different only in kind from whoever had shot the climber at the base of the cliff. He shook his head. He had never worried much about such fine distinctions and had seen enough of the world in thirty-eight years to be persuaded that some men were good and others were not and that the confrontation between them was as old as the world itself. If he had changed at all it had been sometime during his last tour when he had stopped thinking of the other side as evil but simply as shrewd, dedicated adversaries. As it turned out there had been good people on both sides, and bad. Maybe he had been in the military too long. It had been, finally, a rotten war, screwed up by everybody—the politicians, the joint chiefs, the liberals, the conservatives—fucked up, bungled and botched, and too many good men dead because of it, too many he had flown with and fought beside.

The prospector's shack was a twenty-by-twenty foot square building with warped, weathered board siding and a corrugated metal roof. It hunched between the headwaters of the stream that boiled up out of the ground in front and the wall of the canyon that loomed behind. The ramshackle structure was dwarfed by the immensity of the cliff. Whittaker went up onto the rock slope again, moving warily, his eyes fixed on the door of the shack, the small single-railed porch and steps. He was still afraid, but it was a cooler fear now, tempered,

as it had been on the missions he had flown, by an un-
compromising instinct to survive.

He approached the west side of the shack on an
oblique angle, counting on the noise of the wind and
stream to cover any noise he might make as he came in.
It was dark. The sky overhead had already begun to fill
with clouds; there was no sign of the three-quarter moon
of last night. The yellow light that came through the
single small window in this wall fell upon the ground in
a neatly articulated rectangle that he was careful to avoid
as he moved along the wall to the rough frame and
looked in.

The first person he saw was a young woman, mid-
twenties he guessed, though he could not be sure. She
was seated at a table, back to him, just inside the window.
She wore high-cut black Levi shorts, a long-sleeved ceru-
lean blue jersey and a pair of Kletterschuhs, well scuffed
as if she had taken them with her on many high climbs.
Her hair was black and straight and fell below her shoulders. Her legs were tied to the legs of her chair, and her
hands were tied behind her with a short length of hemp
rope, and in the brief seconds it took for him to receive
these impressions he saw that she was working steadily
but patiently at loosening the knot.

Three girls sat at the same table. The youngest of
them, sixteen, maybe seventeen, was a chunky, plain-
looking girl with short, collapsed brown hair and a ma-
roon sweatshirt across the front of which in bold white
letters was printed the name MYKE and below that a
phrase in smaller letters which he could not make out.
This girl was facing the window, staring at it, her expression half stunned, half stoic, as if in the absence of courage she was trying hard to be brave.

The other two girls, who sat facing each other in

profile from his point of view, appeared to be identical
twins. Their blond, bobbed, curly hair, large eyes, bright
cheeks and parkas suggested to him they were college
coeds, cheerleaders, sorority girls; but now one of them
was crying openly and the other was moving her lips as
if to comfort her, and each of the twins and the other girl
and the young woman with her back to him had their legs
tied to the rickety chair legs and their hands tied behind
them, and, as far as he could tell, only the young woman
was trying to get free.

He pressed close against the outside west wall of the
shack, the wind rattling the corrugated roof above him.
Another person inside attracted his attention now, a fat,
pale slug of a man in gray twill pants and a filthy T-shirt
who knelt on the floor near the far wall, blowing into the
grate of a wood-burning stove as if to rekindle a fire that
had recently gone out. His blunt head had been shaved
and in the light that fell upon it from the two kerosine
lanterns hanging from the rafters it looked as though it
had been rubbed with charcoal. His shin-high boots were
new, an inexpensive brand of simulated leather and
ribbed rubber soles that Whittaker recognized at
once. A foot-long bowie knife hung from his belt. The
knife and scabbard also looked new, as if just before
coming into this wilderness the man had shopped at the
discount stores in a large city. He blew into the stove
angrily, apparently having reached the end of his
patience.

Whittaker exhaled softly. This had to be one of the
two men who had crippled the deer. He wanted to locate
the other one, but from this edge of the window frame
he could not see the north half of the room. Crouching
under the sill of the window, he moved to its other side
and from this new position he could see two still heavily

laden packs leaning against the wall beyond the wood-burning stove and between them what looked to be a high-powered rifle with a scope. An army-issue blanket hung from the back rafters of the room, apparently to conceal a cot, its aluminum lower frame just visible. He guessed the other man might be back there, lying on the cot perhaps. Seated on the floor near the hanging blanket was another figure, a young boy he thought, no more than fifteen, very slender with closely cropped red hair, climbing shoes, Levi's and a faded blue denim shirt. The boy was not tied, though there were two short lengths of rope by his feet as if he had been tied until recently. His knees were drawn up, his arms folded across them, his head resting facedown on his arms.

That was it then. The four at the table, the one at the stove, the one on the floor and the other one on the cot perhaps, behind the blanket which moved in the drafts that came in through the chinks in the north wall. He wiped his forehead with the sleeve of his parka. In spite of the increasing cold he had begun to perspire. He wanted to do something, knew he would have to do something, but he could not decide what. It would have been clear enough with his revolver in hand, but he had left that behind. He had his pocket knife, a Swiss Army model with a short blade, and in addition to that the advantage of surprise; but that was all and right now it did not seem like very much. If he could lure one of the men out of the shack, or, better, simply wait until one of them came out to piss or get wood, he could probably take him; but that would leave the other one and the rifle inside. He rubbed his face with the palm of his right hand, felt the still unfamiliar roughness of his beard as if it were part of the face of a stranger. He needed to act but could not decide what to do, aware that until recently such indecision had not been a part of his character, not until his marriage had failed, not until the war had gone sour.

You've got your own skin to think about, he reminded himself. You better go back for the gun.

And that might have been all right except that the young woman was still working patiently at the knot that locked her hands behind her. He could see her long finger teasing the center of the knot, picking at it again and again. She had made progress since he had last looked; the knot was beginning to open.

He liked the idea that she was trying to get free, but wondered what good it could possibly do. She must have some sort of plan. He tried to imagine himself in her place. He would go for the rifle that lay propped between the packs on the far wall; but she might not be sure how to use the rifle. She could not count on help from the other girls all tightly bound and not, as far as he could tell, making any efforts to work themselves free. She might be able to count on something from the young boy who was not tied up, but he was very slight and had not moved at all since Whittaker had first noticed him.

The roof of the shack clattered in the wind which blew hard against his left side, causing him to shake with cold. He thought that the moon should have risen by now. Last night he had first seen it through the highest branches of a hundred-foot spruce where he had rolled out his sleeping bag, had tried to sleep, had dreamed of his old friend Ike, of how Ike had died, of what it must have been like to die that way. . . . When the moon did finally rise, if it was not too much obscured by cloud, it would illuminate the canyon floor, making it difficult for a man to hide. You should go back for the gun, he thought again. But the woman inside would have freed herself and made her move long before he could hope to return.

He decided finally that once she had freed her hands and eventually her legs, she would most likely bolt for the door, hoping to escape in the dark and go for help. If she did do that, at least one of the men inside would come after her, probably not the fat one, who did not look capable of much more than raising an alarm, but the other one, the one he had yet to see. Would he pick up the rifle as he came? Or leave it where it was propped between the two packs? Would he have a pistol as well? No way to be sure, but it would probably be smart to assume that he would. A lot was going to depend on how much lead time the woman had in getting away from the shack, how much moonlight there would be by then, who came after her and whether or not he brought the rifle with him. If the rifle and the fat man both stayed in the shack, Whittaker thought his own chances might be good. He would have to finish the fat man quickly and quietly. That was something he knew how to do. Then, with the rifle, he would be able to go after the other one.

But there were a lot of *ifs.* Too many. And he had begun to shake his head when behind him he heard a sudden sound unlike the sounds he had become accustomed to in this place, not the rush of the wind and the water in the stream, but a sharp click, the tick of a stone, perhaps, that had been dislodged by the end of a boot. He went rigid, chest locked, breath stopped in his throat. Before he could turn he heard the sound of a man's voice. It was a soft, whispery voice all but empty of inflection.

"I knew you were here," it said. "I was out to get

wood and I had a look-see around like I always do and I saw you coming up the trail."

Whittaker felt the painful beating of his heart. He forced himself to turn slowly, hands at his sides.

"What's going on here?" he asked as easily as he could, as if he were only curious.

At first the man did not reply. Instead, he gazed intently at Whittaker as if he were the curiosity. The man was tall, lean, not unlike Whittaker himself except that his hair was darker and shorter and his beard was only that of a man who had forgotten to shave for a weekend. He wore faded olive-green fatigue pants and a blue and black checked mackinaw, collar raised against the wind. His right hand held a large-bore automatic. In the light that came through the window, the muzzle looked large enough to fire a golf ball.

"I had a brother looked like you," he said finally.

This time Whittaker did not reply.

"You got to get up pretty early in the morning to slip up on me," the man said. "You like to drink?"

"Sometimes. . . ."

"Well, I've got some good whiskey inside, couple of bottles, good stuff. We might just as well have some before I shoot your balls off."

"There'll be some other people here before long," Whittaker said. It had not sounded convincing. The man ignored it.

"Course," he said, indicating with the pistol that the pilot should move in the direction of the front of the shack. "Course I could get Johns to do it with his knife."

9

When the door of the shack banged open and the tall blond man came through it instead of the dark one she had expected, Kate O'Rourke assumed that he was a friend of the other two, the men who had murdered Neil. Terrorized, half numb from shock, still she had been working as hard as she could to free her hands and knew now that eventually she was going to get them free and after them her feet as well; and the slight hope these certainties had triggered was crushed by the fact that instead of having to get past two of these men to the rifle at the far wall, she would now have to get past three.

Paul had been devoted to guns, had insisted on teaching her how to shoot. He had kept rifles and shotguns in locked racks in the basement of their home and a loaded pistol under his side of the king-size mattress they had shared. For what had seemed to her an interminable chain of Sunday afternoons he had taken her to the practice range, had methodically explained to her the differences between the pump-action, lever-action and bolt-action rifles, how to work these actions, how to line up on close and distant targets, how to hold her breath and squeeze off her shot.

At first she had resisted him as strongly as she knew how, telling him precisely what she thought about guns and bullets and violent death of any kind, how she would rather suffer the worst kind of injury from another human being than do him bodily harm. She called it having a reverence for life. "What about rape?" he had asked, incredulous. "What if some S.O.B. came piling into this bedroom with the clear intention of assaulting you and you were here alone? Are you telling me you wouldn't use this pistol?"

"Yes," she had said, she was telling him that, trying to get into the thick meat of his male skull what was to her the uncomplicated notion that if all the guns and bullets in the world were dumped forthwith into the sea, the world would be a finer place. "Don't murder a deer," she had said. "Write a poem."

It was not funny, he replied. It was not funny at all. There were nights when he would be away; one never knew about these things. She told him she would actually feel safer if his own guns were out of the house; at least then no one would be able to use them on her. She cited statistics to back up her case. "I'm asking you to do this for me," he replied. "Oh, all right," she said finally. And she had done it for him.

She wished desperately that he were here now, wished he and that ex-GI gang of his who played poker and drank beer and talked endlessly about bullet trajectories and muzzle velocities would appear suddenly at the doors and windows of this drafty shack with their weapons drawn. She closed her eyes. She did not in truth want anyone to be hurt: not herself, not the girls, not even these men whoever they were, these sick, filthy men who had done what they had to Neil Markham without warning or provocation; no, if she had to, if they gave her no choice, she would shoot for their legs, cripple them somehow, make them believe she knew how to work the gun and would use it on them if she had to, would kill them if she had to, even though she doubted that she could.

Their rifle was a bolt-action type. She had practiced

with that kind for hours because Paul had told her it was the most accurate. She had gotten pretty good with it too, had even managed to outshoot him one or two times before he finally announced he thought she could handle herself all right and if she really did refuse to go hunting with him—which she assured him she really did—then there was not much point in her practicing all the time.

She wanted to weep thinking about him, remembering how he looked, what an able, good, decent man he was. He had always tried to warn her about just this kind of thing, how it didn't always happen to the other guy, how it happened to nice people like herself, how it was happening more and more often these days. "Katherine, you are being naïve as hell," he had said during one of the last exchanges they had had on the matter. "What if we had kids? What if some cretin came into this house, threatening our kids?" "We don't have kids," she had reminded him. "And if we did, if we ever do, one of the first things you are going to do is get rid of those damnable guns. . . ." *Oh, God, Paul,* she thought. *Neil? What am I going to do? What can I do with three of them now . . . ?*

But as the door slammed shut and she opened her eyes, she saw she had been wrong about the blond bearded man, for now the tall dark one with the decayed teeth, the one called Karpus, had come in just behind him and was holding a pistol at his back.

"Got us a snooper," he said huskily. He seemed pleased, as if he had gone out to fish and had come back with a big one. The fat man who had been fussing with the stove stood up and wiped his hands on his trousers. He was repulsive. Whenever Kate looked at him she felt something rise in her throat.

"Look—" the blond man started to say.

"Shut up," Karpus said. He put the muzzle of the

pistol against the man's back and moved him a couple of steps into the room. Kate could see the twins watching from the corners of their eyes. Myke had craned her neck to look.

"Where did *he* come from?" the fat one wanted to know. His voice sounded as if it had never quite finished a change begun in puberty; and, unlike his companion, he did not seem at all pleased at the prospect of having more company.

"Outside," Karpus said.

"What was he doing outside?"

"Snooping in the window. I told him we were having a party and he should come in and have a drink." Karpus laughed in the same toneless way he spoke. "Get his wallet out," he said. "See who he is."

"I came here to climb—" the blond man started to say, but Karpus cut him off by exerting more pressure with the muzzle of the pistol against the small of his back. The fat man came over until he was close to Karpus, but not too close to the blond man, and then he reached out and lifted the blond man's wallet from the left rear pocket of his pants.

"He's got about fifty *bucks* in here," the fat man said. He began counting. "Sixty, sixty-three, sixty-four . . ."

"What else has he got?"

"I don't know. . . . Credit cards. Bunch of them. Matthew Whittaker . . . APO . . . Some kind of military I.D. Air Force. Major . . ."

"Major?"

"Yeah. Right. Major Matthew Whittaker. Retired. U.S.A.F. Air Force, right?"

"I'll be a sonofabitch," Karpus said. He had caught a fish with rank.

"Pictures, couple of kids, some lady, probably his

wife I guess. Nice-looking cunt." Johns laughed. "Nice-looking house. Fucking plane. Look at this. . . ."

Kate watched the tall man who held the pistol in his right hand take the wallet with his left and look at what the fat man had told him to look at. In the half-minute of silence that followed, the owner of the wallet turned his head slowly until he was looking at the table, at the twins and Myke, and at her. His expression was gaunt, as if he had not slept well recently, and she thought he looked too thin, had suffered some debilitating sickness perhaps and was still on the mend. She looked back at him critically, wondering if somehow he might help them, wondering if there were others who had come here with him. He had indicated he was a mountaineer; there were not many who climbed alone.

"You pilot fighters, do you?" Karpus wanted to know. He had put the wallet into the breast pocket of his mackinaw.

"I used to."

"What?"

"I used to. I got out. . . ."

"Johns and me do some flying too," Karpus said. The pilot did not answer. "We fly pretty high when we want to," Karpus said. "Don't we, Johns?"

Johns smiled, but he did not seem very happy.

"What are we going to do with him?" he wanted to know.

"Tie him up," Karpus replied.

"Chrissake," Johns said. "He probably saw those tents. . . ."

"He didn't see anything," Karpus said.

"What if somebody's with him?"

"Nobody's with him. Tie him up. Make it tight."

Johns did what he was told. Kate had already noticed that. He was someone she could handle. It was the other one who would be dangerous, the other one she would have to shoot if she had to shoot anybody. But if they ate and drank enough they might fall asleep, pass out even, and she would have her chance. At her right side, Dietz was crying again, shaking her head at the same time as if she were ashamed of her crying but could not help doing it. At her left the other twin whispered more words of comfort. Kate had written to their parents, telling them about the trip, reassuring them. Now she worked carefully, intently at the knot of the rope that bound her wrists. Across the table Myke stared back, her face expressionless, as if she had managed to deliver herself finally into some hypnotic state. And now this pilot, this gaunt-looking man whoever he was: One more to worry about. She closed her eyes, prayed.

Please help me, dear God.
Please help me, dear God.
Please.

10

Sitting on the floor not far from the bound feet of Katherine O'Rourke, Whittaker strained uselessly against the ropes that had been knotted around his wrists and ankles. Nearly an hour had passed since the man whose name was Karpus had brought him into the shack, and the only things that had changed in that time were the fire blazing up from the grate of the stove and the fact that the two men now seemed to be drunk. They sat on the floor, comfortably close to the stove, passing a quart bottle of whiskey between them.

The tall man Karpus did most of the talking. The fat

man Johns with the filthy shirt and the bowie knife would listen. As he listened he grinned incessantly, and now and then would burst out in a shrill giggling laugh that, whenever he heard it, chilled Whittaker to the bone. The metal roof of the shack banged and clattered in the wind; the two lanterns burned silently; the fire in the stove snapped and popped. The army blanket, suspended from a rafter, moved steadily now in the drafts that came through the chinks in the walls.

When the men were not looking his way, when the overall noise in the room was loud enough to cover his whisper, Whittaker tried talking to the young woman who sat bound in the chair above him. She was the chance they had.

"What happened?" he said.

She glanced at him impatiently, as if in the face of this transparent disaster she found his question absurd.

"We were climbing the east face," she replied finally, her voice so low he could barely hear what she said. Her words were clipped. "Practicing. They shot one of us and brought the rest here." Even before she finished saying it, she returned her gaze to the two men who sat across the room by the stove. The tall one was lighting a cigarette from the end of a flaming stick. Whittaker watched him.

"Any reason?"

"No. None."

"Why is he untied?"

"Why is who untied?"

"The boy," Whittaker said. He nodded in the direction of the blanket.

"She's a girl," the woman replied. "Pam."

Whittaker nodded. "But how come she's not tied up?"

"Because he untied her. The tall one."

"What for?"

"You can probably figure that out."

He looked at the two men. They were still passing the bottle between them, taking sips, sharing the cigarette. He could smell the smoke, could distinguish it from the oily smell the lanterns produced and the clean smell of the burning wood. They were talking, but not loud enough for him to hear what it was they were saying over the rush of the wind. The fat one looked as if he were listening to something he had once been told was obscene. Whittaker glanced at the young girl who sat on the floor by the blanket. For an instant she caught his eye, her lips parting slightly as though she wanted to tell him something, as though in the space of that moment she thought he might be able to help. Then she lowered her eyes, and he turned to the dark-haired woman again.

"Are you going to get loose?" he asked her.

She looked at him, frightened, as if she thought he might betray her.

"Yes," she said finally.

"What's your plan?"

"Look, it's not going to help if they figure out you're talking to me. . . ."

"If I know what you're going to try," he started to say, "I might be able to help. . . ."

"Why did you come here anyway?" she broke in. Her voice had risen and he thought she might be on the verge of losing control, but he saw she continued to work at loosening the knot, her lower lip caught sharply between her teeth, her breasts pushing against the soft blue fabric of the jersey.

He took a breath. "I found your friend," he said. "The one they shot, up by the start of the east-face route."

"Why didn't you go for help?"

He did not reply, understanding the criticism, angered by it. He had come here to see if he could help, had long since had a stomachful of righteous women telling him what to do. *All right*, he thought. *You do it yourself*.

He began to work at loosening his own bonds. The fat man had tied him so tightly his hands tingled. The twin at the side of the table closest to him glanced down; he tried to smile at her. She looked like a nice girl, wholesome, the kind who in maybe one more year would fall in love with the president of the student body, would get married and raise about six kids—one more year if she made it through this. The chunky girl in the sweatshirt had tipped back her head, her eyes were closed; he guessed she might be trying to sleep. MYKE the large letters read, the smaller letters lost in the folds of the shirt.

"Kate," the closer twin whispered to the young woman. *"What are we going to do?"*

Whittaker glanced up, saw that Kate was about to reply, then saw her shake her head. She was looking past the twin, toward the far wall.

"I'll show you how," he heard Karpus say, the husky voice abruptly audible. He watched the man get unsteadily to his feet. The fat one grinned up expectantly, as if he had been waiting for this. "Come on, Johns," Karpus said. "If I'm going to do it, you're going to watch. Get your tail up."

The fat man laughed. When he made an effort to rise he burned his hand on the stove and the tall man reached down to help him up.

"You hurt?"

"Son-of-a-damn-bitch," the fat man said. He looked at his palm, rubbed it on his trousers, grinned again.

Karpus shook his head. "Johns, aren't you ever going to learn?"

"I am. I'm all right."

The tall man laughed. Whittaker thought he seemed
relieved. "You never watched me do it, did you?" he
said.

"That?"

"Yes, that."

"I saw what you did in Salt Lake. . . ."

"I didn't do anything in Salt Lake."

"Sure you did. The one in the filling station . . ."

"That was a him."

"I know. . . ."

"I don't believe you're ever going to learn, Johns.
You know I really don't?"

"I'll do whatever the fuck you tell me to," Johns
admitted.

"Pick one of 'em out."

"We already did that."

"I did. But you didn't. I don't know about you,
Johns."

The fat man blushed. Whittaker could see the color
rise from his cheeks up into the grayish skin of his shaved
scalp.

"You didn't," Karpus said huskily. He put his arm
across his friend's shoulder, let his hand drop down until
it covered the man's plump breast. "We've got a bunch
of 'em here. You can have any one you want except the
major and the one I picked out for my own. You can even
have her when I get done."

Johns laughed, but it was not a confident laugh. "I
don't know," he said.

"There's a first time for everything," Karpus told
him. "Isn't that right?"

"You said I could watch. . . ."

"Come on," Karpus said. He kept his arm around his friend's shoulder, guided him to the table where Kate and the three girls sat. The men stopped next to the chair of the girl whose name was Myke. Her eyes were still closed, but Whittaker could see her jaws tighten when Karpus put his hand in her hair.

"Please leave her alone," Kate said. "She's just a kid."

"Now this one is just about as fat as you, Johns," Karpus said, ignoring what he had heard. "You both get on that cot we trucked in here you might bust it."

"Cut it out," the fat man replied. He seemed to be genuinely hurt, as if Karpus's cruelty had been unexpected. "I'm going to lose weight," he said. "I've *been* losing some."

"You don't want to lose too much," Karpus told him. "If you lose too much it's not good for you. You like these twins?"

"If you have to bully someone," Kate said, "why don't you bully me?"

"Take it easy," Whittaker told her.

"We like 'em young," Karpus said. "Isn't that right, Johns?"

"I don't like these twins," Johns put in. He was looking at the woman who had spoken out.

"You like her?"

"Sure. I like her all right."

"You do?"

Johns nodded. He had put his hand up inside his T-shirt, scratching his belly.

"She's got a big mouth," Karpus said.

The fat man laughed. "She's got big fucking *things* too," he said.

"How do you know she has?"

Johns looked worried. He brought his hand out from under his T-shirt and pointed.

"You can see," he said.

"They could be fake."

"Fake?"

"That's right."

"They're not fake. . . ."

"How do you know they're not?"

Puzzled, the fat man scratched his scalp, then looked at his nails which were gnawed and lined with grease. "I don't know for Chrissake," he said. "They *look* big. You can see the ends. . . ."

"That's because she hasn't got her underwear on, Johns. She's some kind of whore I guess."

"At least I'm a woman," Kate said unevenly. "At least I'm not a child."

"Look, take it easy," Whittaker said.

"I'm not afraid of them," she replied; but he knew that she was, just as he was himself. To talk up that way was like shaking a stick at a snake.

"Okay, Johns," Karpus said. "Let's have us a look."

The fat man laughed. Karpus came over and put the toe of his boot in Whittaker's rib. "Roll over," he said. His voice was quiet. There was no edge to it, but it carried a threat. "Face the other way."

"How come?" Johns wanted to know, as Whittaker did what he was told.

"You and me are going to see it, but he's not. That's all."

"How come?" Johns said. "How come he can't see it too?"

"He didn't do anything to get a free show, did he?"

"I don't know. . . ."

"He didn't do anything. You and me did something. We shot the belly button out of that one on the cliff."

"*You* did," Johns said.

"Go ahead," Karpus replied. "Lift up her shirt."

Whittaker felt the pulse of blood at his temple, beating too fast. Behind him, he heard the rustle of fabric, then a soft whistle of satisfaction.

"That real enough for you?" he heard Karpus ask.

"She's a fucking beaut," Johns admitted.

"Give her a feel."

"I don't need to, I can see she's a beaut. . . ."

"Go ahead. Give her one."

"*Don't,*" Kate breathed.

The fat man laughed. "You do this one," he said. "I'll watch, okay?"

"I don't like 'em built like her," Karpus explained. "Too floppy, see that? I already picked mine."

"*Her* you mean?"

"Yep."

"*Jesus,*" the fat man complained, "she hasn't got *any*-thing. . . ."

"She's got plenty for me."

"I thought she was a boy at first. . . ."

"So? What's wrong with that?"

Johns was silent.

"What's wrong with that?" Karpus asked him.

"Nothing."

"When it's your turn, you can have whatever you want. All right?"

"Sure," Johns said. "I didn't mean anything."

"I'll do her and you can watch, pick up some pointers, then we'll have a drink."

"You said we had to go and get those tents . . ."

"We will."

". . . before morning."

"We will. Come on," Karpus said pleasantly. "I'm ready for it."

"Don't," Kate whispered. But they were not listening to her. Whittaker saw their boots pass close by him, heard the squeak of the floor. They went to the place where, just in front of the army blanket, the slender girl sat.

She had gathered herself into a tight ball.

11

It went on for a long time, so long that although the girl had not made any sound that Whittaker could hear he thought he was the one who would scream as he lay on the rough floor, straining against his ropes. The fat man stood just outside the blanket, looking in. At first he asked questions, and Karpus, quietly and carefully, answered them; but after a while Karpus told him to keep still and so he did. Then there were no other sounds in the room except the wind against the metal roof and, when that would die, the soft hiss of the lanterns, audible for the first time, and the breathing of Karpus which had become labored until it resembled that of a man attempting to move too large a weight.

When at last the breathing rose methodically and ended in a husky cry, Johns smiled at Whittaker as if this were something only men would understand, as if he had known from the start that Karpus would accomplish what he had set out to do. Then he looked behind the blanket again.

"See that?" Whittaker heard Karpus say.

"*Jesus,*" the fat man breathed. Then, after a while, he said, "You want me to get you the whiskey?"

"I'll get it. You tie her up."

"Like she is?"

"Sure," Karpus said. "Like she is. You can get her clothes back up if you want."

The fat man got some rope and went behind the blanket and the tall man came back into the room. He looked the same as he had before except that his hair was damp and the right side of his cheek inflamed as if he had rubbed it against something. He went over to one of the two packs, got out a new bottle of whiskey, fumbled the cork out of it and took a long drink, looking at Whittaker as he did.

The pilot clenched his teeth. "Did you really enjoy that, you prick?" he said.

"Pam!" Kate called.

"You keep quiet," Karpus told her. One of the twins was crying again and he went over and slapped her face. "You keep quiet too," he said. When she went on crying, he slapped her face again, harder this time. Then, in the silence that followed, he took out a pack of cigarettes and lit one, tossing the spent match into the stove. Johns came out from behind the blanket looking worried.

"What's the matter?" Karpus wanted to know.

"We better get those fucking tents. . . ."

"I told you we would."

"You can see them for miles. . . ."

Karpus laughed.

"Nobody's going to take us in this canyon, Johns," he said. "Not unless they bring the marines."

"I know," the fat man replied, but he did not look persuaded. He rubbed his hands on his shirt, then took a drink from the bottle. "I know," he said. "But if we don't go pretty soon, we're going to freeze our asses off. . . ."

"You going to take her back there?" Karpus wanted to know. "Now I showed you what to do?" He was looking at Kate.

Johns shook his blunt head. "I don't feel like it," he said. He looked at the floor. "Not now."

"You told me before you did."

"I know. . . ."

"What's wrong then?"

"I don't know. . . ."

Karpus draped his arm around the fat man's shoulders. "You got horned up watching me, didn't you?"

"Sure. . . ."

"What's wrong then?"

"I just don't feel like it, that's all. Chris*sake,* Karpus . . ."

"You worried about me being here?"

"No."

"You know it's not good for you, Johns," Karpus said. "You can't always leave things to me. What are you going to do the first time I'm not around?"

"I don't know. I'll get along all right. I got along all right before."

Karpus went to the wall and picked up the rifle. His pistol was in a holster at his belt.

"What are you going to do?" Johns asked.

"I'm going to take down those tents."

"Good," the fat man replied. He hurried to his pea jacket which lay on the floor next to his pack.

"I'm going alone," Karpus told him. "You stay here."

"I don't want to stay. . . ."

"You stay here and keep your eye on things. I'll be back in a couple of hours. I'm going to have a good look-see; be sure no one else is out there poking around."

Karpus took down one of the lanterns and raised its wick. Johns hovered next to him. "I better go with you," he said.

"I don't want you to go with me. I want you to stay here."

The tall man went for the door. The fat man hurried beside him. "Look, I don't want to stay here," he complained.

"I can't always do everything," Karpus explained patiently. "You've got to learn how to get along. You'll be all right. Take care of her. Do what you want."

"What if somebody comes?"

"I'm going to be on the only trail in here. Nobody's going to come."

Karpus opened the door. The room filled with the sounds of the creek and the wind. "Take care of that one," he said good-naturedly. "You can do it just as good as I can. Take her behind the blanket if you feel like it. Keep her hands tied is all. Put her belly-down the way I did."

Johns rubbed his hands together as if he were trying to wash them. "At least let me have the pistol," he said.

"You've got your knife," Karpus told him. "That's all you need. They're not going anywhere."

"Well, how the fuck long will you be?" Johns sounded worried, but a little pleased too, as if Karpus had complimented him unexpectedly by his willingness to leave him in charge.

"It's a couple of miles out and a couple back," Karpus said. "I'll have to break down that camp, bury all their shit; then I want to check the trail through the meadow, have a good look-see. . . . Figure a couple of hours, maybe a little more."

"What are we going to do tomorrow?"

"How should I know? What do you care about tomorrow for?"

Johns lowered his voice. "They'll be looking for us," he said.

"Sure they will," Karpus replied. "They'll always be looking for us."

They went out onto the porch then. Whittaker could hear the sharp squeak of one of the porch steps, like a nail being pulled out of green wood. He had rolled onto his back and now he turned onto his side, facing as he had been before Karpus had made him turn the other way. Kate was working hard at the knot that secured her hands.

"Are you going to get it?" he whispered.

"Yes. . . ."

"Before he comes back?"

"No, I don't know. . . ."

"If not, talk him into untying your feet. . . ."

"Look, I know what I'm doing. . . ."

"Give him some time first. The other one may hang around for a while to be sure his friend is holding up. He's smart."

"Pam," she called quietly, ignoring him now. "Are you all right?"

"I think I heard her crying," the closer twin said.

"Pam? Can you answer me?"

"She's probably too scared," the twin said. "After . . . I mean after what happened."

"Dianne, listen. I may be able to get loose. I don't know what I'm going to do, but whatever I do I won't leave you here. Dietz? Myke? Can you hear what I'm saying? Just keep your eyes open, all right? Be ready to move as quickly as you've ever moved in your lives." She paused for a moment, as if to consider whether the rest of it needed to be said. "I think I can fool him," she said finally. "I'm going to try to get him to take me back there. He's interested in me. . . ."

She trailed off mid-sentence. The chunky girl started to say something, then, apparently, thought better of it.

"Kate?" the close twin said softly. "Can we . . . can we do anything?"

"No, Dianne," she said. "I'll be careful."

"Get his knife," Whittaker said.

She looked at him, where he sat now on the floor. The young people looked at him too.

Kill him with it, he was going to say. *Put it hard right into the middle of him.*

The four who sat at the table looked down as if he had already said it.

12

The room was darker now that Karpus had gone away with one of the two lanterns. The fire had died to coals on the stove grate and with the door open the heat was going out of the shack. Whittaker could feel the cold, especially where it came through the floorboards, and he was glad for the fact he still had his parka on. His hands and feet had felt numb for too long a time; he had made no progress at all in loosening the ties.

There was not much chance that Kate would be able to handle the fat man. If she was smart enough and lucky enough, she might manage to get hold of his knife, but though Whittaker had seen she was possessed of a certain toughness, he doubted it went deep enough to allow her to use the knife. There would not be time to screw around, to run a ladylike bluff. If she got the knife she would have to use it quickly. Otherwise the man called Johns would take it away from her, and he did not like to think what might happen after that.

The girl on the cot behind the blanket was crying quietly now, he could hear her. The chunky girl called to her that things were going to be all right. The others called to her too in a chorus of reassurance. Then one of the twins also began to cry. Were things going to be all right? He doubted it very much, and felt within him, as he swelled his wrists and forearms against the tight circle of rope behind him, a rising of helpless rage. Why was the fat man taking so long to come back into the shack? He shook his head in disgust. Why had he, Whittaker, allowed himself to be taken so easily? With all his experience, he should have done better. He should be out there now, undetected, ready to move.

Karpus was smart. He was quick, obviously strong. Six hours with a dentist and he might have passed as the vice-president of a suburban bank. Then why had he done the things he had? Something in the chromosomes, Whittaker thought, some genetic foul-up that had started with Cain. Easier to understand the other one, grotesque, unsure of himself, neither smart nor quick, nor strong, he could not have passed for anything except what he was: a misfit, a man whose change had always been short. What was he capable of if the circumstances got right? Raping a child? Shooting a man in the back?

"Christ, be careful" he said suddenly, glancing up at Kate. "Don't take any chances with him."

She shook her head, looked away toward the door as if steeling herself for what she knew was about to take place.

The fat man came in finally with a load of wood in his arms, grunting and wheezing as if he had taxed himself in the gathering of it. He built up the fire, slammed the door shut, took a long pull from the bottle of whiskey.

"I'd like some of that too," Kate said. Her voice was not strong.

The man looked surprised. He lowered the bottle, looked across the room at her as if he had not expected anyone to speak to him, especially not this one.

"Take it easy," Whittaker warned.

"Your name is Johns, isn't it?" she said.

He nodded.

"Well, Johns," she said. "May I have a drink too?"

He glanced at the bottle, then at the woman who was talking to him. Whittaker thought the fat man was trying to make up his mind what to do. He looked as if a small steel ball was rolling around the convolutions of his brain, waiting to drop into the right hole.

"You better be sure your friend is gone first," the pilot said.

"Shut up," Johns told him. "If I want to give somebody a drink I'll do it. I don't need to ask anybody." He went to the door and opened it, looked out, closed it again. Then he hitched up his pants, unsnapped the leather loop that secured the upper handle of his knife and came over to the place where Whittaker sat, but not too close. "You shut up," he said. "I've cut the nuts off a bigger man than you." He took the knife out and pointed it at the pilot. Whittaker could see the lantern light glint along the blade which looked clean, unused.

"Don't bother with him," Kate said. Her voice this time held until the end of what she had to say. "I really would like a drink."

When Johns returned the knife to its scabbard, his hand shook. He wiped the neck of the bottle on his T-shirt and held it for her while she drank. Whittaker could see the whiskey spill down the side of her mouth and neck. *Jesus, be careful,* he thought.

"You're a whore," Johns said when she had finished. "Karpus said you were. You drink like one and you don't wear anything under your shirt. That's why you're different than these other ones."

"All right," she replied, as if she had not heard him. "Please untie my feet."

He laughed. "Why should I?" he wanted to know.

"Because I would like to get it over with, that's all. I'd like to go behind the blanket. I don't want . . ." She looked at the girls at the table. "I don't want them to see us."

The fat man seemed to be puzzled. Then, slowly, he began to grin. "You *are* one," he quipped. "I saw them in Mexico. They do it for four bucks there. American."

"Look," she said, as if to let him know she understood something about him that the others did not, "at least take me back there and make it look good. Otherwise your friend . . ."

"I don't have to make anything look good," the fat man said. His mood changed abruptly. He slammed the bottle on the table in front of Kate and then went past the pilot and behind the blanket. When he came out, he had the young girl in his arms. He held her the same way he held the firewood, carrying her to the place where his pack was leaning against the wall and setting her down. Kate cried out to her, but she did not reply. Her eyes were closed, her cheeks still red and wet from crying, one cheek redder than the other. "I don't have to make anything look good for you or anybody else," Johns said. "And I don't have to do things the way Karpus does, either. I've got my own way of doing things."

Whittaker could see the fat man's agitation. His face and scalp had reddened in blotches. He knelt down in front of Kate's chair and quickly untied her legs. She watched him, her expression detached, as if he were not untying her legs at all but rather the legs of someone whom she only distantly knew. When the man told her to stand up, she stood and flexed one ankle, then the other. He looked at her legs which were long, slender and smooth where they showed below her high-cut shorts; but he did not seem especially interested in them. He took her by the arm and shoved her along toward the blanket.

"Please don't be rough," she said, glancing once without expression at Whittaker as she passed. "I'm not going to cause you any trouble."

"You bet your ass you're not," Johns said. It sounded odd whenever he talked that way, for his voice was high-pitched and did not quite carry a threat.

As they went by the place where he sat, Whittaker could see that Kate was holding her hands together as if they were still tied behind her, but both ends of the rope hung loose and he prayed the fat man would not notice; he held his breath as the two of them disappeared behind the blanket. Almost at once, he heard the ripping of fabric as if Johns had taken the jersey by the collar and ripped it to her waist; then he heard the same whistle of satisfaction he had heard before.

"You'll have to take down my shorts," he heard her say quietly. Her voice, he thought, was not strong now. He pulled his knees up, tried to reach the ankle rope with his teeth, could not.

"I don't care about that," Johns replied. "That's Karpus's way. I told you I got my own way."

"All right, what?" she whispered. "I'd like to get it over with."

"You'll figure it out," he told her. "You're smart."

For a moment it was quiet except for the wind slamming against the corrugated roof, and the soft hiss of the fire across the room that once again had died to embers. Whittaker twisted to look at the girls at the table. In profile the shocked faces of the twins were alike: eyes slightly wide, lips slightly parted; looking as if each were holding her breath. *We're finished,* he thought. But then, as he was about to look away, he saw the girl Myke bring her hands in front of her, rub them briskly, then bend forward in her chair and begin to untie the knots that secured her ankles to its front legs. He thought she must have been working at it as long as Kate had, and he felt a brief surge and then a falling of hope, for there was no real chance, no time.

He tried to get the girl's attention, but she was intent upon what she was doing. She seemed to be having trouble with one of the knots. Now the twins were watching her too. Their expressions were somber as if they assumed that whatever it was she was trying to do was not at all likely to work. He writhed against his own bonds, glancing at the blanket. He could hear the fat man's wheezing breath, conspicuous now and angry. Suddenly, the chunky girl was free. She stood up, wobbled, looked as if she might fall. The floor squeaked under her weight. When he saw she was going to come to him, he shook his head, tried to indicate she should go out through the door, get out and away, but she came stolidly toward him and the floor squeaked loudly under her and even before she began to kneel at his side and work at the rope that fastened his hands he heard the fat man's hoarse voice say something from behind the blanket and heard the woman's urgent reply.

"*Hurry*," the pilot breathed. "*I am*," she told him. Then his hands were free and he snapped forward and together he and the girl tore at the knots that fastened his legs, working furiously in the half-dark and chill of the room while the north wind came through the chinks with enough force now to brighten the embers in the stove and cause the lantern to flicker and move the blanket behind which the fat man's voice again was heard, a quizzical, angry and impatient whine. Then the young woman blurted suddenly: "*Please finish it, please . . .*"

Then he was free. He stood, legs so numb beneath him he too thought he might fall as he half ran, half hobbled across the room, stooping to snatch from the pile near the stove a solid length of wood, not pausing on his way to the blanket which he tore from the rafter with his left hand, raising the chunk of wood with his right, bringing it down with all the strength he had in a glancing blow against the side of the fat man's scalped head; and under the impact of that blow, the man, who had been straddling the narrow cot, groaned and rolled back from the half-naked woman who knelt before him; and when Whittaker saw she held the bowie knife, its glinting, unused blade an unfamiliar extension of her small hand, he said, with his blood pumping a red rage through him, "Give that to me, *give it to me. . . .*"

"*No,*" she breathed, covering herself with one arm, holding the knife out of reach with the other.

"Finish him then. . . ."

"No. He can't hurt us now. Can't you see that? He can't do anything now."

He turned to the body of the man who now lay on his back on the cot, unconscious; turned and planted his feet and gripping one end of the length of wood he raised it with purpose above his shoulder.

13

Horrified, she saw what he meant to do, saw the thick vein that leapt along his neck, the livid color that suffused his face. *Don't,* she thought, stunned to immobility by her own conflicting needs: the need to cover herself, the terrible need to be sick, the need to place herself somehow between this murderous man and the man he meant to kill, the fat and now injured form that lay unconscious at her knees. The wind blew in a fury against the cabin wall; she felt her skin crawl, tried to move, could not.

Her own plan would have worked, had been working until the pilot had interfered. She had done what she had to do with the fat man, had done it as well as she knew how, and after the first uncertain minutes when he had resisted her, had looked down at her with such contempt as she had not seen before in her life, he had begun to go along, had begun to work with her. And once he had, she had done it the way her husband had taught her, with the same seriousness of purpose he had taught her to work the moving parts of his guns; had finally found the handle of the knife, had begun to draw it free of its scabbard, had heard sudden noises from the other room, had heard him grunt, seen him turn to gaze into the opacity of the blanket, had redoubled her efforts to bring him back, had begun to sense he was ready as she had always been able to sense it with Paul and the others, the few there had been. Then, at the penultimate moment she had slipped the blade out of the scabbard, had pulled back from him, and the blanket had been ripped away. . . .

Now she did move to put herself between the fat man's body and the pilot's poised club.

"Don't," she said hoarsely. *"Please."*

He looked as if he might destroy her as well. She was still kneeling, but now her torso was over the unconscious man's, and close, as if she had been surprised in the act of mounting him. Her left hand was flat on the cot, touching the man's thick neck; she had raised her right arm to deflect Whittaker's blow.

For what seemed an interminable moment, he looked down at her. Then at last he lowered the club, his hand shaking; lowered the club and walked away, going to the door, opening it, gazing out. Kate got up, hurried to Pam where Myke already knelt, working at her ropes.

"How is she?"

"Okay I think. . . ."

"Pam honey," Kate breathed, helping her stand, putting her arms around her. "Oh, Jesus, baby . . ." She could feel the girl tremble, feel her tears run between her own breasts. She closed her eyes.

"Kate?" she heard.

"Yes, Myke."

"I untied Dianne; she's untying Dietz now."

"Good."

"Dianne thinks we should climb the mountain and get away before that other man comes back."

Kate shook her head. She felt weak, embarrassed under Myke's somber gaze. She wondered if she would be able to do anything more now than go outside and be sick and then come back and wash out her mouth with some of the whiskey that was left. Across the room she saw Dianne on her knees, working at the knots that bound her sister's legs.

"We'll see," she said tiredly. "There's a knife on the cot. Take it to Dianne. She needs it. I can't leave Pam."

"Sure. . . ."

"Tell the others to come here as soon as they're free."

"Okay."

Myke waddled away. Kate felt dizzy. Whittaker was rummaging in the packs. She wanted to sit down, wanted to sit with her knees drawn up, her elbows resting on them, her face in her hands as she had once liked to sit under the willow tree in the backyard of the house where she had lived with Paul before she had left him. *It's not over,* she thought. When she heard the odd but unmistakable sound of cellophane tearing she looked to see the pilot standing next to her, pulling the pins from a store-new red flannel shirt.

"Put this on," he said abruptly, as if he did not approve of her standing there half dressed as she was. "I found it in one of their packs. I thought they might have another gun, but they don't. No bullets. Nothing. He didn't take any chances." He looked at the girl who had been raped, put his hand gently on her head. "I'm going outside and look around," he said. "Whatever we do, we're going to have to move fast."

She nodded. He turned and walked away. Pam shuddered against her. "It's all right," Kate whispered. "We'll be all right."

When she put on the shirt it was much too large so

she had to roll up the sleeves and leave the tails outside
her shorts. She tried to collect herself. Already it seemed
they were wasting time. Dianne had said what? They
should climb the mountain. Hurry to it and climb it and
be gone before he came back. But they had no idea when
he was coming back. He had said a couple of hours.
Already some of that was gone. Twenty minutes? A half-
hour? She glanced at the window in the cabin's west wall,
was startled to see quite clearly the tall form of the pilot
who stood with his back to the window, looking at something or for something out there in what had become the
bright light of the moon. She watched him briefly, then
shivered and turned away.

The twins appeared at her side, breathless with sobs
of relief that this much of the ordeal had come to an end.
Myke hung back with an expression that hinted their
excitement was only partially shared. Pam stood quietly
now, her small hands clasped in front of her. Kate
wanted to hold her again, but the twins were bursting
around her—they had looked at the fat man who lay
motionless on his back on the cot, trousers still open,
mouth open, blood seeping from his ear; they had
looked at him once, then averted their eyes.

"It's the only way we can get out," Dianne insisted,
gulping breath as she tried to deliver her plan. "We can't
go the way we came, or along the stream, because he'll
be coming back that way and see us for sure; and even
if he didn't, even if we hid until he went by and then
tried to run, he'd only catch up to us, only come after
us. . . ."

"He'll never think we're on the mountain," her sister put in. "Dianne and I can each lead a rope if you want
us to. . . ."

"All our stuff is up there," Dianne went on. "And
there's plenty of light with that moon. One of us can take

Pam, and the other can take Myke; and maybe you and that man . . ."

Whittaker, who had circled the shack, returned. He walked quickly past them and when he reached the cot he put his hand along the thick neck of the man who lay unconscious there. *My God,* Kate thought. She had started toward him when she realized he was only trying to find the man's pulse.

"Is he alive?" she asked weakly.

"Yes."

"Is he badly hurt?"

"I don't know. Frankly I don't care if he is."

She nodded. *Yes,* she thought. *You've made that clear.*

"There's no sign of the other guy," he said. "Not yet anyway."

Myke looked at him. "Dianne thinks we should get away from here by climbing the mountain," she said tentatively, sounding to Kate as if she might abide by whatever judgment the man made, as if the chunky girl thought he were by virtue of his sex the rightful leader of the group.

"I think it's a good idea," Kate said. She thought her voice might have sounded all right, but she did not feel strong. "If we hurry we should be well up on the face by the time he gets back here. If we're lucky, he won't suspect what we've done until it's too late. We can cross the summit, find a place to hide below the ridge. . . ." She had not thought what they would do then.

"If it were up to me," Whittaker said, "I'd try setting up an ambush, try hitting him somewhere along the creek trail."

"But we couldn't be sure he'd come back that way," Dianne said quietly, not to Whittaker but to Kate. "He's got those guns. . . ."

"What chance would we have?" she said to Whittaker. "Doing it your way?"

He shook his head. "I don't know. He's smart. He's not going to be easy to fool, that's for sure. The moon's in and out from behind those clouds. . . . An even chance maybe . . . Maybe not that good. It would depend on a lot of things."

"Then I think we should climb out," she said. "I agree with the girls."

"I thought of that too," he replied.

"Do you think it will work?"

He had seemed apologetic for a moment, as if he had not meant to butt in. He was tying the fat man up, stretching his legs along the cot, feet together, and she winced when she saw how tightly he drew the circle of rope.

"It will work fine if he doesn't spot us," he said. "But if he does spot us, if he gets himself in range with that rifle of his . . ."

She watched him turn the man over, pull his arms together, cross his limp wrists behind him. More blood had collected around the man's ear.

"Please don't hurt him," she said.

"Look," he said, "I don't give a damn whether I hurt him or not. I'm going to tie him tight and stick a rag in his mouth. . . ."

"All right. . . ."

"If it bothers you, why don't you take these people and go outside. . . ."

"Are you going to come with us?"

"When I'm through here."

"You don't have to be harsh. . . ."

"Go on," he said. "Get going. I'll catch up."

She helped Pam up, took the bottle on their way past

the table, went out onto the porch, stood by its single rail in the ice wind, rinsed her mouth with the whiskey, spit it out, rinsed again, swallowed this time, felt its warmth descend to the pit of her stomach. She had never taken that much in one time in her life.

The twins had followed her and Pam; they were already hurrying along the creek trail. She started to call them back, but stopped herself; they were old enough to take care of themselves, knew where to go, where the rucksacks were. *Where* Neil *was.* But they knew that too, they all knew that.

Pam was standing next to her at the porch rail, silent, shocked, her eyes fixed on the farthest bend of the moonlit trail as if she expected to see the tall man returning, his light coming toward her, his obscene whisper filling her ears.

"Take some of this," Kate said.

"I don't want any. . . ."

"Take a sip. It will make you feel better." She held the bottle to the girl's lips, heard her swallow and cough. "Are you all right?" she asked. "Did he hurt you very much?"

"I bled. . . ."

"A lot?"

"I don't know. I think it stopped. . . ."

Kate held her close. "You were brave," she whispered. "I love you. Don't cry. Not yet. We can't cry yet."

We can't, she thought. *We've got to run now. We've got to get away from this place.*

Then they were hurrying along the creek trail, she and Pam, running with the wind at their backs. After they had gone a mile, they turned up onto the talus and the wind came along their right sides. The moon was bright when it showed, but it did not show as often as it had, for the clouds were coming in from the north like sleek black ships. She guessed there would be a storm; higher up, it might even snow. Take everything that's warm, she thought. She helped Pam find her way through the treacherous maze of rock that had fallen from the face, heard the scrape and thud of boulders shifting under them, tried to be careful but move quickly too, tried to think what had to be done, tried to keep cool. She had lost sight of the twins. And where was Myke? Had she come out of the shack? She could not remember. She felt a sudden sinking in her heart: She was following reck-lessly a plan that had not been her own; the pilot had been right; maybe some sort of trick would have worked. But he had not seemed at all sure either, had said the odds were no better than even. And these girls were hers, not his. Myke! She wanted to shout. Answer me! But the wind was stopping her breath almost, and now the light of the moon falling off, Pam stumbling, almost falling beside her. . . .

"Hold tight to me," she said.

"I can't. . . ."

"Hold on to my shirt. . . ."

"I'm *freezing*. . . ."

"There are clothes in the packs. We're almost there. I can see Dianne, see, see up ahead? Hold on to my shirt. Hold tight. . . ."

Don't cry. Not yet.
We can't cry yet.

14

At first Whittaker thought everyone had fled the shack except for himself and the unconscious man whom he had bound and now gagged, turning him belly-up on the aluminum-frame cot. He took no comfort in knowing this man was still alive, a fact he had been prepared to alter had it not been for Kate. His own survival and that of the others depended as far as he could tell on the elimination of the two similar if unequal factors that had threatened it: the tall man with the guns who had gone away from the shack; and the fat man with the knife who had stayed behind.

When the tall one returned he would free the fat one, give him the automatic perhaps, and such hopes as the rest of them had of escape would have been reduced by a certain percentage. Five? Ten? Fifteen? Depending on the situation. Whatever, it was not anything that Whittaker wanted to give away, and even now, although his rage had diminished to a level where the killing, were he to do it, would have to be cold-blooded, he wondered briefly whether he should not do it anyway, do it and say nothing to the others.

But it was here he realized they had not all left the shack: One of them had remained behind; the stocky one in the sweatshirt and bedeviled hair. She stood in the center of the drafty room, having watched him, apparently, at his work at the cot.

"I could help," she said, shrugging. "But I don't know what to do."

"I thought you were off and gone with the others."

She shook her head. "If you're going to stay, I'd like to stay too, if that's okay with you. If I wouldn't be in the way or anything."

"What, are you worried about doing that climb?"

"Yeah," she said as if disgusted by the fact.

"Come on," he replied, clapping a hand on her shoulder. "Let's get out of here before the rest of them get too far ahead of us. You and I'll stick together, all right?"

"Sure."

"Is Kate a good climber?" he asked.

"Oh, yeah, she's one of the best in our club. Some of us think she *is* the best. The twins are good too. . . ."

He nodded, threw Johns's pea jacket over him, the man still unconscious on the cot.

He let Myke go through the door first, out onto the porch; then he went after her, pulling the door shut behind him, following her down the rickety steps, following her down the narrow creek trail.

He tried to estimate how long it might take the six of them, climbing in three ropes of two, to reach the summit and descend to the snowfields below the west ridge where they could hole up until the storm that was evidently coming in had time to do whatever it was it was going to do and go away again. They were going to need time.

Already it troubled him that he had not made his own decision as to the best means of escape but had, instead, persuaded himself there was not much difference between the options available—all of which were poor in his view; had been unwilling to take upon himself the responsibility of choice; had simply gone along. Used

to leading in combat, he was discovering now that he
could not lead here. For Christ's sake why? he wondered.
Because of what happened with me and Marie and the
kids? Because of that rat's ass of a war? So far, it had been
Kate and Myke who had done the work.

So maybe going up the east face was the best chance
they had. He knew they were no match for Karpus and
his guns. If the man had been less canny, an ambush
could have worked, something set up along the trail, a
diversion, the bowie knife used as he had been taught to
use it. But Karpus might make his approach to the shack
indirectly and would not be easily fooled. The fact that
he knew about the loggers' road out of Morgan indicated
a knowledge of the basin which, coupled with his
strength and the range of his rifle, would give him the
advantage in pursuit even if they were simply to hide
themselves until he passed on his return to the shack and
then make a run for it.

But the mountain was vast, and only a practiced
climber would be able to negotiate its precipitous face.
Here he and Kate and the four girls would have an advantage. If they made the ascent safely, their prospects,
he thought, would be good. Once they had roped down
the west ridge, Karpus's chances of finding them would
be small. The others could remain holed up. With luck,
he could make his way to his truck and the revolver he
had left in the glove box. Almost certainly Karpus would
waste time looking for signs along the creek trail, for he
had no way of knowing that the pilot had come in over
the pass or that he or any of the others knew of its
existence.

But he was extremely tense now as he followed
Myke up the forty-five-degree talus to the start of the
thousand-foot wall, wondering if what he was doing

made sense, wondering now if it might not be better for the rest were he to remain behind, to do what he could in stopping Karpus or, at least, in slowing him down. But the idea of escape was a lovely idea. He wanted very much to believe in it. Needed to.

He peered ahead. The light of the moon was lost behind clouds. The east face was immense now and close; the twins, he thought, must have already reached it; Kate too, and Pam. In front of him Myke's silhouette swayed and pumped against the demands of the slope. Even with the wind as brisk as it was he could hear her labored breath and guessed that although she was trying hard to keep a good pace she knew she was falling behind.

"You're doing fine," he told her, his own breath coming fast.

"Sure. . . ."

"Just keep it slow and steady, watch for loose rock."

"I'm the kind who doesn't live through these things."

"I wouldn't bet on that," he told her. "It was you who got free of those ropes."

"They didn't tie me as well as the others. They said I was too fat to run away. . . ."

"The hell with them," he said.

"They were sort of right," she admitted. "I joined the Scramblers to try and make friends. . . ." She stopped, breathless, apparently unable to both talk and climb. "I thought I could cook for them or something. I almost died those two days hiking in."

"It's going to be easier going out," he said. "I've got a truck a few miles from here. You can ride in front with me, all right?"

"I'd *ride* anywhere," she said. "I'd *ride* on the roof!"

He smiled.

"Keep it down now," he reminded her.

"Jeez, I forgot. . . ."

"You're doing fine."

"Sure," she replied. "I'll be okay."

But when they finally reached the others at the foot of the wall he saw that she looked up, craning her neck to see its vast reach, and shook her head. Kate had said this one and the young girl Pam were the only ones in the group who had not done the climb at least once before. The twins had already roped up. They stood at the base of the wall, listening as Kate gave them instructions in a low, businesslike voice.

"There should be plenty of pitons already in place," she said. "Otherwise try to use chocks and slings. This wind is going to carry every sound we make so you'll have to signal each other. Do you remember the signals?"

"Yes," one of the twins said. "One tug if I want more rope, two tugs if I want less. Whoever's leading tugs three times at the end of a lead. . . ."

"Four times when the belay is set," the other twin finished.

"Good," Kate said. "If anyone has any trouble, stay right where you are. We'll get to you as soon as we can. You two can alternate leads. You'll make better time than we will so when you get to the traversing ledge just wait for us. Don't try the exit crack by yourselves, all right?"

"We did the crack last year," one of the twins complained.

"Never mind," Kate said. "You do what I say. Understood?"

They nodded. Whittaker saw they were eager to be

off. He wanted to tell them to be careful, wanted to say he liked them, admired the courage they had already shown. But he felt reluctant to speak, reluctant to intrude. Kate, who had smiled briefly at his arrival, hugged each of the twins quickly and they hugged her in return.

"Who's going to lead the first pitch?" she asked.

"I am," one of them replied. Her name was Dianne, apparently. Her sister's name was Dietz. The only way Whittaker could tell them apart was by the color of their parkas: Dianne's was yellow, Dietz's was blue. He smiled, keeping an eye, as he had from the start, toward what showed of the open end of the canyon. "Good luck," he said.

"Thanks," they replied.

"You can take turns carrying this pack," Kate told them, having managed to sort out their gear. "We've got three ropes in all, and three ice axes. I've divided up the climbing iron and slings as evenly as I can. Keep the iron in your pockets; don't let it jingle around."

Then the twin in the blue parka established a belay, sitting astride a boulder at the base of the wall; and the twin in the yellow parka began to climb, following a route that took her a little to the right of the fixed rope that moved to her left on the wind. Whittaker saw at once she was capable and quick. By the time he had stripped his own pack to what he thought were essentials, she had gone a hundred feet up the wall and was, from a standing position, taking in the rope while her sister climbed up to join her.

He began to feel better, began to think maybe these people had been right, maybe this was the best way, the best chance they had. Intermittently the light of the moon fell upon the mountain's face, illuminating it as brightly as day; but otherwise its surfaces were shadowed.

"The twins are good," he said to Kate.

She smiled and asked him if he had led the climb before and he told her he had. "I'll take Pam if you like," he said.

"No," she replied. "I'd rather take her myself. Can you and Myke . . ."

"Sure. We'll be fine."

"All right, I guess we're ready," she said. She had put a blue parka and blue windpants on over the red flannel shirt and shorts. When she put her arms around the girl, she kept them there for a longer time than she had the twins, saying finally: "Do the best you can. I'll be with you all the way up."

Whittaker saw the girl cling for a moment to the woman who tried to comfort her. "Please," he heard her whisper in a voice so uncertain that he felt a tightening in his own throat and looked away as if by looking on in this moment he had unwittingly violated the privacy of a trust. He squinted up at the dusky wall. The twins had already gone up another lead; he was having difficulty locating their position.

"Goodbye, Myke," Kate said. "Be careful, all right?" Then, she began to climb.

She finished the first hundred-foot lead in quick time, and he was relieved to see by that that she was indeed very good—her movements swift, certain; her feet and hands shifting from hold to hold as if she had studied this route, had practiced it as she might have practiced a simple sonata on the violin, over and over until her performance was without flaw. But when she signaled with the rope to indicate she had established her belay, he had to speak to the young girl, Pam, tell her it was time to start and how she should begin. She fell twice as she went up slowly. She uttered no sound either time, and both times Kate held her slight weight easily from above until she had regained her holds.

Then Kate went up another lead, and Whittaker tied in to one end of his own rope and shouldered his red pack. "Okay?" he said to Myke, who had tied the other end of his rope around her stout waist and sat now astride the same boulder where the others had sat, ready to belay.

"Sure," she replied cheerfully, but that was all she said. She had found her parka in one of the packs, had given it to Pam to wear. She hugged herself and shook her head as if to say it was pretty cold, but not too cold.

"Give me plenty of slack," he said. "When it's your turn, you do the best you can. If I think you're having trouble, I'll give you some help on the rope."

"I've practiced a lot," she told him. "I'm just not very good."

"You'll be an ace by the time we finish this."

"That's what I'm worried about."

"You'll be fine," he said.

But he was not at all sure. It seemed to have taken much too long to get under way, and between here and the traversing ledge he remembered at least a half-dozen exacting pitches which were bound to slow them down. Just before he began to climb, the moon appeared briefly from behind the clouds, and he looked over his shoulder, across the talus and down to the place where the canyon began to curve and the creek trail wound out of sight. By his watch it had been just forty minutes since they had left the shack. Karpus had been gone over an hour. There was no sign of him now, but Whittaker knew even if they were lucky it would not be long before the man returned. If he heard nothing suspicious as he passed, he would go to the shack first, see what had happened there, attend to his friend. Then he would start to look for them. Would he guess the route they had taken in their attempt to escape? He tried to imagine himself in Karpus's place.

He'll come here, he decided finally. *He'll check sooner or later to see if we picked up the gear.*

Then he put his hands on the rough solid granite of the wall and made his first moves up. The wind hummed against the fixed rope that had been left earlier that day; he could see that rope, lighter in color than the wall, its graceful length blown in an arc by the wind to the left of his way. At the top of the talus, not far from the boulder where Myke sat on belay, the body of a man named Neil lay under the pilot's neoprene tarp.

He had died instantly, a bullet through his back.

15

At what had been the site of the climbers' camp, Karpus sat cross-legged on the ground in front of a small, smokeless fire which he had kindled within a circle of stones atop a thin bed of old coals. A casserole of Spam and baked beans was warming in a two-quart aluminum pot which he had balanced on a stone along the windward edge of the fire. Whenever the contents of the pot began to simmer, he would stir them idly with an army-surplus mess-kit spoon. The Weatherby rifle lay on the ground at his left; the automatic, out of its holster, on his lap. He had positioned himself in such a way that he could watch both trails that led into the canyon: the game trail, which went high along the top of the east-wall talus and the regular trail which went low along the west bank of the stream. Some bad weather that had bred in the North was on its way here: wind gusting up; blown clouds under the moon.

He had reconnoitered the basin and found it deserted as he had expected to find it. There had been no fires visible, no winking of flashlights or lantern glow. The pilot had tried to lie about some other people coming into the basin, and Karpus counted it against him that he had lied badly.

Some people could lie well, others could not. The pilot obviously could not, and that made him vulnerable to those who could. Vulnerability was a condition that Karpus had avoided since he had been a child. Johns could not lie either. Whenever he tried to do so he would look over the head of the person to whom he was talking as if to say, I am about to tell a lie. If I were not about to tell a lie I would not be looking over your head. Karpus smiled, put a handful of dry sticks, one by one, onto the small, wind-whipped fire he had made.

Johns had lied to him about what he had done in Truth or Consequences, and about Senator Montoya, and about some other things as well. But it did not matter, because every time Johns had lied to Karpus he had looked over Karpus's head.

The people who had pitched their tents in this place would not be good liars either. The one Johns liked, maybe, but maybe not even her. If she was married she might go out on her husband once in a while, get herself laid in a motel somewhere and lie about that when she got home—because that was what married men and women did—but her kind would not do much else. She had not bothered trying to pretend some people were on their way up here, and that, as far as he was concerned, made her smarter than the pilot.

These people who had come here to climb had outfitted themselves with very fine gear. He had gone over it, item by item. It was not like the crap he had gotten out of that store in Salt Lake, the kind he had always been used to: army surplus mostly, bulky, lead-heavy, tough to haul. Their stuff was compact and light. Two of their sleeping bags rolled tight took up less space and weighed less than a single one of the kind he and Johns had carried in. One of their two-man tents folded down to the size of a seat cushion and he doubted that even with its poles and fly it went more than seven or eight pounds.

He stirred the casserole, put some more small sticks on the fire, yawned, scratched his face, which, he reminded himself, needed a shave. Johns might ask him why he had not known about this good equipment. If so, he would say he had known about it, but the store they had shopped in had not carried any. Maybe it had, though. The pistol in his lap was a Colt Gold Cup National Match .45 which the guy had told him (before Karpus had hit him and taken it) listed for about $140. The Weatherby had gone for over twice that, so maybe the store did have this kind of gear and he had walked right by it because he had not known how much better it was than that army-surplus crap he had always depended on before.

Well, he thought, we've got ourselves some good outfits now. He could see them across the fire, two of the climbers' rucksacks fully packed and ready to haul, plus one of their orange tents. The rest of the stuff he had taken down into the timber a ways and stashed under a ledge of rock that blind-sided the trail, where it was not likely to be found any time soon. He did not personally care one way or the other whether it was found or not.

It was Johns who cared. He really was a pisser when he got on to something like that. He'd worry it to death. He'd think he was not bringing it up very often, but he would bring it up about every fifteen minutes or so. "What about those fucking *tents?*"

Karpus shook his head, smiled, lifted the pot away from the fire. The pot was scalding hot, but he dealt with it as if it were not hot, holding it deliberately in his bare hand, placing it to cool just where he wanted it, on the ground by his right side. The wind kept the center of his fire a bright red-orange, and if he had been the sort of man—which he was not—who regularly recalls events out of his past, this fire might have reminded him in miniature of a smelting furnace he had looked into once when he had been a boy in Morenci.

His father had been shop boss on the graveyard shift and had brought him in one night, had opened the door to the big smelter and shouted at him over the din of machinery that he should take a good long look because that for a fact was what hell looked like.

Karpus had been eleven years old at the time. His brother had been sixteen, and just before his father had opened the furnace door, his brother and the other men around him had tied handkerchiefs over their mouths and noses, but his father had not and so young Karpus had not either. When the door had flung open he had taken in a large quantity of sulfuric smoke which had seared his lungs and shut off his breath until he had thought he would faint. But he had given no indication of the distress he felt. Instead he had concentrated on the terrific inferno within the smelter itself, had imagined what it would be like to walk slowly into such an inferno and turn and stand while his flesh melted from his skeleton, stand without uttering a sound, looking out at his father and brother.

He ate the Spam and beans as he ate all of his meals, slowly and without irritation or pleasure. He did not review the events of the day. Occasionally an image would come to him: the child belly-down on the cot; the climber falling back from the cliff; the deer in the moment before it was struck. But these were simply pictures in his mind, so many unnarrated slides flashed at random, provoking in him no special sense of satisfaction or consequence. And although he was capable of laying intricate plans for the immediate future, he did not typically do so and did not do so now. Instead he sat comfortably cross-legged before the small fire he had built, alert, confident that he would prevail in whatever might befall him, even if what befell him might include the end of his life.

He finished the Spam and beans, put the spoon and pot on the ground beside him, then took out his cigarettes, lit one, flaring the match to life under the nail of his thumb. When he saw that a mouse had come into the small circle of firelight, he watched it while he smoked. The mess-kit spoon, lumpy with bits of casserole, was still lying on the ground next to the pot, and it was evident the mouse had gotten wind of that spoon and wanted to eat from it. But it was also evident that the mouse was wary of the man who sat so close by.

"Go ahead," he said hoarsely. "Get yourself some food."

The rodent, as if it had understood him, darted in, took something from the spoon and streaked away again. It did this several times, filching all of the best that was on the spoon.

"You got yourself a set of balls," Karpus said.

The deer that morning had not. It had stood for what he had done to it as if that had been its proper fate. So had the girl on the cot. She had not uttered a sound, and although he had not been troubled by her passivity in any way—it was her concern, not his—he had wondered briefly what accounted for it.

Whatever accounted for it, it seemed to confirm what he had always believed anyway: that the meek were not going to inherit the earth. At least the fat, homely one in the sweatshirt had been trying to get her hands free. She had been steadily picking away at the knots Johns had tied. This had been, in fact, one of the reasons Karpus had decided to leave the shack. Somehow, Johns was going to have to learn how to deal with things like this. If he did not learn, he would have to spend the rest of his days holding the same short end of the stick he had always held until Karpus had stood up for him.

Because he had never cared for anyone—not even for himself in a way—the fact that he had begun to care for Johns had become a matter of curiosity to him, and he had tried to account for it. Part of it was in the nature of challenge, something he had always liked. Throughout the prison, among inmates and guards alike, he had discovered Johns a subject of ridicule, contempt, the lowest on what was an intricate, brutish and unusually fixed pecking order. He had taken Johns out of that pecking order in a single evening and had kept him out of it. He had used Johns too, of course, but only in the beginning; only before he had begun to realize that his feelings toward the fat, hapless man had become for him unique. "I like what you've done for your cellmate," the warden had told him when he had finally granted the joint furlough. And although this had changed nothing in his overall view of things, and quite to his own surprise, Karpus had found that he liked it too.

He finished his cigarette, reached for another, felt the pilot's wallet in the breast pocket of his mackinaw. Idly, he took it out and, turning so the firelight might fall upon them, he began to look at the pictures of Whittaker's family and home. Here were two children, a boy and girl, looking into the camera with pensive expressions as if whoever had posed them had tried too energetically to get them to smile. After he had gazed at it for a moment, he removed this picture from its clear plastic folder and lay it on the fire where it slowly began to curl, its surface becoming brown and bubbly and then gray-white and cratered as the distant surface of the moon.

And here was a picture of the pilot's home, an expensive-looking house with what appeared to be a half-acre or more of lawn and trees. He laid this picture on the fire as well, and also the picture of the pilot's pretty wife, a woman with brown hair and brown eyes who looked to be younger than he was.

He kept the picture of the pilot himself who sat in the uncovered cockpit of a sleek fighter plane, his helmet off, his expression that of a reliable man who liked what he did and who knew he was good at it. In the secret compartment of the wallet, behind the many denominations of bills, he found a yellowed newspaper clipping which he removed and read, unfolding it carefully so that it would not tear along its several worn creases. A headline in boldface that ran across four columns of what apparently had been the front page read:

U.S. PILOT HELPS A.R.V.N. IN AMBUSH

And below that, in smaller type:

112 VC DEAD COUNTED

Karpus read the article twice, then folded it carefully and put it back into the wallet in the open compartment with the bills. He studied the credit cards briefly, then

put them one after the other on the fire, keeping the
military I.D. that indicated the pilot had retired with the
rank of major.

Karpus's brother had looked remarkably like this
pilot, a brother who had been preferred by both parents
and who had for a period of time beaten young Karpus
up on a daily schedule, coming home from school,
finding him, taunting him and, when that failed to pro-
duce the desired result, beating him. Because the parents would not intervene on his behalf, Karpus had
learned how to absorb that punishment, how to shift his
awareness away from the point of pain until the pain no
longer existed. His brother, having derived no satisfaction, finally gave the beatings up.

This had been an object lesson for Karpus, and he
had thought of it often until he had managed to kill his
brother and then he had not thought about it anymore.
He had killed his brother many times. He had also killed
his father and mother, had killed them over and over
until at last they had left his mind. Now with this pilot it
was as if one of them had come back.

He raised the globe of his lantern and, using a burning stick, he fired the wick, shielding the flame from the
wind with one hand until the wick flared up and he could
lower the globe again. He covered what was left of the
fire with the stones that had contained it. He put the pot
and spoon in a place where they could not be seen, but
where the mouse could find them.

There had been a line strung between two of the
tents before he had taken it and the tents down, a line
that earlier that day had had some towels hanging from
it. Some of them had blown down, apparently, for when
he had returned here he had found several of them
neatly folded under a rock by the fire. He had also found

each of the tents zipped shut though he remembered they had been open when he and Johns had first arrived. He guessed the pilot had stopped here.

He took the two rucksacks he had prepared down-slope and strung them up where they would not be seen. Then he returned to what had been the site of the climbers' camp and stood for a moment, looking out over the basin in the direction of the high pass three miles distant through which he and Johns had come. The pass itself was not visible at this moment, nor were any of the distant high peaks; only the close downslope of trees through whose branches the sound of the wind rose and fell as if the trees were in mourning, as if they had taken root in the burial place of their dead.

When he made his way down to the stream and began to follow it into the canyon, he carried the lighted lantern in his left hand and the Weatherby rifle in his right. Once he was in the canyon, he looked for a place where he might cross the stream and he did cross the stream finally, picking his way carefully after that over terrain that was rough and had not been worn to a trail.

16

From the start it had been a cold, silent climb except for the noise of the wind. The route was familiar to Whittaker, most of its pitches easy enough that he did not have to take the time to protect himself as he went. In the difficult pitches he usually found pitons already driven into the available cracks and left by climbers who had passed this way in previous years.

Whenever he reached one of these pitons, he would remove an aluminum carabiner from the cargo pocket of his combat trousers and quietly clip it to the eye or ring of the driven piton, and would pass his rope through it so the piton might hold him in the event that he fell. Myke, as she came up after him, retrieved these carabiners and gave them to him when they met briefly at the belaying positions he established.

The first 850 feet of the wall were rated 5.3 to 5.6 on the Sierra Club scale, only moderately difficult for practiced climbers, but very exposed and requiring the use of ropes and pitons or chocks for protection. This, the longest sustained section of the climb, consisted of a series of vertical cracks and small ledges complicated by several smooth pitches with small but well-situated holds. Eight hundred and fifty feet up the wall, a steep fifty-foot chimney led to a broad traversing ledge from which they could exit via a hundred-foot-long vertical crack. That final crack, Whittaker knew, was the most difficult pitch on the wall. Once it was behind them the face tilted back and up to the summit and they would be able to negotiate that part easily without ropes.

Twice, in difficult pitches where there were not pitons, he found loops of sling that one of the twins or Kate had tied off around a projection of rock, and, testing them first, he clipped his carabiners into these. Myke climbed slowly and awkwardly, but did not complain. He would anchor himself to the wall above her as best he could, then turn and bring up the rope as she made her ascent. When it was difficult or impossible to see the progress she was making, he would keep the rope tight, and whenever she seemed to have paused too long at any given place he would lean forward and put his back to the rope and, leaning back again, would help bring her up until he could see or sense that she was moving on her own again.

The temperature continued to drop. He guessed it was in the low forties now, perhaps even colder. Except that his fingers would grow numb at times, he felt warm enough as he climbed, but whenever he stood motionless in a belay position, facing the canyon itself, he would shiver in spite of his wool shirt and parka and think, *I could use Sister Agnes's shawl.* He knew Myke could use it too.

"Keep coming," he told her.

"Wow!" She replied.

She had just reached the narrow ledge where he stood belaying her, 400 vertical feet above the place where the talus began its more gradual drop to the canyon floor. The twins, leapfrogging their leads, had long since climbed up and out of sight into the dark shadows of the upper wall. Even when the moon showed, he was unable to locate them, but he guessed that by now they must be nearing the traversing ledge that crossed the face at 900 feet. Kate and Pam had kept a single lead ahead of him. He could hear the muted sound of the girl's boots scraping the wall as she went up.

"How about a drink?" he said to Myke.

She nodded yes, and he handed her his canteen which he carried on a clip at the lower frame of his pack. When he looked north he could see, at a distance of one mile, the small yellow squares of light that marked the windows of the prospector's shack. He knew that smoke no longer rose from the chimney. The fire had died even before they had left. Karpus would spot that. Although Whittaker repeatedly looked for him, there was still no sign of the man.

"Cold?" he asked.

"A little I guess. I'm all right. *Jeez*," she said, glancing up. The wind tugged at her hair. "Doesn't this thing ever end?"

"It does for a fact. We're making good time."

"Neil said . . ." She paused as if she wasn't sure it was appropriate to mention their dead co-leader's name. "Neil said," she continued finally, "that the last hundred feet are awful."

"No," he told her. "They're not all that bad."

"Dianne and Dietz said so too. They did it last year. . . ."

"Climbers who have done a route like to bug the ones who haven't," he said.

She nodded, but he saw she was still tense.

"And," she said, "once we *got* to the top we were supposed to be able to walk down. I guess we won't be going down that way now."

"If he knows anything about the mountain, he'll expect us to come down that way."

"I know. I guess we'll have to rappel then."

"We'll rope down three pitches. You've done that kind of thing before."

"Yeah, I know, but I'm terrible at it. The first time I tried it I turned upside down. Neil . . . Neil had to get me."

He smiled. "I'm ready to climb now."

"Okay," she said, already paying out rope though he had not yet turned to face the wall. "Am I supposed to call you Major Whittaker or what?"

"You call me Matt. You're Myke, right?"

"Right."

"What else does that shirt say?"

In the half-light of the moon, she stuck out her chest so he could read the smaller letters. TRY IT, YOU'LL LIKE IT, they said.

"Beautiful," he replied. "Why did you have to join a club to make friends?"

"I don't know," she said. Then, after a moment, added: "I've always been the kind of person . . . I don't know . . . the kind who people sort of don't look at when they're talking, know what I mean?"

"I look at you, don't I?"

"Yeah. But most people don't. If we're ever in a busy room someplace you'll notice it."

"Hey," he cautioned. "Not too much slack . . ."

"Ooops," she said, and took in some of what she had let out. Then he began to climb again. He had not gone far when he heard her call his name. It was the first time she had done that.

"What?" he answered hoarsely.

"Look," she said.

The moon was not shining on the face just now, but it was shining on the stream. He could see small white clumps of foam whisking south on their way to the fall. Because of the bend in the canyon he could not see the fall, but he could see what it was that had attracted the girl's attention: a bobbing pinprick of light moving north toward the blind end of the canyon and the prospector's shack.

He's coming back along the opposite bank, he thought. *I might have figured that.*

He did not say anything for there was not much, really, to say. The wind was furious and very cold as it blew against him; his fingers and toes were numb. He hoped that Kate and Pam and the twins had noticed the light too and that they would keep quiet as they climbed up toward the traversing ledge.

That ledge was 500 feet above the place where he now stood, balanced on small but comfortable holds, looking over his shoulder, watching the progress of Kar-

pus's lantern as it bobbed along across the creek from
the standard trail. It was closing the distance but was still
a mile at least from the yellow-lit windows that marked
the location of the abandoned shack where before long
he would discover what had happened to the man who
was his friend.

"*Jeez, now I really am scared,*" Myke whispered.

"So am I," Whittaker said. "There's nothing wrong
with being scared."

Then, without saying more, he began once again to
climb.

17

He had had two planes shot out from under him—one
in South Viet Nam, the other in Laos. He had been lucky
both times, although one of his backseaters had not. In
Viet Nam the choppers had come in and picked them
both up before they had been on the ground an hour. In
Thailand, commanding a squadron of night-fighters
flying missions over the Laotian Trail, he had come
down alone in karst country too rough for a pickup, had
had to make his way to a rendezvous sector, traveling at
night, holing up in caves during the day. On the first
night, with the trail still in sight, he had stumbled onto
a small gun emplacement: two men in a camouflaged
revetment. That was the time the revolver had saved
him.

In situations of danger there was nothing wrong
with fear; it was, he knew, an appropriate and understandable response. He also knew that for him, at least,
it had to be tempered in equal parts by his anger and his

will to survive. The balancing of these three elements, delicate and often subtly at odds within him, was something he had learned, had had to learn, in the mountains and in the war.

He had also learned—and this had been more difficult for it was in his nature to care—not to become too fond of the people with whom he climbed or flew in combat. Too many of them, often the best of them it seemed, were lost. As a younger man he had been impetuous, even sentimental, in his relationships with most people. But when he had seen what loss and grief had extracted from him, he had withdrawn, had become in spite of the required conviviality of military life a rather isolated and lonely man.

He thought, as he continued his climb toward the traversing ledge, that he had already begun to care too much for Myke, who payed the rope to him as he went. *I'm the kind who doesn't live through this sort of thing,* she had told him. He thought she might be right, too awkward, too good-natured, too much without cunning to survive in a world across the surfaces of which men like Karpus had always walked.

The man's lantern had stopped bobbing now, the wink of its light distant and steady as if it had been placed on a flat stone. Whittaker watched it over his right shoulder, the wind full against his face, taking his breath, numbing the lobes of his ears. He could not see the trail or the stream or the opposing walls of the canyon or the place 450 feet below him where he knew the young man's body lay under his tarp. The moon was lost behind a schooner of cloud; only the yellow lights of the shack windows showed, and the smaller light of the lantern. He judged the distance between these lights now to be less than half a mile.

He wondered what Karpus was doing. Perhaps he

was resting, but that seemed unlikely. Karpus had not struck him as a man who would pause by the side of a stream in the midst of an oncoming storm, not with a warm shelter in sight. Probably he had noticed something, the fact perhaps that smoke no longer rose from the shack's chimney. He would not be able to see that now, but he could have seen it the last time the clouds had broken in front of the three-quarter moon and the moon's fluorescent light had illuminated the canyon in the ghostly way it did. If Karpus had noticed the absence of smoke, Whittaker knew he would wonder instantly why it was so. Then he would be even more careful as he came in, and that fact, which might have caused an ambush to fail, might now give them just a little more time as they made their way up toward the exit crack and the high summit of Wolf Mountain.

"Why is he just stopped there?" Myke whispered as she joined him at the next belaying site. She sounded afraid, but annoyed too, as if Karpus had somehow disappointed her.

"Don't worry about him," he said softly. "The wind's in our favor now; it'll be harder for him to hear us. Just pay attention to the climbing. If we get off this face before he spots us we're going to be fine."

"That other one—that one called Johns. He was bleeding, wasn't he?"

"Yes."

"Golly," she sighed.

"You're not worried about him, are you?"

"I guess not. It's just that before he went with Kate . . . I mean, he didn't seem as bad as the other one. . . ."

"I'm ready to climb," he told her.

"I guess I felt sorry for him for a while. . . ."

"I don't think he felt sorry for you."

"I know. . . ."

"Watch the rope now."

"I didn't mean I exactly felt sorry for him. . . ."

"Keep still now and watch the rope."

He had not meant to be curt and, realizing that he had, he again put his hand on her shoulder.

"I can't believe Pam is climbing this thing," she said, as if to forgive him while peering up. "I can't believe *I'm* climbing it either."

He went up then another hundred feet, brought Myke to him, went up a hundred more. The point of light from the lantern showed steadily from its place by the creek and he knew, was certain, that Karpus had left it there, had gone up onto the talus either on the east or west side of the water and was moving in on the shack in the same oblique way Whittaker himself had approached it just before Karpus had taken him so easily. He thought Karpus would not take him that easily again, not if they were off the face by the time the man learned what it was they had done.

18

Oh, Jesus, Johns thought. At last, he had managed to open his eyes.

In prison, the therapy guy had loaned him a manual; it had been well thumbed and had had to do with sex. "Look into it," he had said. "Let me know if you have any flashes."

The therapy guy was always talking about "flashes"

and "awarenesses" and "sociopathic behavior," none of which meant anything at all to Johns. The therapy guy wore turtleneck sweaters, and Levi's that looked as if they had been washed in an acid vat, and he always kept an unlit pipe in his hand while he talked.

"Take it with you," he had said, as if the loaning of a sex manual to Johns was comparable to giving Johns a parole. "Look into the chapters that delineate the various classifications of impotence. Let me know if you have any flashes."

The first flash Johns had had was to take the unlit pipe and shove it up the therapy guy's nose, but instead he had simply stood up, trying not to notice the drill bit that was beginning to turn at the top of his skull; had stood up and said, "I don't *like* reading these fucking books," whining away, of course; and the therapy guy had smiled and replied, "I'm not asking you to read it, Johns. All I'm asking you to do is to look at it."

And so Johns had. He had not looked into the chapters delineating the various classifications of impotence because he thought there was a chance he might find something there that could humiliate him. He did skim through the chapters that delineated the various positions of intercourse and actually looked into the material the book contained regarding the nature of wet dreams.

He had heard about these before and like most other areas of his life he was pretty sure he had suffered a malfunction in this one. Periodically, he would have an intense erotic dream during which he would enter a poorly furnished room in a derelicts' hotel in an unfamiliar place where a female—these were always submissive creatures who ranged in age from six to sixty—would, after he had slapped her around a bit, go down on him and lead him to the brink of what promised to be a satisfactory climax, and then he would wake up, erect but quickly subsiding, and there would be no trace of what the therapy guy's manual referred to as a "nocturnal emission." Sheets and shorts dry as a bone. Sometimes he would crawl under the covers in a groggy state of rage, trying to find some sign of what the manual said was routine, particularly among pubescent boys and among men who had marginal sex lives.

The dreams were often so vivid they would live in his mind's eye for days, even weeks, after the event, creating within him a nagging, chronic frustration that nothing he knew would relieve. He had never liked to handle himself down there. His nuts had only partially descended, they ached whenever the weather was cold; he thought his unit was too thin, too short, that it hung oddly and did not look much like the rest of the units he had seen in the foster homes and reform schools and prisons where he had spent a lot of his time. Around other men, he tried to keep himself covered. Urinals intimidated him; he preferred wearing shorts to the shower.

Oh, Jesus, he thought.

He had been ready, knew he had; he had been all set. It was going to work right for once, pretty quick and without a big hassle. He had felt the onset of joy, not for the relief this was going to be—it had, for him, never lived up to its billing—but for the relief it was going to be to be able to say *Fine* when Karpus came back from burying those goddamn tents and asked him in his McKuen voice how everything had gone. Be able to look right at him and say FINE! EVERYTHING WENT FINE! *Did you fix her?* YOU BET YOUR ASS I DID! *That's good, Johns. What do you say we have ourselves a whiskey and a smoke?* SURE! WHY NOT! YOU BET YOUR ASS!

But instead, in the instant before the instant that mattered (just as in his dreams), sitting astride the narrow cot in the poorly furnished room, looking down at a whore's face, something had exploded along the side of his head and he had fallen into a black pit of nothing and every time until now he had tried to crawl up out of that pit—which was many times indeed—he had only gotten dizzy and fallen back in.

Now at last he opened his eyes, saw above him a cobwebby rafter, above that a segment of corrugated roof, the roof segment moving as though buffeted by wind, but he could not hear this wind except remotely, as if the sound of it came to him through a complex of tunnels underground. He could not move his hands or feet. His jacket lay like a small dark blanket over the rise of his belly and chest. He could not speak, could not close his mouth; the muscles in his jaws had tightened in a spasm of pain that was endurable only because the pain in his head was so much more severe and unendurable. It repeated itself in electric waves that began above the left hemisphere of his brain and ended below the socket of his left eye. He could only breathe through his nostrils and these were congested, giving him the constant and horrific sensation that he might drown in his own mucus. He shook with cold.

For an hour he lay in the grip of his pain and a rising terror, even more formidable, that he had been left in this place he despised to suffer and die alone. He wanted to scream and would have except that his mouth had been stopped with something that felt like the butt end of a log. He wanted to sit up, but whenever he tried, a Ferris wheel of brightly colored lights would begin to turn in his brain, would turn faster and faster until he lay back again, feeling an impotent fury that any of this should be his fate. The single rafter-hung lantern was consuming what was left of its fuel in silence. The sound of the wind came to him distantly through its deep tunnels. Tears rolled into the numb wells of his plugged ears.

When Karpus finally appeared, he appeared as a dimly focused vision beside the cot, his rifle caught in the crook of his left arm, his stoic face gazing down. Johns blinked, his surge of relief, of gratitude, touched at once by a flash of fear that he would be blamed for what had happened in this place, and by a pulse of anger as yet indistinct.

Then Karpus was carefully removing the gag from his mouth, gently turning him onto his side, freeing his hands and feet.

"Jesus, I can't hear," he whined, his voice sounding hollow inside his skull. He sat up on the edge of the cot. The Ferris wheel of lights began to turn. He put his hand to the side of his head where it was swollen and crusty, saw Karpus go to their gear (strewn on the floor by their packs); watched him return with a bottle of whiskey and some gauze and a roll of tape. Karpus sat down on the cot, the rifle beside him, and began to work on the head wound, cleaning and bandaging it. Then he soaked some gauze with whiskey and swabbed out Johns's ears until Johns could hear again, but not as well as he had before.

"What the fuck happened?" the fat man whined.

"Somebody got loose and whacked you one."

"Somebody got loose? Who, for Chrissake?"

"That pilot most likely."

"But he was tied up *tight*. . . . I *tied* him."

"Well, he must have got loose somehow."

"Jesus, he really hit me."

"There's a chunk of wood over there's got blood on it."

"What did they do? Fuck up our stuff?"

"Looks like they went through it. That red shirt of mine's gone. Nothing else I can see."

"We better clear out of here," Johns said. "They'll *really* be after us now. . . ."

"You're cold. Stick out your arm and I'll help you get into your coat."

"You know what I mean? They'll be up here in fucking helicopters. . . ."

"Better zip your pants too."

Johns looked down, Ferris wheel turning. "You must have really got your rocks off . . ." he heard Karpus say. *Must have really what?*

". . . 'Fore he whacked you."

"Yeah, well I don't remember. . . ."

Karpus smiled. "It was me," he said, "I'd have remembered that one."

"Yeah but he *hit* me," Johns said. "Jesus, we better get out of here." He tried to stand but could not manage it and sat, finally, with his face in his hands. Karpus sat next to him, smoking a cigarette. *You shouldn't have left me,* Johns wanted to say. *Why the fuck did you leave me here?* He wanted to say it, but his head felt as if someone had pumped it full of molasses, and what was more, he had never said a really critical word to Karpus in all the months he had known him.

"Hurt?" Karpus asked.

"Yes!"

"I got hurt like that once."

"It hurts like a *son*ofabitch."

"There was a deputy sheriff in Morenci—"

"Jesus Christ," Johns said, "we better get out of here. That fucking pilot's probably halfway to town."

"He's not halfway to town."

"Well where the fuck *is* he then? Do you know where

he is?" Johns insisted. And before Karpus could reply, before he himself really knew he was going to say it, he said: "You shouldn't have left me here like you did, you know that? Jesus Christ, if you'd been here it wouldn't have happened, he wouldn't have done anything like this to you. I told you I didn't want to stay here with those fucking people by myself, remember I told you that?"

Karpus did not reply. He smoked his cigarette, and when he had finished it he extinguished the coal between the forefinger and thumb of his left hand and flicked the butt in the direction of the stove. Then he picked up the rifle and walked to the door of the shack and looked out for a while. "Storm coming," he said. "Looks like it's going to settle in pretty soon now."

"I *hurt*," Johns said.

Karpus did not reply. He stood, framed in the door of the shack, looking out where the stream boiled along the canyon floor between the angled talus and the thousand-foot walls, illuminated now under the moon.

"I hurt like a sonofabitch," Johns said quietly. "That's all."

19

Whittaker was establishing his belay stance at a delicate position he estimated at 700 feet above the top of the talus when he heard the hiss of something falling past him, a stone he guessed, dislodged by one of the climbers higher on the wall. He flattened himself against the face, heard another hiss and then another, as if someone were in trouble up there, off route perhaps, scrambling for holds. *Christ, be careful,* he thought. *Don't come off of there now. . . .*

Only the three stones fell, one after the other; then, when he thought it was safe to do so, he looked up. At first he could see nothing, the vast slab of the mountain lost in shadow; but then as the moon began to appear once again from behind its cover of cloud he saw the youngest girl not fifty feet above him, hanging from her rope, swinging in a small arc back and forth. A hundred feet above her, near the start of the chimney below the traversing ledge, Kate, anchored to the wall and facing out, had stopped the girl's fall easily with a standing belay.

The girl was trying to find some purchase on the nearly vertical expanse of rock, but there was, he thought, something halfhearted about her moves, as if she might have reached the end of her ability to go on. Finally, he saw her drop her arms at her sides and hang motionless except when the wind blew hard enough to move her, which was not very hard for she was a slender, fragile girl.

Ordinarily he would have called out; Kate would have called out too. They would have urged her on, tried to give her the encouragement she needed to get herself together again, to find the holds she needed for her feet and hands. But this was no ordinary climb and he knew, and Kate must have known too, that even with the wind howling around them their shouts might be heard, might give them away; and he knew how little time it would take for Karpus, once he had a fix on them, to reach this place. They were high on the wall now, but if he was good or even just lucky he might very well reach them with his long rifle and scope in the intermittent light of the moon. And so he and Kate watched helplessly, he looking up, she looking down, waiting for the young girl to try again, but the girl did not try again.

"Pam," he called hoarsely. She was closer to him than to Kate. *"Can you hear me?"* The girl's body moved in the wind, turning slowly until instead of facing the wall, she faced in the direction of the shack. The moonlight that had been quite bright against the slate-gray surfaces of the mountain was suddenly eclipsed by cloud, and Whittaker, balanced on small holds, peered up, waiting for the pupils of his eyes to dilate. *"Pam,"* he called, *"can you hear me?"*

There was no reply.

Securing himself to the wall by means of a piton already in place and a short length of sling fixed to his waist loop, he brought Myke up to him. She too seemed to take longer than usual. Several times he had to assist her, giving her enough tension on the rope to enable her to climb past a difficult section. The lantern still burned in its place on the trail, as did the light in the windows of the shack. Karpus had to be close by now. Maybe he was already inside.

"What's wrong?" Myke wanted to know when she finally arrived at a spot just below him.

"Pam took a fall," he said. "She'll be all right. I want you to climb up next to me now." He showed her the route she should take. "This is a pretty tight place," he said. "But there's a good solid piton and once you're in position and tied to it you won't mind at all."

She looked for the holds he had told her to use. "I can't see," she said tiredly.

"The moon will come out again. As soon as it does, you make your moves up. Once you're set, I'll go up and help Pam. That may take a little while so don't worry if you think I've been gone too long."

"Like who *worries?*" she croaked.

"You're doing fine," he said.

"Can I hold onto your foot?"

"Sure."

"The book says that's not too cool."

"The hell with the book," he said.

In the next light she came up and he anchored her to the wall. Then, quickly, he made his way up the fifty feet that separated him from the youngest girl. The wind had turned her another quarter-turn so that she now faced directly out from the cliff. Her eyes were closed.

"Pam," he said, climbing up next to her.

She shook her head.

"Let's go," he said. "We're going to be off of here soon and won't have anything to worry about from him. Come on," he said, helping her face the wall again. "There's a hold just above your right shoulder, a good one. Kate will keep the rope tight, so you don't have to worry at all. Put your left foot here on this nubbin, a little to the left and up, let it take most of your weight. That's it, you're doing fine. Reach out with your right hand now. . . ."

"I can't," she said. It was the first time she had spoken directly to him. Her voice was high like the voice of a small child.

"Yes you can," he said. "You're already doing it. Put your right foot on my shoulder if you like; I'm in a good place here. That's it, that's it. . . ."

He talked to her this way, and, with agonizing slowness, she began to move again while a hundred feet above her, not far from the start of the chimney that led to the traversing ledge, Kate took in the rope. He sighed his relief. Of all of them, this girl had suffered most, and he was touched by the courage she had shown, by what she had managed to climb so far and now by her willingness to go on.

She continued to move up very slowly. He moved up just below her, keeping an eye on her small, booted feet as they shifted hesitantly from hold to hold, the left toe pushed into a wide crack now, the right toe testing a nubbin, rejecting it, searching for something more stable, her small form lost in Myke's parka, reaching, stretching a little higher, a little more, the edge of the right boot scraping, holding, the left toe coming out of the crack too quickly, going back into it, but a few inches higher up, always a few inches higher up, always reducing the distance between herself and Kate who never let slack develop in the rope as she took it in from her stance on the wall above while the north wind blew its promise of a storm and the light of the moon rose and fell against the mountain's face.

"You're just about there," he told her. "I'm going to help you now with my right hand. I'm in a good place and you can put all your weight on your right foot and step up. . . ."

"You're doing wonderfully," he heard Kate say above him. She stood on a ledge a foot and a half wide by six feet long, her back to the wall, anchored by a short length of webbing that went from her waist loop to the ring of a driven piton behind her. She brought the climbing rope up from Pam with her gloved right hand, running it across her back just above the short length of webbing that secured her to the cliff, letting the slack rope gather in a pile by her left foot.

"Come on up," she said to the girl. "There's plenty of room for two on this ledge. I'll tie you in as soon as you're here. You're doing wonderfully well, Pam, you really are. Come on now. I'll give you some help with the rope. We're almost out of this mess."

"I couldn't go anymore," he heard the girl say when she had gained the narrow ledge. "He had to help me. . . ."

"That's all right, you're here now, that's all that matters."

He found his own holds and stood facing the wall just below the fifty-foot chimney that began to the right of the belaying ledge. The chimney would be the next obstacle: He remembered it as not being difficult, looked up at it, then looked at the woman a few feet to his left as she secured the girl to the anchor piton. Her blue parka and windpants were as dark as the wall itself when the light of the moon fell off, and her pale, tightly drawn face seemed almost disembodied, betraying an apprehension that had not been betrayed by her voice.

"Thank you for helping," she said. Her tone was formal.

"How are the twins doing?" he asked.

"All right. They've been on that traversing ledge for a long time."

"Myke's doing well too."

"I'm freezing," Pam said. "I feel terrible taking Myke's parka. I'm more trouble than anybody. . . ."

She began to cry. Kate held her, the two of them standing on the small ledge, 850 feet above the talus, just to the left of where Whittaker stood below the start of the chimney. The young girl never looked down.

"Myke can have my parka," he said. "Any time she wants it."

"I have more clothes in this pack," Kate added. "Two ponchos, some socks, gloves, insulated shirts and pants. I can get them. . . ."

"Let's hold that up until we're off the face," he said. "Let's keep moving."

She looked at him in the way she had that made him feel like an intruder, as if, because he was a man and the rest of them were not, she did not quite trust him.

"What do you think he's doing?" she asked finally.

"I don't know."

"He left his light on the trail."

"He may have noticed something. No smoke from the chimney, nobody moving in front of the windows. Whatever it was, he's been a long time checking it out."

"The weather is getting worse. I'm afraid we're going to get rained on. Maybe even snow."

"Probably. Once we get off the face, we'll have to make one hell of a run for the summit. Have you done the west ridge?"

"Yes. Once. It's steep, I remember. Quite a few rappels."

"Just three. Two off the ridge itself and one down a pitch of steep snow below the ridge. We'll have to shoot for that and dig a cave and hole up if this turns out to be as bad as it looks."

"Pam and Myke haven't done much rappelling."

"I wouldn't worry about them. If they've gotten through this much, they shouldn't have any trouble with the ridge."

He shifted his shoulders under the weight of his pack, gripped the hold he had found for his left hand, leaned back, glanced to his right in the direction of the shack. He thought something had changed: a wink of light visible that had not been visible before; the door open now, perhaps; Karpus going in or coming out. Kate had noticed it too. She gazed past him as if to deny that what she had feared for a long time might finally be about to take place.

"I don't think he'll look here first," she said.

"I hope not."

"He'll think we hid, and then ran for the trail."

He did not reply. Still leaning well back from the wall, he craned his neck, tried to see past the broad ledge where the twins, apparently, were waiting for the others, tried to locate the thin, jagged hundred-foot-long crack that provided the only retreat from the face at this elevation and was in its upper reaches the most difficult pitch of the climb.

"It's to the left," she told him. "Sixty feet or so down the ledge."

In half-light he found it, scarcely noticeable from here: a dark, vertical scar.

"Have you led it?" he asked.

"No. But I've done it several times."

"It couldn't have been part of somebody else's climb, could it," he said dryly.

"No."

He blew into the cup of his right hand, hoping to warm it a little; wiggled his toes; kept his face turned from the wind which was blowing grit along the wall.

"I'm going now," she told him. "I'd appreciate it if you'd come over here and stay with Pam. I'll put her as close to the chimney as I can. The chimney is easy; I won't need a belay."

He nodded. It seemed to him that given the emotional state of the younger girl, her lack of experience handling the rope, Kate had come up 850 feet already without a dependable belay.

"Can you manage with that rucksack?" he asked.

"Yes."

"My truck is parked a few miles from here," he

started to say; then he heard a shot, a flat explosive sound that gained dimension as it echoed again and again between the narrow canyon walls. Instinctively he crouched, reducing himself as a target, waiting for the whine of the bullet, the high-pitched ricochet off the wall.

"It came from there," Kate said. She was holding Pam with one arm, pointing with the other; this time the tension was sharp in her voice.

As Whittaker looked in the direction of the shack, all of its lights winked out.

20

He made his way to the belaying ledge, quickly tied himself in to the anchor piton. The ledge was crowded with three of them; it was difficult to maneuver. Once, in his haste, he came close to losing his balance. His breath came in spurts. Kate was trying to reassure the girl who, at the sound of the shot, had frozen in place, her eyes clamped shut. Whittaker set up his belay, standing the way Kate had stood, facing out from the wall, tugging hard on the rope four times, taking in slack as soon as Myke began to climb up.

"Get going!" he called over his shoulder.

"Pam's terrified. She needs somebody. . . ."

"You get up there; set up the belay. Myke and I will help her. . . ."

"She's *my* responsibility. . . ."

"She's the responsibility of all of us, now get up there will you!"

She did not answer. The wind sliced through his

fatigue pants; he was shivering badly now. "We need you up there," he said. "I'll look after Pam."

"All right. Fine," she said. "But I'm not going up there to sit on that ledge doing a basic belay. One of the twins can do that. The other one and I can start the last lead. . . ."

"No, negative. . . ."

"I can handle myself; I know what I'm doing."

Angrily, he glanced to his left, saw she was already in the lowest part of the chimney, her back against its far wall, her feet against its close wall, her rucksack resting on her lap, her knees bent sharply, ready to move up. But she was not moving up; she was looking at Pam who stood on the belaying ledge, facing the wall not far from the start of the chimney.

Whittaker could not see the young girl's face, but he could tell from the way she held herself, the clutch of her hands on the rock, the tension in her legs, that she was on the verge of losing whatever control she had left. Kate was talking to her. He could not make out what it was she said. He went on taking in the rope as Myke continued her slow ascent, a shadowy bulk now that moved imprecisely in the giddy dark below his feet.

"All right, I'm going up," Kate said finally. "One of the twins can belay you, the other can belay me. It doesn't make sense to waste any more time, not now."

He shook his head. *No, I'll do it,* he thought. *You belay Myke for me. I'll do the chimney and the exit crack. It won't take five minutes to change this around.*

But again he found he could not assert himself, could not take over the climb, and this angered him, suggested he had lost his nerve, was thinking of his own pride, thinking *If all this goes wrong, or even any part of it goes wrong, I don't want anybody coming to me. . . .*

"It gets worse as it goes," he told her. "The last pitch is 5.7, 5.8. . . ."

"I can handle that," she said. "I remember the moves. I told you I've done it before."

"Then do it. We're damn well running out of time."

"What was he shooting at?"

"Nothing probably. Maybe just letting us know he was back."

"I talked Pam into coming here," she said, her words carrying to him clearly on the wind. "She's the daughter of a man I teach with. She wasn't happy about coming. Neither was he. I talked her into it because she's very shy. . . ."

"Look don't tell me about that now."

"I'm telling you because it's why I feel responsible. Neil and I were responsible for all of them; but Pam . . ."

"We'll have cover on the ledge," he broke in. "And we'll have cover above the crack. But we'll be exposed as hell in the crack itself. We may have to wait for this storm to open up before we can risk following you."

"All right."

"Use pitons if you have to. He's probably going to find us soon anyway. It's worth the risk, I think."

"I'll decide when I get up there. I'm going now. Pam, you do what he says; do exactly what he says, all right?"

"Yes."

"I'll see you soon."

But it was only just after she had begun to move up the chimney that Whittaker, still belaying Myke, happened to glance up in the direction of the final hundred feet and caught at the periphery of his vision a splash of color against the wall, a splash of bright yellow revealed in an increasing light as the wind swept clouds away from the moon: one of the twins, he knew at once, already high in the exit crack.

He looked away. The belaying rope passed across his back from his right hand to his left, and he gripped both hands tightly against the rope as if against the realization of what he had seen. Until now he had sustained a hope they might all make it safely off the face. *Now*, he thought, *we've really bought it.*

He guessed how it must have happened: the twins waiting on the broad traversing ledge above; Karpus's single shot; a quick decision to move out, to go up that long final lead while there still might be time. In a way he did not blame them; had he been in their place he might have done the same thing. But the splash of bright yellow had not moved up or down since he had first seen it, had not moved at all, and was as visible now as a bright balloon that had managed to rise nearly a thousand feet up the canyon wall, only to catch its string just below what would have been for it the liberating sky.

Move! he thought.

He looked past the young girl who stood facing the wall next to him, on up past her to the chimney where Kate must still be working her way toward the higher ledge. Then he looked down to see Myke, twenty feet below him now, peering up, hands searching deliberately for holds. The canyon was dark again, the windows of the shack no longer lit, the lantern no longer burning by the trail.

Move! he thought. But the yellow balloon did not move.

"*Myke?*"

"*What?*"

"*Are your holds good?*"

"Like right now, you mean?"

"Yes, can you stay where you are?"

"I don't know. . . . I guess I can."

"The twins are in trouble. I'm going up to the ledge. Pam will take your rope up when she goes, then Kate will give you a belay. All right?"

"What's wrong?"

"You just hang tight. Wait for the signal and when you get it come up as fast as you can."

He untied the rope where it circled his waist and tied it to the rope that circled the waist of the youngest girl. "You'll be going up in a couple of minutes," he told her. "The chimney is short, not hard to do, you've done much harder pitches already. The ledge up there is at least six feet wide. Once we're on it and lying down, there's no way anybody in that canyon down there is going to see us."

Her eyes were closed, her small, vulnerable face pressed against the cold granite of the wall. Wisps of her closely cropped hair moved in the wind. He touched her arm. The name on her borrowed parka said MYKE.

"Don't quit now," he told her, his heartbeat quickening. "You've toughed it out all this way. Just hang on a little longer. Myke's counting on you. You'll be bringing her rope as you come. Kate's counting on you too. Don't think about anything except chimneying fifty feet up to that ledge. She'll be waiting there for you in a place that's safe as a bunker, all right?"

"Yes."

He made his moves past her and into the chimney and then up the chimney, back against one wall, feet against the other, the Kelty pack across his lap, careful as he went not to interfere with the rope that joined Kate above him to the young girl on the ledge below. He had

been very cold, but now as he exerted himself he began
to feel warm again. The chimney was like a laundry chute
in a four-story building with one wall pulled away. It was
dry and deep, and the wind sounded lost when it came
in.

"What's wrong?" Kate asked when he came up just
below her. She was still in the chimney, a few feet below
the traversing ledge.

"The twins are climbing the exit crack," he said.
He was winded from having come up so fast. He had to
work for his breath.

"They're *what?*"

"They're climbing the crack, at least one of them
is. They must have started when they heard that
shot. . . ."

"Oh, my God. . . ."

"Get going," he said. "As soon as you're up there
set up a belay and bring Pam up. Pull her into the chimney if you have to. She'll be bringing Myke's rope with
her. Get Myke out of there too, as soon as you can."

"What are you going to do?"

"I don't know. She's way the hell up there."

"Which one is it?"

"The one in yellow."

"Dianne. It *would* be Dianne. She's good, but she
hasn't got any sense. . . ."

"She better be good," he said. "She better be goddamned good."

Kate climbed out of the chimney and onto the ledge.
He climbed out after her, breathing better now, his
adrenaline up. The wind seemed even more furious
here; it blew as if to take the two of them and shove them
along down-ledge in the direction of the start of the final
lead. The moon was behind the clouds. Against the puls-

ing heat of his face, he thought he felt the first flakes of snow.

"Bring the others up," he said. "As quickly as you can. Then coil one of the ropes; I may need it. If that sonofabitch starts shooting at us, get Pam and Myke to lie flat on the ledge as close to the wall as they can. You keep down too. Don't let him know where you are and don't make any moves unless it's dark."

She stood next to him in her blue windpants and parka, bracing herself against the thrust of the wind at her back, thinking for the first time since Neil had been killed that the rest of them were not going to make it, that her decisions had been wrong decisions, that this pilot had known better, that she should not have stopped him from killing the man in the shack or from trying to kill the other man as he returned, that she should have trusted this older man with her own safety and that of the others. But he had seemed unsure of himself, hadn't he? And these were her people, not his. And now Dianne was doing something she had been told not to do, and Pam was by herself on that ledge below the chimney, and Myke somewhere below that, and Dietz . . .

Oh, God, she cried silently, over and over, as if the repetition of that phrase might alter somehow this narrowing and hopeless circumstance which she, out of her perfection and pride, had contrived to bring upon them all. Her body felt numb. Her hands were distant, prodigious weights at the ends of her limp arms. Her feet were leaden, immobile. Her voice was locked in her throat.

Oh, God. Oh, God.

As if in a dream, she saw the slant of the pilot's gaunt face, contemptuous of what she had done in the shack though it might have saved them, judgmental as a father

of what would now prove to be the disastrous consequence of her mistake.

*If it were up to me, I'd try setting up an ambush, try hitting
him somewhere along the creek trail.*

Then why hadn't he done it? Why had he left it to
her? Why had he followed along as if waiting for this
moment, this inevitable moment, preordained, when he
might take charge and salvage what he could from the
ruins of her failure, proving again what her father and
Paul and every man she had ever worked with or known
or heard or seen all finally believed whether they said
they believed it or not, whether they even knew they
believed it or not: that they were better than she, always
would be better than she, no matter how good she was,
no matter how hard she tried, no matter what her accom-
plishments, no matter what her endeavor or role (except
as brood mare, something to be fucked, something to
clean snot from the noses of the young).

*Katherine, this is your father's chair. . . . Your father knows
best about these things. . . . We'll do as your father says. . . . You're
his only child, of course he is proud of you. . . . We will wait until
your father comes home. . . . Ask your father. . . . Do as he says.
. . . Do as he says. . . . Do as he says. . . .*

And for as long as she had lived in his house, she
always had done as he said, meekly almost, dealing with
what in her adolescence became a deep, inarticulate rage
by screaming terrible things at her mother.

Now on this ledge, in this wind that blew, in this
half-minute of time when she could not bear to think
what might happen to the twins or to Pam or to Myke,
she saw the pilot's hand come slowly toward her until it
rested on her shoulder, gripping cruelly there, saw his
judgmental face, heard his clipped voice, his authoritar-
ian tone.

"Bring the others up!"

"All right," she said, scarcely aware she had said it.

Then she was setting up her belay, and he was making his way unroped along the broad ledge to the place where it gradually narrowed, ending finally at the start of the exit crack.

He groped along the wall, staying away from the edge, trying to see into the gloom ahead, trying to locate the figure of the second twin who, he knew, should be seated at the last comfortable spot on the ledge, her feet dangling over, paying the rope to her sister as her sister went up the crack. But even after he had gone for what he guessed to be fifty feet, the wind slamming against his back in gusts so strong he sometimes had to brace himself to keep from toppling forward, he could not make out anything in front of him except the indistinct outer lip of the narrowing ledge.

The second twin's parka was blue. That would make it hard to see in the shadows against the slate-gray cliff. But he knew he was close to the end of the traversing ledge, close to the place where it tapered to a width of less than half a foot, and that whatever she wore he should have seen her by now.

He paused, one hand on the wall, his fingers curled tightly into a small fissure at a point just above his right shoulder. Once, he thought he heard voices above him, then again. He squinted up into the blackness, saw nothing, heard voices again; this time they were more distinct, though he could not make out what it was they had said. He decided finally that for some reason both of the twins were on the exit crack now, though he could not understand why. The crack was a hundred feet long, a single lead. It was standard procedure for the belayer to remain anchored to the traversing ledge while the leader made his way up the crack. Once the leader had done the crack, he would anchor himself to the more gradual slope above and would belay his second man up. There was no reason for two people to be in the crack at the same time, and all he could think was that the twin in the yellow parka had managed to climb the crack with astonishing speed and was up and out and already belaying her sister. But as much as he wanted to believe that this was so, he could not, for he had seen that lead twin climb, and although she had been good, he had not thought she had been that good.

He located the start of the crack, boot-wide and rough-edged here, and he peered up.

"*Dianne!*" he called. "*Dietz!*"

The wind cut off his cries. He glanced behind him. Soon there would be a division of clouds and the light of the moon would come up slowly and he would be able to see. He waited impatiently, looking along the ledge to the place where, sixty feet away from him now, Kate should be anchored to the wall, taking in rope as Pam came up. He could not see her, but he could hear her: steady phrases of encouragement brought to him on the wind. She was tough, and he admired that, understood something of what she must be going through, how it was different from what he was going through because she was a woman who had probably never been shot at before and who was responsible for these young people in a way that he was not.

Until now he had hoped for the storm to hold off. Now he hoped it would not; not if Karpus knew where they were, not if he had caught a single one of the sounds they had made, not if he had spotted them during one of the moonlit periods and was even now on his way to this place, hurrying along the trail, the fat man stumbling behind him, picking his way up onto the talus, perhaps on the opposing side of the canyon, finding the right elevation of rock to steady his rifle, to pick them off one by one as they tried to get up that last stubborn crack after which they would be, for a long while at least, beyond his reach.

He closed his eyes. The weight of his pack seemed to have doubled. He was tired: flat bone-weary now. When he opened his eyes again, he saw that the light of the moon had begun to appear. He jacked up his head, squinted up at the last of the great east face of Wolf Mountain that rose vertically above him under a dizzying rush of cloud. The lead twin was just below the final pitch. She stood motionless, her feet jammed into the crack below her, her hands jammed into it above. He thought that in this section her feet should not have been in the crack at all but balanced on small nubbins of rock that were available on either side; that was the way he remembered it. The second twin was, as he had feared, climbing steadily up toward her sister, climbing to help her, and this meant neither one of them had the protection of a belay.

The light of the moon kept coming on until it was incredibly bright. He saw that Pam had reached the ledge, saw Kate untying the rope that led from Pam to Myke who waited on the wall below the chimney. Sixty, maybe seventy feet above him, the second twin had stopped climbing. The crack would be more difficult now: without a belay it would be tough for anyone to commit himself to the required moves. Climbing down was out of the question, impossibly hard, even if he might have persuaded the twin in blue to try.

He took off his pack, leaned it against the wall, clipped a half-dozen pitons and carabiners to a loop of rope at his side; but he was not at all sure what he should do, not at all sure that even if he climbed up to a point just below the second twin he would be able to pass her somehow and reach the lead twin and get her moving again.

He had reached no decision when he heard suddenly the flat explosive sound of a second shot: this one much louder, its crescendo of echoes rising around him, the high whine ricochet of a bullet slamming off the wall somewhere below him and to his left. Instinctively he crouched, seeking the shelter of the ledge. He heard another ricochet, then the sound of the shot, then the echoes; and he could not keep it all together: how many shots there had been or what he would hear first, the crack of the gun or whine of the bullet. Everything was distorted by the echoes that filled the canyon now as if a whole platoon were firing rather than a single man.

Agonized, he looked at the sky. It was filled with clouds except in a poollike place from which the moon sent its unwelcome light. There had been two shots, he decided; the echoes they had begun were already dying away, lost in the wind. He looked up-ledge, saw Kate and the youngest girl lying facedown. Kate still held the rope that ran to the lip of the ledge where it bent sharply over the lip and down as if at the end of it there now hung a dead weight. She looked at Whittaker, shook her head. He closed his eyes. Had Myke been the first then? Nailed by Karpus on the wall below the chimney? He remembered how she had worked herself free in the shack, how when she might have run she had made her stolid way across that squeaking floor and risked the untying of his own ropes.

But he had to be sure about Myke and so he moved rapidly along the ledge, using his belly and elbows and knees, covering a little less than half the distance that had separated him from the others before he turned briefly onto his back and lay looking up the illuminated wall to the place where the lead twin still stood motionless, high in the exit crack. The second twin had gone up another ten feet, but she was holding precariously now, stopped by either the difficulty of the pitch or the sound of the shots or both.

Move! he thought.

But he knew they could not. He remembered his nights in the F-4 over the trail, jinking and weaving and dodging through the tracers and multiple clips of 37s and 57s and all the smaller stuff that came up from the revetments and caves and pits and holes. But the twins were immobile in their place on the wall, unable to twist or bob, unable to move a half-foot in either direction, holding tight and praying, he knew, that the clouds would cover the moon very soon and give them a blessed cover of dark. And the light did begin to fade just then, just as a third bullet whined off the wall somewhere high and he heard the blunt crack of the explosion and the echoes rise.

"Climb up!" he shouted before they had died away. *"Put in a piton! Use your slings! Get the hell out of there!"*

In glimmering light, before the next shot, he saw the second twin begin to climb. He had not heard her drive a piton, but she must have done that or found one in place, for he could see she had clipped a short loop of rope to the wall at a point above her waist and was now trying to raise her left foot, trying to bring it up and into the loop and, by doing that, gain a more secure and higher position in the crack.

She had gotten her foot into the loop and had begun to step up when he again heard the sound of the gun.

This time there was no ricochet and at first he thought
Karpus, trying to hit the lead twin, had simply missed the
wall, had aimed too high, the bullet lost somewhere in
the more gradual angle of ground that led to the summit.
Then he saw that one of the lead twin's feet had come
out of the crack, that she seemed to be hanging at arm's
length by one hand. Her sister screamed. Whittaker
rolled to his hands and knees.

A thousand feet above the talus, a hundred feet
above the ledge on which the pilot crouched, the lead
twin fell back and away from the crack she had nearly
managed to climb. She seemed to fall slowly and silently,
turning in her fall end over end; and when her weight at
last hit the end of the long rope that was fastened to her
sister's waist, it wrenched her sister from her holds and
her sister fell too and in the same slow and turning and
silent way.

Then it was quiet except for the wind. And it was
dark. And for a while there were no more shots.

21

Halfway up the talus across the stream, squatting intently
behind a pulpit of rock, Karpus worked the action of the
Weatherby rifle, ejecting a spent cartridge, sliding a
fresh cartridge into its breech, trying without success to
locate through the powerful magnification of its scope
yet another of the climbers high on the dusky wall of the
mountain's east face. He managed the gun with the instincts of a man who had been bred to it, allowing for the
flattened trajectory of such high-angle shots and for the

effect of a crosswind gusting now in excess of twenty miles per hour.

He had missed his first shot, made his second, missed his third, made his fourth. Two of the climbers had fallen from high on the wall; he had watched them come down. One of the others, the first he had hit, still hung from a rope below a wide chimneylike gap that led to a higher ledge where the three remaining climbers were keeping out of sight.

It was too dark now to see much of anything, and as far as he could tell it would be a while before the moon would reappear from behind its cover of cloud. He decided to smoke a cigarette. His legs were cramped from having squatted so long in one place, and he felt aroused by the shooting too, not for having killed three of these climbers in their attempt to get away, nor in anticipation of killing three more—though he was aroused by these things—but more by the requirements of the shooting itself, the several factors that had to be taken into consideration before he could hold his breath and squeeze the trigger and feel the brisk recoil of the cushioned butt plate against his shoulder: the unusual trajectory, the effect of the wind, the brief periods of time available in which to shoot, the uncertain light.

"You want a smoke?" he said.

"*What?*" Johns cried. He was sitting on a rubble of stone not far from the pulpitlike rock Karpus had been using to steady the rifle. An unlit lantern and a quart bottle of kerosine were on the ground at his feet. He sat with the tall collar of his pea coat up, holding his bare and bandaged head gently in his hands as if it were a large cracked egg which if he did not hold carefully might fall in pieces to the ground. He had been making high-pitched groaning sounds since arriving here, and every

time the rifle had gone off he had cried out as if it had
gone off in the center of his injured head.

"*What?*" he repeated.

"I asked if you wanted a smoke."

"*No!*"

"I figured I'd have one now while it's too dark to see
anything."

"I don't give a fuck about seeing anything," Johns
said. "I want to go back and lay down."

"We'll go back pretty soon."

"My ears keep filling up, I can't hear."

"We'll go back."

"*When?*"

"Soon as we get the rest of them."

"Jesus Christ, I don't care about them; I don't care
if we get them or not. . . ."

"You don't want that pilot going into town do you?"

Johns groaned. He seemed to have changed since he
had been hit on the head, seemed to have gotten cranky
as hell, and this worried Karpus for he felt somewhat
responsible for what had happened to his friend. He had
not imagined the fat girl in the sweatshirt capable of
hurting Johns in any way. Apparently she not only had
managed to get herself free but also freed the pilot who
slipped up on Johns and brained him with a chunk of
wood. It was not one of the two scenarios Karpus had
written on his long walk to the climbers' camp and his
supper of Spam and beans.

The first of his scenarios had had Johns discovering
in time what the fat girl was up to and simply tying her
up again, slapping her around a little first, or maybe
putting her belly-down on the cot. The second had had
the fat girl escaping into the night whereupon he himself
would recapture her and would walk her back to the

prospector's shack as if walking her back from a date. The second scenario gratified his ego. He had imagined the expression on Johns's troubled face when the fat girl who had gone galloping off suddenly reappeared, contrite and as if by magic. But he had liked the first scenario too, had liked the idea of Johns excitedly telling him how the fat girl had almost gotten away and how he had stopped her in the nick of time. Johns needed that kind of satisfaction.

Instead, something had gone wrong. Johns had been hit on the head and from all the noise he was making, it was clear he thought he hurt pretty bad and clear he was not going to handle his pain well.

Other things had gone wrong too. Karpus had told Johns to wait in the shack while he went after the climbers, but Johns had refused, had said he would not stay there or anywhere else by himself, that he would rather cut his own throat or stick his head in the fucking stove. It was the first time Karpus could remember that Johns had refused to do something he had asked him to do. Then, with Johns still inside taking care of the lantern, Karpus had gone out to look around again and had put his boot through one of the rickety porch steps. He had dropped the rifle, which, to his embarrassment, had fired; and, unable to pull his foot free from the broken step that held it like a fox trap, he had had to wait until Johns had come out and freed him.

Karpus had not liked any of this. And finally it had been Johns and not he who had spotted the climbers high on the wall, Johns walking along the creek trail with his head in his hands, groaning his dirge of discomfort, looking up, seeing them, while he, Karpus, had worn himself out searching the talus on either side of the stream.

"They're up *there* for Chrissake," Johns had said. And there had been something in his voice that Karpus had not liked either: a trace of disappointment as if Karpus and not he should be making such discoveries.

"I can't tell if it's going to rain or snow," Karpus remarked now, exhaling smoke from his cigarette. "It feels just about cold enough to snow."

"We should go back," Johns said. "We should get the fuck out of here."

"This is a good place to steady up the rifle. I may try going a little higher, but this is a damn good place right here. Your average sonofabitch couldn't hit a Mack truck on that wall; not with the light always up and down and the wind blowing like this."

"I'm not going to make it," Johns said. "I need a fucking doctor."

"Did you take those aspirin?"

"Aspirin! Jesus Christ, aspirin isn't going to do me any good for Chrissake! My head's busted! I'm bleeding out my ears!"

"Did you take them or not?"

"Yes. . . ."

"You didn't look too bad to me, Johns. Just a knot and a gash is all. Head cuts always bleed a lot; they always look worse than they are."

"Yeah, well, he must have hit me with everything he had. He must have stood up on his fucking *toes* for Chrissake. *Jesus.*"

"You see those two come down?"

"What?"

"Those two I picked off up there just now. Did you see them?"

"No."

"You ever stand in a blind and shoot ducks?"

"No!"

"Well, that's how they came down. Like a couple of ducks."

"I've got to go back to that fucking shack and lay down," Johns said. "Light this lantern for me, will you? I can't even *hear.*"

"Just wait a couple of minutes. Wait until those clouds blow out from under the moon."

"What?"

"I said, just wait a couple of minutes. I've already got three of them. I'll get the other three and then we'll go back. You don't want that pilot making it to the top of that cliff, do you? We'd just have to go after him if he did, and you'd be worse off than you are now. He's probably the one who hit your head."

"I don't *care.*"

"I'll get him, and the other two, and then we'll go."

"Fuck that," Johns replied. "Fuck all that, I'm going back now."

Karpus looked at him. He was holding his head in both hands and trying to get to his feet at the same time. Then he barked his shin on a rock and cried out and held his head with his left hand and his shin with his right.

"Sit down," Karpus told him.

"I *hurt!*"

"Just sit your tail down," Karpus said. "You remember the Candle Man don't you?"

"The *what?*"

"The Candle Man?"

"Yes. . . ."

"You just sit your tail down and think about him while I wait for that pilot to make some kind of move up there. He'll have to do something pretty soon or he'll wind up spending the night."

Karpus could not be sure what Johns was in fact thinking about: He looked unhappy enough to still be thinking about his head. At least he was sitting down again, next to the unlit lantern and the bottle of fuel, his tall collar up, his back to the wind.

Except for the fat girl in the sweatshirt whose unmistakable bulk hung like a sack of meal from a rope high on the wall, Karpus had no special feelings for any of the people he had put to sleep with his rifle. If the therapy guy had come toiling up the talus in this moment and asked, "How do you feel about what you have done? Do you feel any regret? Any remorse?" Karpus would have thought for a moment and then replied in all honesty that he felt no regret or remorse, that he felt very little in fact.

"What about pleasure then? Was it fun? Was there a kick to it?"

Not really. Well, it had been interesting making shots that were as tough as these shots had been; and some kind of sight to see those people come down the way they had. But not fun exactly.

"Were you . . . aroused by it?"

I don't remember.

In the case of the fat girl there had been a moment of gratification for she was, he knew, the one who had hurt Johns; he had seen her loosening her ropes. He wished he could tell Johns that, because he thought Johns might experience some gratification too if he knew the person who had caused him such unhappiness was now dead.

The surface of the pulpitlike rock was wet to the touch as if a dew had fallen, and when he looked through the rifle scope he discovered that moisture had collected on the oval lens which he had to wipe clean with his handkerchief. He assumed it had been the pilot's idea to try and climb the mountain, and at first he had not been very impressed by it. But the fact was—and it was not a fact he found easy to accept—that if Johns had not spotted the climbers up there on that wall, they might have gotten away.

I would have gotten them sooner or later, he thought.

But he was not really sure, and knew that in any case it would not have been as easy as this.

22

For one interminable moment, Whittaker had remained on his hands and knees, paralyzed in a complexity of emotion: of grief, fear and shock at what had happened to the twins and what had apparently happened to Myke; and then, and not at all too soon, these feelings were contained by a swift and rising anger, and he stood up and walked into the wind forty feet up-ledge to the place where Kate and Pam still lay flat and now close to the wall.

He saw Kate look up at him, stunned, her finely boned face sheet-white, framed by her dark parka and hair.

"Tell me about Myke," he said. His voice was hoarse.

She did not reply.

"Tell me about Myke," he said.

"She was just starting to come up, had just gotten into the chimney or was just getting into it. . . ."

"Did you try signaling?"

"Yes. After the first shot."

"Did she signal back?"

"Yes. One pull. Then the second shot came and the slack went out of the rope. . . ."

"Have you tried calling her?"

"Yes, but there's too much wind. . . ."

"I'm going down there," he said.

She looked at him as if the world in which he moved were not her world, as if she alone knew the twins had been killed and what it meant.

"I may need a belay coming up," he said, lying on his stomach now, crawling across the ledge to the place where the rope bent sharply and the chimney began. "If she's alive and hurt, I'm going to need all the help you two can give me."

The last thing he saw on the traversing ledge was Kate uncoiling a rope. She was doing it, but in an odd, slow way as if she were not sure that it mattered. Then he was in the black well of the chimney, reversing the moves he had used coming up, discovering at once that it was more difficult to go down, even without the nuisance of his pack. As he went, he could look out from his place in the chimney and see what he knew was the stream running south out of the canyon toward the fall, and the talus many hundreds of feet below him, and the opposing talus and opposing wall of the canyon. But in the absence of any clear light from the moon and under what was becoming a more cohesive layer of clouds, everything that was visible to him of the rough terrain was visible only in a way that was shadowy and unarticulated and depended to a considerable degree on his prior knowledge of this place.

The wind sounded in the chimney, slow and flute-like; the chimney reduced the thrust of the wind to a chilly but acceptable breeze. When he guessed he had descended thirty feet, or about half or a little more than half of what he would have to descend to reach the girl, he paused and tried to see down the rest of the way, but everything below him was very dark and he could distinguish nothing except the two jagged vertical lines of rock that indicated the outermost corners formed by the chimney and the wall.

He guessed that Karpus would be concentrating on the ledge and the exit crack now, and even if the moon showed again there would be enough shadow here in the chimney to keep the man with the rifle from seeing much, or, even if he did manage to see something, to keep him from getting off as clear a shot as he had when he had hit the lead twin high on the wall, and when he had hit Myke on the wall below.

He found that his anger had begun to subside and his fear had begun to rise again, as if these two emotions shared a precarious balance within him. He moved down five feet, then five feet more, hunching awkwardly against the rock, warming his hands alternately by blowing on them and by opening and closing his fists. If Myke was alive, he knew he would have to get her up this chimney. If she was conscious, able to move but scared to death by what had happened, he thought he could manage to talk her up; but if she was unable to move or was hanging unconscious from her rope somewhere below the start of the chimney in a place exposed to Karpus's view, he knew it was going to be very hard to get her into the chimney, and, if he was able to do that somehow, even harder to bring her up the chimney to the traversing ledge.

It occurred to him that he had not been at all explicit in his directions to Kate. He remembered telling her that he might need a belay as he came up, but he had not told her how he would communicate this need or how she was to get the rope to him. She could try lowering it, perhaps tying her piton hammer to it as a weight; or she could throw it out from the ledge, keeping hold of one end, hoping the other end would fall somewhere within his reach.

He was thinking about this and making his awkward descent when he sensed the light begin to change, and when he glanced out of the chimney at the sky above the canyon he saw the moon was going to show itself again and he pressed himself as far into the chimney as he could and held himself motionless there.

The light came up quickly. It reached toward the place where he waited until it lay along the fabric of his trousers and parka. He was scared now, but the light did not reach all the way into the chimney and he thought if he did not move, Karpus might not notice him here. He held his breath. The light went up, and then it went down, and then it went up again even brighter than before. He closed his eyes, heard the flutelike sounds of the wind piped through the chimney, waited for the sound of the shot.

Make it, he thought. *Get it over with if that's the way it's going to be.*

But the sound of the shot did not come, and after what seemed a long period of time, he opened his eyes and craning his neck slowly, a half-inch at a time, he forced himself to look down.

The chimney ended fifteen feet below him. Ten feet below that he saw Myke. She hung from her rope, facing out from the wall. Her arms were at her sides, her head tipped sharply forward. In the stronger gusts of wind she would move slightly, but not much, and when he saw this he felt his throat tighten, and he looked away. "I didn't know the other two," he said quietly. "But I knew you. At least I was beginning to know you. . . ."

Then, startled by something, he looked down. She was still hanging there, exactly as she had been before, but he was certain he had heard her call to him, her familiar, half-apologetic voice quite distinct in the chimney as the light began to die.

"Myke?" he said hoarsely.

"Is that you, Matt?"

"Yes. Christ, yes," he said. "Are you hurt?"

"I'm freezing!"

"Did he hurt you? Did he hit you?"

"No. He was trying to, but he didn't."

In the accumulating dark, Whittaker breathed his relief, prayed thanks to a God in whose powers he had years ago lost faith.

"I fell," she explained. "Then I couldn't get back up. He thinks I'm dead. When it's light," she said, "I just hang like this. He doesn't shoot here anymore. . . ."

"Don't move," he said, "until I tell you to, and then move as fast as you can."

He had time in the last of this brief period of light to locate substantial holds in the chimney from which he thought he could help her with the rope; and when it was dark again, he positioned himself on these holds; and when he was ready he told her to climb. He could feel the rope twist in his hands, hear her soft exclamations as she struggled to face the wall and get into the chimney, saw, as he took in the rope tightly, the hump of her shadow rise below him.

"I *peed,*" she said. "I couldn't *help* it."

She talked to him breathlessly, looking up, as if he were her father.

"I was so scared I just peed and then I shut my eyes and hung there and I think my pants froze because I wet them like that." She stopped a second for breath. "Is everybody else all right?"

"We'll talk when we get up there," he told her. "Let's get out of this chimney while it's still dark."

"Gosh," she blurted, still working to breathe, *"you look terrific!"*

23

After they were up, he went down-ledge and brought back his pack, telling Myke to open it and put on the thermal shirt and pants he had brought and whatever else she could find that was warm. She was silent now; he had told her what had happened to the twins. He tied Pam in to the wall, then told Kate to follow him down-ledge to the place where the exit crack began, and he prepared himself to climb.

He set up the belay in such a way that Kate would be able to handle the rope while seated on the ledge and anchored to the wall, without presenting herself to Karpus as a target should the moon come out again. There had already been a brief shower of snow; the surfaces of the ledge were slippery, the rock wet. He knew this would make it harder to ascend the last 100 feet of the face, but he also knew the storm was imminent and if the moon came out at all, it would not come out for very long.

"Maybe . . ." she said, glancing up at the sky, speaking as if in a trance, ". . . maybe you should wait. Maybe we should all just wait here. . . ."

"If this weather is going to be as bad as it looks," he said, "I don't want to have to sit it out here. We don't have any shelter at all."

"I keep hoping I'm going to see the lights in that shack again. I keep hoping he's as cold as we are and he'll decide to give up for a while."

"He's not going to give up, not him. I doubt if he's hurting at all down there, wherever he is. He's enjoying it probably: I picture him praying for something like this all his life, ever since he was a kid with an air rifle maybe —he and his fat friend."

"I can't think about what's happened," she said. Her dark hair was tied behind her. Wisps of it stood in the wind. "I can't believe it or think about it. . . ."

"Don't."

"Dianne and Dietz . . ."

"You start thinking that way, you may as well quit."

"What would you think about, if you were me. . . ?"

"Handling this rope. Going up this last hundred feet. Taking care of the other two."

"It's easy for you to say, isn't it? You don't let your feelings show, do you?"

"Not when they get in the way of staying alive."

She was silent.

"I found some cigarettes in the rucksack," she said finally. "They must have been Neil's. Do you want one?"

"No," he said. "Maybe once we're up there . . ."

"I'm not as brave as I thought I was," she said. Her voice was unsteady. "I seem to hold on for just so long and then I fall apart. . . ."

"Send the young one up after me. Then Myke and then you. Tie the packs to the second rope. We can haul them up after us; there's no sense trying to lug them."

"What are we supposed to do if something happens . . . ?"

"To me you mean?"

"Yes."

"Then you try it alone."

She nodded, and he would have liked in that moment to put his arms around her as much to comfort himself as to comfort her. He would have liked to say: *Listen, I'm not what you think I am. I'm flesh and blood and bones like you, sick to death of what's happened like you, tired and afraid.*

"I wish I could cry," she said.

"Keep it together, will you?" he said. "I can't do this without you."

She nodded, but for the first time he was not sure she would be able to hold up; nor was he sure of himself.

He made his first moves up into the crack, felt the rough wet rock under his hands, felt his heartbeat quicken, his skin slip along his spine as he left the protection of the ledge and came into the range of Karpus's gun.

"It's going to go," he called, but she did not reply, and he supposed he had not said it loud enough or the wind had taken what he had said away.

He went up the first fifty feet without finding a piton, then he found one, an angle-ring piton with a carabiner in place. He clipped his rope into this and went up twenty feet more, finding four more pitons, each with a carabiner in place, and he clipped his rope into these carabiners as he reached them.

He assumed that the first twin had placed the carabiners and had clipped her own rope to them as she had climbed up. Then, with the rope all but run out between them, the second twin had had to unclip from them in order to come up from below. That had been a foolish and brave thing to do, he thought; and knew that if she had made it it would only have been thought of as brave.

But remembering the twins now would do no good, and so he stopped remembering them and climbed as swiftly as he could, but carefully too, jamming his fingers and toes into the crack when the crack was deep and wide enough, balancing up on small holds on either side of the crack when it was not. The wind blew steadily. It was cold. There were times when he had to blow on his fingers to warm them, times when he had to pause for long minutes, peering up into the shadows above, trying to work out his next series of moves.

Don't let that moon show, he thought. *Give me a little more time.*

Then, he heard the explosion of the gun.

The first explosion was followed in quick succession by two more; he heard bullets ricochet off the wall somewhere below and to his right. The canyon filled with echoes which seemed to rise in waves from its floor, up the talus, up the thousand-foot wall, ever louder as they came, deafeningly loud as they reached him and passed him and were driven off by the wind. Then, except for the wind, it was quiet.

He pressed himself as tightly as he could against the crack, tried to pull himself into it, but it was much too small. Just above him something moved like a flag, something scarcely visible in the dark that enveloped the face.

He closed his eyes. He had pressed himself so tightly to the rock the beating of his heart had become painful.

Get it over with, he thought. *Get it over with if you're going to.*

It puzzled him that Karpus had started shooting again, for there had been no apparent rising in the level of light. When he looked down toward the ledge it was lost in shadow; he could not see Kate or either of the girls. He glanced up again, discovered then that what was fluttering beyond his reach was the ribbon of rope left by the second twin, the loop she had clipped to a piton and into which she had tried to step just before she had been torn from her holds.

He began to inch his way up. The crack was deceptive here: large enough to take the toe of a boot, but smooth-sided and slippery. He put his hands into the crack as far as they would go and balled his fists, letting his arms take his weight as he changed the positions of his feet, stubbing his toes a little higher in the crack, pulling himself up toward the loop of rope. The wind was strong. It blew in gusts. When it was blowing hard the loop would flutter in an uncertain arc up the wall above and to his left until it was horizontal; then, when the wind died for a moment, the loop would drop again closer to his reach.

Just keep it together, he thought. His legs were shaking badly. *Just do it, get it done.*

He had paused for a moment, and now as he started to inch up again he felt a pull at his waist as if the rope had caught somewhere below him. Although it was only a slight pull, it was enough to unnerve him even more in this exposed, precarious position, and very carefully he eased himself back down until the sense of pull was gone.

He did not want to trust his feet to take all of his weight, but he did trust them to take most of it, keeping his left fist balled in the slippery crack above, reaching with his right hand to grip the rope where it left his waist and followed the crack straight down to the ledge. Then, with a hand that trembled, and very gently, he tried to pull the rope toward him.

It was possible, he knew, that the rope was jammed.

If so, he would have to climb down somehow and free it and then climb back up again. The thought of having to do that made him weak. It was also possible that the three shots had distracted Kate and she had forgotten to keep some slack in the rope.

"*Come on,*" he breathed. "*Come on!*"

When he tried to pull the rope toward him and it would not come, he yanked it once sharply and then it did come, and he said, "*That's it,*" and began to climb.

He had just started when he heard a bullet whine off the wall to his right and felt a sharp pain in his upper right thigh. He almost did come out of the crack then, his leg jerking reflexively, his hand snatching for the hurt place, his fear rising and joining with the echoes of the shot until he was disoriented and dizzy and felt for one moment as if he were in fact beginning to fall, turning slowly and clockwise out of the crack until he was upside down and then rightside up again, and then the whole upper wall of the mountain seemed to turn in the same way as bullets ricocheted on either side of him now and he felt the slippery feel of blood against his palm and swore and felt his balled left fist still in the crack above him begin to slip and his left foot click down in the crack as if something essential to his position had broken out from under it; and against the pull of his own weight that seemed to be dragging him down and out of the crack, and against the driving force of the wind, his teeth bared and face uptilted, large wet flakes of snow melting against it, he no longer moved carefully or even skillfully, but lunged rather, driving his boots and hands into the crack, up toward the loop of rope that fluttered indistinctly in the shadows above, lunged and kicked and reached until at last he felt the grace of the loop in his right hand and trusting it to take all of his weight he pulled himself up, his feet kicking angrily at the wall, pressing down on the loop with his right hand until the loop was at the level of his groin, reaching as far up into the crack with his left hand as he could reach, pulling himself up past the loop, standing finally not in the loop but on the exposed tip of the piton to which it had been clipped, finding the small clean holds on either side of the crack, moving to them carefully now, first one, then another, going up, inching up, with the explosive sounds of the gun multiplied and amplified and deafening now, bullets whining and pinging off the wall first to the right of him then to the left until in what had become a gentle light he saw where the wall ended its steep rise and began its angle toward the summit, and scarcely aware of how he was doing it or of how difficult it might be or of the terrible risk he was taking, he trusted his hands alone, jamming and balling them into the crack, first one and then the other, his legs exhausted and dragging uselessly behind him, knowing he was going to make it now, reaching beyond the angle of the wall, finding solid holds, bellying up and over, pulling himself then dragging himself beyond the reach of Karpus's gun.

You sonofabitch, he thought.

After what seemed to him a long time, after a period in which there were no more shots and the light of the moon that had risen began to die again and then did die and left him in shadow lying facedown full-length along the rocky uptilting place he had reached, he sat up, wiping his wet face with the sleeve of his parka, and gave three sharp pulls on the rope that circled his waist and then, once he had established his position, gave four more.

He sat with his back to a large, comfortably shaped boulder, his feet braced solidly in front of him, looking out across the canyon in the direction of its opposing wall, invisible where it bulked below a dark, all-but-solid overcast of sky. He could not see the floor of the canyon, or the stream, or the prospector's shack at the headwaters of the stream, toward which, he knew, Karpus and his friend Johns might already be making their way.

"You've gotten three of us," he said. *"That man Neil and the twins. You're not going to get any more."*

24

As far as he could tell, his leg had not been hit by a bullet, but it had been hit by something: a fragment of bullet, perhaps, or a sliver of rock. It had bled freely, but now the bleeding had stopped. Once they were safely holed up, he would clean it out and bandage it up and hope it would not interfere with his ability to move.

While snow fell intermittently and the sky remained dark, he helped the others come up the exit crack, putting his back to the rope.

Pam came up first. She brought the carabiners with her, and as she sat down next to him and he untied the rope from her small waist, he thought she looked very bad and might have to be carried before they got off the west ridge. She had a listless, vacant stare. When he tried to comfort her, tell her the worst was over, she did not reply.

Then he lowered the rope and Myke came up, quite well he thought.

"Whoosh!" she gasped, appearing at last over the edge. "Can I grab your boot again?"

"Sure. You're doing fine."

"Are we like safe now?"

"You bet we are."

"Kate said he was just shooting. She didn't think he really saw you or anything, at least not until the very last part. . . ."

"Maybe he saw you weren't dead anymore and it made him mad."

"I know."

"Could you tell where the shots were coming from?"

"Across the creek, I think. He moved sometimes. How's Pam doing?"

"All right."

"She was freezing down there so I gave her the bottoms of your longjohns."

"How about you? Are you warm enough?"

"I'm hot," she said. "My boobs are sweating."

He smiled.

"I had the tops of your longjohns over my sweatshirt and I was still cold," she said. "And then Kate told me to put them on under the sweatshirt and I've been frying ever since. Gee," she said, glancing up, "I don't see why it has to snow."

"It's not much yet," he replied. "We've got some time."

"I can't believe . . . I mean about the twins," she started to say, but that was all she said.

Kate brought the second rope with her as she came. She stood while Whittaker untied the knot, whispered to him she thought Pam might be in shock or close to it: Once, on the ledge below, the girl had untied herself from her anchor rope, had gotten up and wandered close to the edge before Myke had seen her and jumped up and brought her back.

"She'll be all right," Whittaker said.

But he was not at all sure, nor was he sure about Kate herself who had sounded unsteady, not confident in the way she had seemed in the shack, and whose legs had trembled as he had helped her untie from the rope.

"We're all going to be all right now," he said. "We're going to find a place to hole up and sit out this storm. We're going to eat what we have and stay as warm and dry as we can, and as soon as the storm is over we're going to get the hell out of here. There's a café in Morgan that has plank steaks and draft beer, and as soon as we get there we're going to eat and drink until we fall out of our chairs."

"Wow," Myke said quietly.

"There's a motel too," he said. "It's not much to look at, but the water's hot and the sheets are clean. . . ." He heard Kate begin to cry. "Think about those things," he said. "Keep them right up front while we do what we have to do."

"I left my money in my tent," Myke allowed wistfully. "Pam and I shared a tent and we both left our money stuck in our sleeping bags."

"When we get there," he told her, "all you're going to need is an appetite."

"Boy," she croaked.

"You're not hungry are you?"

"When I was waiting on that ledge," she said, "I thought about eating my shirt."

It was good to talk that way, it helped reduce the pain of what had happened, the anxiety of what was to come. He found his sack of chocolate bars in one of the outside pockets of his Kelty pack and he gave one full bar to each of them and passed around the canteen. Then, when they were ready, he started up toward the summit, the two girls behind him, Kate bringing up the rear. She carried her rucksack and one of the ice axes; he carried the other. Myke carried the two coiled ropes. He had offered to carry one of them, but she had said no, she was feeling all right everything considered. The candy, she said, had tasted terrific. Pam said nothing. She had only eaten when Kate had insisted, then she had eaten slowly and without interest.

He guessed the distance between the place where the wall ended and the summit itself to be no more than half a mile. The ground was rocky at first, but soon became snow-covered, the snow old and well consolidated, the angle of climb gradual enough not to require the precaution of ropes. The visibility in the rocky area was poor, but once they were on the snow it improved somewhat and he found he was able to make his way steadily and without pausing to be sure of his bearings.

The wind died for a while, and he hoped they would be lucky and not have to endure the storm after all. But then the wind came up again as suddenly as if it had blown open a door, and he felt great wet flakes of snow along the right side of his face and neck and knew they would not be lucky that way. If it snowed hard and for a long time it would be difficult to move through the new snow and there would be for a while the danger of avalanche. But it would be difficult for Karpus too, and his fat friend, until he located their tracks. Then it would only be difficult for them.

The Wolf Mountain summit was shaped like a hand, tilted abruptly toward the sky. As its angle increased during the final fifty yards, he kicked steps into the snow and went up slowly, finding it difficult to breathe. Then, when he had reached the place beyond which he could

climb no higher, he turned and stood quietly with the
wind in his face and felt, as he waited for the others to
join him, what had become in the recent years of his life
a familiar complexity of sorrow and relief.

Four of us made it, he thought. *Four out of seven.*

PART TWO

JUNE 5 AND 6

DESCENDING

1

The summit cone of Wolf Mountain dipped a thousand yards to a long serrate ridge linking the mountain with Gaddis, a higher summit to the west. Quickly, Whittaker led the others to the start of this ridge and along the ridge itself until he came to the first substantial ridge tower, where, he knew, other climbers had placed an expansion bolt and descending ring. When he located this ring and tested it, he began uncoiling one of the ropes, making one of its ends fast to the ring, dropping the other end off the ridge, down into the night of its steep south wall.

Speaking deliberately, as if to a class, he said: "Kate will go first. There are three rappels. Each one is a hundred feet long. The first ends at a good wide ledge below here. The second ends on a smaller ledge at the top of a pretty steep slope of snow. The third winds up on the ground below the snow. I'll give each of you a belay with the other rope as you go, so there's no need to worry about falling or getting mixed up in the dark. If worse comes to worst, I'll lower you on down and Kate will be there to help you untie. Just before I do each pitch, I'll lower the two packs. As soon as we're down, we'll dig a cave in the snow and hole up for the rest of the night."

"You'll have to help Pam," Kate replied flatly. She

had fashioned a seat sling out of a short loop of rope and two carabiners. She wore gloves. The rappel rope came down from the tower to her left hand which she held at eye level now as she faced the tower itself. From her left hand the rope continued down to the carabiners of the seat sling, then up through the carabiners to her left shoulder. From that shoulder it passed diagonally across her back and into her right hand which she held close by her right thigh. From there it dropped out of sight off the ridge.

In the time it had taken to reach this place, she seemed to have become even more remote than she had on the traversing ledge, as if the two of them had entered a competition in which after a long struggle he had managed to prevail, as if added to the grief she felt over the loss of Neil and the twins was a resentment at what she took to be his usurpation of her role, his moving from last to first on a rope that was by rights her own to lead. And while he understood why her feelings might be ambivalent toward him at best, he found he was growing impatient with the distance she maintained, found that it riled him more than he would have guessed it could.

He wanted to say, *Look, this is your mess, not mine. I know how you feel about those kids, but don't take it out on me.*

But it was more than this, for had she not kept her distance even in the shack? Even when the twins had been alive? And was it because of what he had almost done to the fat man Johns? Would have done had she not interposed? Maybe so. When he looked at her now, he was aware of a distance of his own in the set of his face, in the tone of his voice as he spoke.

"Do you want a belay?"

"No," she said, backing toward the edge, letting the rope run. "I just want to get off of here. I want this to be over."

"Better take it easy going down then; you've only got one anchor. . . ."

"It's a good one isn't it?"

"Yes. It looks fine."

"Then I don't need a belay."

She leaned back against the rope, out over the edge. She wore her blue parka with its hood up, and wind-pants, and above these bulky clothes the shadow of her face looked small. He suspected that everything had reached her now: the death of Neil, and of Dietz and Dianne, what she had had to do with the fat man, the harrowing ascent of the east face, the fast-approaching storm and here these several dark rappels. But he thought too that she was holding on, as much for Pam's sake as for any of them, perhaps, but for the others also, and for herself. He liked that, and aligned with the anger her coolness produced in him, his feelings toward her had become conflicting, in a way that under these circumstances he did not welcome.

"On rappel," she said. Then she went down on the fixed rope, leaning back the way a telephone lineman leans back against his safety belt, letting the rope slide through her right hand, keeping her balance on the rope with her left, moving her feet catlike down the steep rock surfaces of the upper ridge wall, disappearing into the still deepening gloom below the place where the others stood.

"Okay," Whittaker said, securing the second rope to Pam's slender waist. "You're next."

"I can't. . . ."

"Yes, you can, you've done it before."

He guided her into position over the rope that came down from the rock tower. She wore her gloves and Levi's and his thermal pants bunched under her Levi's and Myke's parka which was much too big for her; when she leaned back over the edge, she looked like a tatter-demalion doll, her form still close but already indistinct from where Whittaker stood on belay. Her movements on the rope were mechanical, halfhearted, as if she no longer cared whether or not she reached the promised safety of the ground.

Snow swirled along the ridge. When he brought up the belay rope and tied it around Myke's waist, he was shivering badly.

"Gosh," she said. "I feel like a jerk wearing your undershirt."

"I'm fine as long as I keep moving," he told her, helping her get into position for the rappel. "Okay, you're all set now. Just back up a little, lean out, and down you go."

"Oh, boy," she breathed, glancing behind her.

"You'll be fine; I've got you belayed. Lean back now."

Very slowly she leaned back.

"More," he said. "Trust the rope."

She leaned back until she was committed, her eyes pressed shut.

"Let the rope move a little through your right hand and start moving down. . . ."

"My dumb legs are shaking. . . ."

"That's all right, move them one foot at a time. Do it the way Pam did. . . ."

"I mean they're like *really* shaking," she said. "I hope I don't faint."

"You're not going to faint. You're doing fine."

She answered him, but he could not make out what it was she had said. He stood in the lee of the rocky tower, snow pelting him now, paying out the rope as she went. When the signal came that she was down, he lowered the two packs and the ice axes, then reorganized the rappel so he would be able to retrieve the ropes once he had made his descent: He untied the rappel rope from the ring, joining it with the belay rope, using a double sheet-bend knot. By the time he had finished, his hands were numb and he had to blow on them and beat the circulation back into them before he put on his gloves and started his own rappel down the now doubled rope.

The wind swept over the ridge, tore at his parka and pants. Snow stung his face. There were times when he had to stop and close his eyes and wait for the drive of the wind to ease. He hoped it would be a quick storm. He hoped it would not take them too long to dig an adequate cave in the consolidated snow below the ridge. He hoped that by eating some food and getting a few hours' rest they would be strong again, would be able to move out at first light if the snow had stopped or as soon as it did stop. He hoped Karpus would not find them easily, would be late getting started from the shack, perhaps slowed up by the fat man Johns, or that he would spend time looking for them in the area of what had been their camp or on the south slope of the mountain or along the regular basin trail. He hoped most of all as he went down the doubled rope that from this point on for the four of them things would go well, for he thought—and knew it was foolish to think so—they had had their share of suffering.

When he reached the first rock shelf where the others were waiting, still 200 feet above the ground, he saw Kate holding Pam as if to keep the girl from moving too close to the edge.

"There's something wrong with Pam," Myke told him quietly, standing close to the wall, hanging on.

"She'll be all right," he said. "We'll be off of here before you know it."

"It's like she's in a daze or something. . . ."

"We can lower her if we have to. . . ."

He hauled on one end of the doubled rope, watched the other end move up the wall until it was lost in a dusky swirl of snow, kept hauling until the rope ran through the descending ring a hundred feet above. As it whipped back down the wall it made the whirring sound of a lariat. At shoulder height above the shelf where he stood, a second descending ring had been placed. Quickly, he separated the ropes and set up the second of the three rappels.

"All right, Kate?" he called when he had finished.

She came to him along the ledge, one arm clamped tightly around Pam's waist.

"Myke, hold her," she said. "Don't let her go for one second."

"I'll hold her," Myke said. "Don't worry. I could anchor a boat."

When Kate got into position on the rope, Whittaker thought she moved awkwardly. Twice she pressed her glove against her face as if to dry her cheek where the snow had melted.

"Let me give you a belay this time," he said.

"No, thank you."

She backed slowly to the edge of the shelf, fussing with the rope.

"The ledge below this one is narrow," he said. "Not half the size of this and it could be iced up. . . ."

"*I don't want a belay,*" she snapped.

He might have snapped back at her, but she was already roping down and he was exhausted, could feel a trembling in his legs, a dizzying pressure in his gut. When he tied the belay rope around Pam's waist, she began to untie it, pulling absently at the knot.

"You listen to me," he said, knocking her hand

away. "I know how hard this has been for you, and I know you think it's never going to be over. But it is. You're going to do these last two rappels. . . . *Listen to me,*" he said, his hand clamped on her shoulder now. "You're going to do them because you have to do them. Kate's already down there waiting for you. She's already done this one, and for her there's only one to go and it's the easiest of all and once she's done it she'll be on level ground. I've got a sleeping bag in my pack. It's a fine down bag and it's warm and as soon as we get down there I'm going to get it out and get you into it, all right? We've got a Primus stove and a bottle of gas and some packets of soup and as soon as we get down and dig our cave Myke is going to cook up that soup and we're going to drink that and eat some tuna and noodles I brought and munch on some more candy bars and as soon as the snow stops we're going to hike to my truck and you're going to be back home safe and sound."

"He won't let us," she said. Her face was wet from the snow. "He won't let us go."

"He's not going to know where we are, believe me. He's going to waste half a day looking for us on the south slope of Wolf Mountain because he thinks that's the way we'll have to come down. By the time he figures out what we've done we'll be long gone."

"You can do it, Pam," Myke said hoarsely. "The sooner we're down, the sooner I can cook the soup. You're a lot better at doing rappels than I am. I mean I'm *really* bad, but I'm going to do it. . . ."

"Come on," Whittaker said. He was guiding her now, helping her back toward the edge of the slippery rock shelf. "The worst part is getting started. Once you're past this ledge you'll be down in no time."

"Let me stay here. . . ."

"No, you can't stay here."

"I don't care what happens. . . ."

"Yes you do."

"Come *on*, Pam," Myke said.

"Lean back. You can do this. I've got you."

"Just let me stay here," she replied. Her voice was reedy and thin. "You can go. . . ."

"Geez, we *can't* go without you," Myke said. "We can't leave you here. Come on. We can eat as soon as we're down. Some of us are pretty hungry. He's got you on belay, you'll be okay. He's got tuna and noodles in his rucksack. And a stove. And *soup*. . . ."

When at last the girl did lean back and commit herself to the rappel, the pilot sighed his relief and payed out the belay rope slowly from a standing belay position as she disappeared below the shelf. *One more pitch after this,* he thought. Then the belaying rope suddenly pulled tight against his back and he knew Pam had come off her rappel, not halfway down he guessed from the amount of rope she had taken so far.

"Something's wrong," Myke said. She was on her hands and knees, peering into the night below the ledge.

"Can you see her?"

"I can't see anything, I hate to get too close to the edge here; I heard something. . . ."

"Call to her. Tell her to hang on. Tell her I'm going to start lowering her. Tell Kate to be ready."

Myke cupped her hands, called into the rush of wind and snow what he had told her to call. He began lowering the rope, letting it move slowly, a foot at a time, feeling the burn of it across his back, feeling the girl's weight above his left hip where the rope passed on its way to the edge of the shelf. He lowered her twenty feet, paused to open and close his numb fists, first one, then the other;

then he lowered her twenty feet more. When he felt the
tension go out of the rope he knew she had reached the
narrow ledge above the steep snow. As soon as Kate had
freed the belay rope, he brought it up and tied it around
Myke's solid waist.

"You be careful," he said. "But get down there as
fast as you can. Kate may need help. Tell her to tie Pam
in, tie her right to the descending ring if she has to."

"Okay, I will," Myke said.

She backed to the edge, closed her eyes, leaned out
and began to go down the rope in the halting way she
had. He belayed her as she went. He was worried now.
When he tried to remember how much room there was
on the ledge above the snow he could not, could only
remember it was small and pitched enough to be hazard-
ous if it was icy or wet. When the signal came, he lowered
the two packs and the ice axes, joined the ends of the two
ropes again, got into position and began his own descent. He did not descend as slowly or carefully this time
but, under the force of his apprehension, went rapidly
down the doubled rope, feeling the heat of its passing
across his shoulder, across the wet palms of his gloves.
The snow swirled around him, a wet confetti that seemed
to explode in many directions and added to his uncer-
tainty as to just how far he had come down from the
upper ledge and how far he had to go.

"*Kate!*" he called. He wanted to hear her voice, let
it guide him to the right place, tell him when it was time
to slow his rapid descent, warn him when he was nearing
the end of the doubled rope. He heard someone answer,
a shrill and frightened cry. He tried to move faster:
Something had gone wrong, something had happened
on the pitched ledge below. He heard shouts, a scream,
heard his name called. When he tried to increase his rate

of descent the burning of the rope across his shoulder and palms became unbearable and he cried out and braked himself, swaying giddily, trying to see to the place below his feet.

"*Kate!*" he cried. "*Myke!*"

"*Hurry!*" someone shouted. He thought it was Myke. She sounded close. He started down again, the heat rising instantly across his palms. Now he could see a figure looming below him just to his left, spectral in what was left of the moon's light as it filtered through the advancing storm.

"*What is it!*" he called. "*What's wrong!*"

"*It's Pam!*"

Then he was on the narrow ledge. He could feel the slick pitch under his boots. He kept one hand on the doubled rope, clawed at the rocky wall with the other, tried to find the security of a hold. Myke was just to his right. Kate was to his left. She had hung the two packs from the last descending ring and now she was tearing at one of them as if to free something she desperately wanted, and when he realized what it was he tried to move toward her, but his boots slipped from under him and he hung helpless by one hand from the doubled rope, his other hand reaching for the wall.

"*Kate!*" he shouted. "*Stay here! Myke! Don't let her go!*"

His mouth was dry. When he tried to shout again, he found he could not shape the words. He felt Myke grope past him on the ledge, trying to go between him and the wall toward the place where the packs had been hung.

"*Kate,*" he said hoarsely, "*Don't . . .*"

But she had one of the ice axes now, and all he could do was watch her, a vaguely articulated shape beyond his reach, as she backed off the shelf, slithering belly down, riding the ax, disappearing without a sound down the slope of snow that measured what would have been the last hundred feet of their descent.

"*Where's Pam?*" he said. "*What happened?*"

"*She fell,*" Myke said. "*She just pulled away from Kate and fell.*"

2

In the timber below what had been the climbers' camp, a freezing rain had begun to fall, driven on an erratic, swirling wind, the rain slashing and ticking against the heaving branches of the trees, lancing into the small puddles it had created along the trail. Johns sat with his head in his hands below a ledge of rock that blindsided the trail, looking as if he had recently fallen from the ledge and was waiting with diminishing hope for the arrival of the king's horses and men. A kerosine lantern burned on the ground between his legs, warming him, lending a jack-o'-lantern aspect to his features with its play of shadow and light. Several feet away, Karpus untied the last of six compact down-filled sleeping bags which he pushed—as he had the first five—into an orange two-man tent that stood erect on a slant of ground, open to the uptrail, concealed from the trail itself by the rock ledge below which Johns sat holding his head.

"You're going to like this," Karpus said. "You're going to like this a lot better than you would have liked spending this kind of night in that goddamn shack."

"*What?*" Johns cried against the wind and rain.

"I said, you're going to *like* this."

"Is the fucking thing ready?"

"Just about. I want to get that stove of theirs primed up and rig a couple of tie-down lines in case this wind picks up any more than it has, and I want to rig a trip line around the perimeter. . . ."

"*What?*" Johns cried.

"A trip line, so anybody slips up on us tonight will fall on their tails. Then we'll get you inside and get the lantern in there to warm things up and I'll make us some hot coffee. . . ."

"I wanna lay down."

"You just hang on there about ten more minutes. I'll have everything set. I've got it fixed up like a nest in there, snug as hell. You're going to like it, Johns. These people had some uptown gear, best you can get. You get dried off and warmed up, little hot coffee with some whiskey and maybe a smoke, you're going to feel fit come morning."

Johns began to moan; otherwise, he did not reply. Karpus busied himself with his tasks, rigging the tie-down lines and the trip line around the perimeter, smiling at the picture that came to him then of the pilot sneaking up to the tent only to trip and fall on his tail. He did not think about having missed the pilot and the others as they had gone up the last hundred feet of the wall. That was over now, behind him, part of the irrevocable past. At the time, he had attributed his failure with the rifle to an unreasonable falling off of the moon's light and an increase in the strength of the wind that had blown steadily across his field of fire. He had felt a brief burning sensation in the area of his heart when he realized the fat girl had risen from the dead below the chimneylike gap, but the burning sensation had expired as quickly as had the realization, both becoming part of the past and hence not to be thought of. Tomorrow would present itself. Right now he had these things to do in order to help himself spend a secure and comfortable night out of this accumulating storm, and in order to help Johns who had been his companion in prison and who had been recently hurt.

I like what you've done for your cellmate, the warden had said. Karpus had nodded solemnly, revealing nothing of the amusement he felt that neither the warden nor the therapy guy nor anyone on the furlough-selection committee had seen a design behind his looking after the fat man Johns.

"I think he's had a bad rap," Karpus had said. "I'm here because I deserve to be; but I think Johns sort of tripped himself up because he's got a temper and he doesn't always understand what's going on."

"The furlough officer tells me that since you've been sharing a cell with Johns, Johns has had no trouble getting along with the other men."

"I'd say that's right."

"His work record has been excellent. Was it your idea to have him transferred to the library?"

"I put him in for it."

"You worked there for a while yourself, didn't you?"

"About two years. Then I moved over to the shop so I could learn how to use some tools. I figure I'm in, and as long as I'm in I'm not going to sit around doing dead time."

"Your work sheet says you reorganized the library, increased its efficiency, recatalogued the history section. . . . Do you like history, Karpus?"

"I like it fine."

"Did you read Gibbon?"

"I read Volume One. It took me a while, but it was good stuff."

"Yes, it is. Can you name me a Roman emperor?"

"Sure, Elagabalus."

"That's not one I've heard of."

"He's in there," Karpus said. "Julian is another."

"Does Johns read too?"

"I've tried to get him to read, but so far I haven't had any luck."

"He's putting in for a furlough. Did you know that?"

"Yes," Karpus said, aware the warden had known that he knew.

"I understand he wants you to go with him."

"He told me."

"Well, we've let some of our lifers out. We've had good luck; a perfect record, as a matter of fact. I'm not saying we can do this in your case, but we can think about it. Would you be interested?"

"Sure. I'll be up for a parole in eight years. I hear a good furlough record can help. . . ."

"As far as we know, Johns hasn't got anyone on the outside. You didn't list anyone, but your sheet says you have an older brother in Morenci, Arizona. Do you keep in touch with him?"

"No. I don't."

"Would he sponsor you on a furlough? He would have to be willing to come up here. . . ."

"He wouldn't. He never liked me much."

"That's a problem then. We can't release Johns without a sponsor. You either, if you qualify."

"I get along pretty good with the therapy guy; maybe he could help out, or tell us about somebody who could."

"All right. Don't count on it, but go ahead and approach him. As far as I'm concerned, I'd like to see you and Johns stay together. He was pretty badly treated before you took an interest in him. You know, you're a puzzler to me, Karpus; I don't mind telling you that. I know just about everything that goes on in this institution, who runs the inmates in each of the blocks, who's got the muscle, who's got his pants down. I can't always do much about it, but I always know. Your block is one of the hardest we've got. We never should have put Johns in there in the first place, but that's the kind of thing that happens when you've got this big a prison to run and too few people to help you run it. Duane Jegalian runs that block; he has for years. The inmates who go in there do what he tells them to do, but not you I hear."

"Duane's all right. I don't bother him and he doesn't bother me. I mind my own business."

"And you get away with it?"

"I guess."

The warden shook his head. He leaned back in his chair, put the tips of his fingers together, looked at the tall inmate who stood politely, waiting to be excused. "All right, Karpus. You keep up the good work. Let me know how you make out."

Karpus had made out fine. The therapy guy had gone along, had agreed to sponsor the two of them himself. They were to be furloughed for twelve hours, were due at his house for supper. Johns had wanted no part of supper at the therapy guy's house. Neither had Karpus. They had gone shopping instead.

"Boy, she's really blowing," Karpus said. He had set the lantern inside the tent whose sides now glowed orange and rose and fell in the wind. "She's blowing like a sonofabitch. Come on, Johns, get your tail inside. She's going to snow before morning."

"I've got pressure in my head!" Johns cried, stumbling up from his place below the ledge.

"A storm will do that to you."

"It's not the storm, for Chrissake, it's my *head,* like my eyes are going to pop out! Jesus, Karpus, I got to get to a doctor or I'm going to fucking well die. . . ."

Karpus took the fat man's arm. "Take her easy now."

"Are you listening to me?"

"You got to whiz, you better whiz now, get it over with so you don't have to crawl out here in the middle of the night."

"I don't have to whiz!"

"Okay. Get on in there then. Careful around that lantern."

"Jesus Christ!"

"We don't want that tent going up like a torch. You take the left side going in. We'll keep our heads by the door."

Karpus went to the outskirts of his camp, relieved himself, looked up at the tossing trees, turned when he had finished to let the sleet sting his face. There were only two ways out of the basin and from here he knew he could cover them both. The climbers who had escaped were high up somewhere; idly he wondered if the storm would kill them. He could see the rotund silhouette of Johns moving behind the tent wall. The wind sucked the orange wall in and heaved it out as if the tent itself were engaged in a labored effort to breathe.

He got the Weatherby from its place under the ledge and took it with him into the tent. Johns was lying on his back where he had been told to lie, on a deep cushion of fine down bags. His mouth was open, his eyes shut, the fingertips of his left hand pressed to his temples as if he would at any moment now give birth to an idea.

"I'll keep one of the flaps open long as we're burning this lantern," Karpus said. "We don't want to use up all our good air. I was going to brew some coffee, but maybe we'll just have a shot of whiskey and a smoke and turn in, what do you say?"

Johns said nothing.

"I wouldn't want to be any higher up on this mountain than we are right now on a buggering cold night like this, would you, Johns?"

"No," Johns said.

"Well, there's four of 'em up there. That pilot and three of those girls. I thought I had that fat one, but she got away."

"*What?*"

"That fat one had her name on her shirt?"

"No!" Johns cried.

"I thought I had her straight off, but she must have played possum on me and now she's up there somewhere with that pilot and the other two." He found the whiskey and cigarettes, reminded himself that he needed a shave. "Keeps up," he said, "maybe this storm will kill them, you know? Maybe it will freeze them up."

"I really hurt," Johns said. "I hope it freezes the piss out of them."

Karpus nodded. He could not tell for sure, but he thought Johns might be coming back to what he had been before he had gotten whacked on the head. "We've done ourselves a furlough," he said.

"*I'm all plugged up. . . .*"

"You and me."

3

It took time for Whittaker to reorganize the ropes, to belay Myke down the final slope of snow, lower the two packs and rope down himself. In the time that it did take, he tried not to think of what might have happened to Kate and to Pam who, Myke said, had suddenly broken loose from Kate's grip and had gone over the edge. It was, Myke said, as if Pam had wanted to fall.

Just beyond the angle where the steep snow ended and the gentle snow began, in a small area free of stone, they found Kate holding the girl in her arms. She did not look up when they approached, the light so minimal now Whittaker could barely differentiate their forms.

"Kate, let me see her," he said.

"No."

"I might be able to help. . . ."

"You can't help her now."

He stood over the crouched, amorphous form of the dark-haired woman, moved his hand tentatively, then let it drop by his side. He stood with his eyes half closed, snow building on his shoulders, swirling in eddies around his feet. He had never been colder than he was now, nor had he been more tired. At what seemed a great distance he heard Myke ask: "Is Pam dead too?"

Kate did not reply. Her arms were folded around the girl as if to shield her body from the storm. Whittaker took off one of his gloves. Instinctively and without much hope, he reached down and took the girl's wrist. He could not find a pulse. When he pressed his numb fingers against the side of her neck, the flesh was cold and clammy to touch; he found no beating of blood.

"Myke," he said, "get my pack."

"Sure," she replied. "I'll bring both of them." The packs were only a few yards away. Myke dragged them over.

Whittaker found his flashlight, switched it on, its beam bright against the white snow. Stiffly, he knelt beside Kate and the girl. "Let me see her," he said. When Kate shook her head, he put his hands on her arms and moved her away from Pam. "Myke," he said, "hold this light for me, will you?" He was shivering badly again, and for almost a minute he warmed his fingers between his legs and then he placed them again along the side of the girl's neck.

"I think she's alive," he said.

"It was my fault," Kate said suddenly.

"It wasn't anybody's fault," he said. "Just forget that, will you?"

"I should have held onto her up there. . . ."

"That's crap!"

"To you maybe it is, you weren't there. . . ."

"Just cut it out, will you? Just cut it the fuck out."

She was silent, drew back from him. He felt a throbbing at his temple, felt her dislike of him as an almost tangible weight now, gratuitous it seemed and unendurable, added as it was to the weight of all that had come down since Karpus had taken him at the prospector's shack.

"What are we going to do?" Myke asked quietly.

"There's a first-aid kit in my pack," he replied. "Get it out, get out my sleeping bag too."

Myke rummaged through the red Kelty pack, found the kit and the tightly rolled bag and handed them to the pilot. Blood oozed from the two cuts at the left side of Pam's face. He used his handkerchief and some snow to clean the area around the cuts. Then he took two large gauze pads from the kit and taped them over the cuts, keeping pressure on them until the bleeding seemed to stop. He asked Myke to shine the beam of the flashlight directly into the girl's eyes and was satisfied when the pupils contracted. He examined her for fractures, going through the motions now as he had in training; and while he did, the wind blew with such force that he had to support himself with one hand and work with the other.

"Her leg's broken," he said finally, and he found it cost him to say it for he knew he was saying it to her, Kate, who watched in silence. "A simple fracture, I think. I can't find anything else."

"She has to have a doctor. . . ."

"I know that. We'll do what we can now."

"She has to get back to town. . . ."

"Myke," he said, "you give me a hand. We'll fix up her leg."

He told Myke what to do, and together they straightened the leg and he fashioned a splint from Kate's ice ax which he secured with a padding of cloth and several loops of web sling. Then he unrolled and unzipped his bag and the two of them covered Pam with it as best they could.

"Try to keep her warm," he said to Kate.

She had crouched again by the girl until her back was between the girl and the brunt of the storm. At once, snow began to build on her parka. Whittaker handed her the light.

"I think she's all right," he said, trying now to gentle his tone. "You should keep a check on her breathing. If you think it's getting shallow, call me. Myke and I are going to dig a cave. We'll need some time."

Kate nodded.

"Call if you need us," he said.

He took his ax; Myke followed him. He walked along the base of the steep snow slope, shielding his eyes with his cupped gloved hands, trying to find some suitable place to begin; and because he could not see at all well, at last he simply began to dig, swinging the ax in short, quick strokes, working until his arms began to ache and then stepping back and handing the ax to Myke.

They worked it that way, taking turns. The storm increased. The wind was dislodging stone from the ridge; it fell like hail around them. Even with his parka hood up, he felt terribly cold, and the tempo with which he swung the ax seemed to increase proportionally to the rising pitch of the storm. Myke, who had given her parka to Pam, worked at a slower, more deliberate pace. The blade of the ax had not been designed for heavy work. Sometimes when they swung it, it would pass cleanly through the snow. They worked hard and said little to each other although his affection for her had deepened: For what seemed a long time now they had shared a rope, and he sensed that she had from the start freely given him her trust. This touched him, particularly when he compared it to Kate whose trust had been, it seemed to him, stubbornly withheld.

He estimated the room it would take to house four of them, and together they shaped the cave to this dimension. At first he had to peer through the slits of his eyes and felt grains of snow build on his lashes, but as they began to penetrate the side hill it afforded them shelter. They stopped using the ax after a while, holding their hands together like scoops, working side by side in unison, widening and shaping the room of the cave.

"My hands are freezing," Myke said. She said it good-naturedly.

"Bang them together," he said. "Get them going again." His own hands felt like lumps of frozen meat under his gloves.

"Pam's really hurt, isn't she?"

"She's alive. That's what's important."

"I don't see why . . ."

"Why what?" he said.

"I don't know. Like why Kate gets mad at you. . . ."

"She's uptight, she's got a right to be; we all do."

"I know. But she shouldn't blame you."

"She doesn't know me from Adam, Myke. Come on now, let's get this done." But he agreed, and was glad Myke had noticed and spoken up.

It took a long time for the two of them to finish the cave. When it finally was finished, they made their way back to the others, holding their hands in front of their faces, blinking against the slap of the large wet flakes of snow that swirled around them. Kate was still crouched over Pam's inert form. Snow had drifted against her legs, was piled on her back.

"Has she come to yet?" Whittaker asked.

"No."

"Is she breathing all right?"

"Yes. . . . I don't know—I think she is."

"We've got the cave ready; it's going to be all right. Come on."

"We made it b-big," said Myke whose teeth chattered when she talked. "It's p-pretty nice out of the wind."

"Come on," he said. "Let's get Pam inside."

Together the three of them lifted Pam and brought her into the cave. She stayed unconscious. Once they were inside, Whittaker and Myke closed up the large center opening with chunks of snow, leaving a small, downsloping tunnel to the outside. With his ax, he poked a vent hole through the roof. Then he stuck the flashlight into one wall of the cave; its light, reflected by the snow, was ample. They covered the floor of the cave with the two ponchos Kate had brought, fashioned a bed out of the ropes and sleeping bag and, with Kate helping now, they moved Pam onto it, on her back with her head raised. Then Myke and Kate took off the girl's socks and parka and gloves, replacing them with dry clothes from the rucksack while Whittaker cleaned the abrasions on her face and hands, painting them with Merthiolate. When she woke suddenly and in pain, he gave her a codeine tablet and soon she was asleep again.

"I'm not sure," he said. "She might have a concussion. . . ."

"What chance do we really have?" Kate said. "Even if Pam wasn't hurt like this . . ."

"We can sit out the storm now," he said, and again he had to work to keep the tension from his voice, for he thought she might be giving up, and if she was he knew he could not abide it, that it would rile him more than her bitterness had, that it would remind him of how he himself had felt on his way to these mountains, on his long drive up from Morgan. "We're not going to freeze. We can dry ourselves out and eat some hot food and take turns getting some sleep. They're not going to find us here."

"What if they do?"

"They won't. They've got no idea where we are; they're not going to find any tracks, not the way it's snowing out there now; and they're not going to see any light or smoke. . . ."

"I'll bet they're in that shack," Myke said. "They

wouldn't be out looking for us now. . . ."

"That's right. Let's get squared away in here and look after Pam. We've got at least a few hours before we can make any move out of here no matter what we decide to do."

"I'm supposed to be the cook," Myke said.

"All right. Let's get into whatever dry clothes we've got; then I'll get my stove going and you can cook the soup."

"Wow," Myke said. "Soup."

Kate said nothing.

4

After that, it was better for a while. The cave, not six feet across, was very tight with the four of them inside. They sat facing the entrance tunnel, the curve of the cave roof close above their heads. Myke and Kate sat on either side of Pam. Whittaker sat on his now empty pack between Myke and the wall of the cave into which he had stuck the light. Myke had found a wool sweater in the rucksack, had insisted he wear it. In such cramped quarters they had to struggle to get it on over his shirt. Then he had gotten his parka back on and for the first time in a long while he felt decently warm. He had checked out the wound on his upper right thigh, thought it superficial, but it was sore; he had cleaned and bandaged it.

During all the time it took for them to dry themselves and sort out gear, to cook what they had and eat and clean up, he and Myke talked only of the little things: how best to adjust the flame of the stove; what should be put first into the pot, the tuna or noodles or soup. He was aware of an atmosphere of subdued cheerfulness which he knew the two of them had contrived in order to keep their anxiety at bay.

Kate remained silent. Twice he tried to have her join in, each time without luck. Myke tried too. Finally, they operated within their small conspiracy to make the best of things.

When Pam next woke, groaning at first, then crying out, Kate gave her another of the tablets, and before it had taken effect Myke gave her some hot soup, holding her in one arm, tipping the cup gently with the other, talking to her agreeably as if within the next hour or so she would be feeling quite well again. Then Pam drifted away into a silent sleep, and outside the entrance tunnel the storm raged. Myke took Whittaker's gloves away and stuck them under her shirt to dry, then lay down on her parka, telling the others she was awfully tired, and she too went to sleep. It seemed to him she went to sleep instantly, her mannish snore filling the cave, her great breast heaving against the writing on her shirt. He found that he missed her at once. Except for her snores and the sound of the wind outside, an awkward silence pervaded the cave.

"She's some kid," he said finally, nodding at the chunky girl who slept beside him. From a few feet away, Kate nodded. "Look," he said, "I'm sorry I got worked up out there. I just don't like to hear somebody with your kind of courage crying in her beer."

"Is that what I was doing?"

"I thought so."

"I'm sorry I disappointed you."

"You haven't disappointed me; even if you had it wouldn't matter much. You've disappointed yourself, haven't you?"

She was silent.

"I know what's working on you," he said. "And has ever since those kids came off that wall. You're capable and smart and probably good at whatever you do, but you couldn't keep that psycho from doing what he did to Pam and the twins and you couldn't keep Pam from falling. . . ."

"Please shut up," she said. Her parka hood was down, her hair untied; she was covering her face with her hands.

"You feel as if you killed Dianne and Dietz, and hurt Pam, don't you? Because you were responsible for them."

"All right, yes."

"And that's crap," he said.

"To you maybe it is."

He shook his head. The flashlight was dimming. He had spare batteries in his pack, but in this moment he preferred the reduced light.

"What could you have done to help those twins?" he asked.

"I don't know. . . ."

"What could you have done to keep Karpus from shooting your friend Neil in the back?"

"I don't know. Nothing."

"That's right."

"Maybe I shouldn't have tried the climb. . . ."

"Maybe not."

"You could have stopped us if you'd been more sure. . . ."

"But I wasn't sure. Any more than you were."

She was silent, as if she had heard what he said but did not believe it was true, as if nothing he said was going to alter the despair that had taken her. She seemed very young to him now. He seemed very old to himself.

"You told me you had cigarettes?" he said.

"Yes. In my rucksack."

"Do you mind if I have one?"

She shook her head, found the pack, handed it to him, their two hands reaching across the inert forms of the two sleeping girls. The matches had been tucked between the cellophane and the package. He saw his hands shake as he lit one, taking a deep drag, letting the smoke escape slowly through his nostrils.

"Want one?"

"No."

"A cigarette isn't much," he said, "but right now it seems like a lot. Are you married?"

She looked at him as if to challenge his right to ask. Her coloring had come back and was heightened by the diffuse light in the cave until, as she faced him now, her cheeks burned as they might have from a fever. He thought she was beautiful, in a way that Marie had not been beautiful, in a way that was more sophisticated, perhaps.

"No," she replied. "I was once."

"Children?"

"No."

"Think you'll do it again? Get married I mean?"

"I don't know."

"You're young," he said. "Were you married long?"

"Just a year."

He nodded, watching the coal of the cigarette pull through its paper cylinder as he inhaled. He had pretty much resigned himself to her refusal to accept him when unexpectedly he heard her ask: "Are you married?"

"No, but I was once too. For ten years as a matter of fact."

"Were there children?"

"Yes, two. A boy, Ben, nine; and a girl, Amy, eight. I didn't get married until I was in my late twenties. My wife was ten years younger. We broke it up about a year ago. What do you teach?"

"English literature."

"Have you got all your tickets?"

She looked at him.

"Degrees." he said. "M.A., Ph.D., whatever?"

"Yes. I have them."

"I'd have bet on that."

She was silent.

"I meant that one as a compliment," he said.

"Do you like your children?" she asked, as if she thought it was quite possible he did not.

"Sure, I like them fine. I haven't seen as much of them as I wish. . . ."

"Because of the war?"

"Yes."

"My husband wanted a brood mare instead of a woman, especially a woman with a career."

"I know that kind of problem."

"Really?"

"My wife wanted me to forget I was a fighter pilot."

"You went over there I suppose."

"Yep."

"Rockets and napalm?"

"That's right."

She pulled her hair back from her damp flushed cheeks, looked up at the close ceiling of the cave.

"You don't approve of that, do you?" he said.

"It doesn't matter what I approve of."

"That's all right. Marie didn't approve of it either. She was an ambassador's daughter; she should have known better than marry a career man."

"Do you think we belonged over there?"

"I did at the time."

"Do you still?"

"No. Not the way it's turning out."

"Are you bitter about that?"

"I wish it had turned out differently, one way or the other. It's screwed up their country and ours too. I don't see it as the white hats and black hats anymore. There were good and bad people on both sides and a lot of them made mistakes."

"It never is the white hats and black hats, is it?"

"Sure. I think it was in World War Two, don't you? I think it was today with Karpus and his friend. I don't think those twins did anything to deserve what happened to them, or your friend Neil either, do you? I think Johns earned what he got, maybe more. I know you could read me a book on all the things that might have made him the way he was, but I'd be happier if he was dead right now, and a hell of a lot happier if Karpus was dead too."

She did not reply, and from her silence he supposed she did not accept his view of things any more now than when she had kept him from killing the fat man on the cot. He had finished the first cigarette and now lit another, cupping his hands around the match. His hands trembled. Outside the cave the wind gusted suddenly; he heard a sift of snow in the entrance tunnel.

"I used to smoke," he said. "A pack of Camels a day. Then the surgeon general's report came out and I gave them up except when I was flying missions over there. I'd usually do about half a pack when I got back from a run."

He thought she had been about to reply when suddenly the injured girl groaned. He pulled the dimming light from its place in the wall of the cave, trained its beam on the left side of her face which was bruised and swollen where it showed around the sterile pads. The right side was unmarked, smooth and pale. He placed his fingertips on her neck and found her pulse, weak but regular, and it was as if he had found something so valuable he dared not breathe for fear of disturbing it.

"How is she?" Kate asked. The vapor of her breath moved between them as she spoke.

"Better."

"Do you really think that? If you don't, you can say so. I can handle it now."

"She's hurt, but she's young and a lot tougher than I guessed when I first saw her. If we can keep her warm and get her out tomorrow . . ."

"I don't see how we can do that."

"We'll rig something."

"I don't mean just finding a way to carry her. I mean getting her out without them seeing us."

"We can't stay here."

"She could. One of us could stay with her. . . ."

"Let's see what it looks like in the morning," he said, returning the light to its place in the wall. "We don't know how long this snow is going to last; we can't decide anything now."

"What time is it?"

He looked at his watch, a Japanese Seiko. The crystal had gotten scratched, a small triangular piece had chipped out, but the watch was still running.

"Four in the A.M.," he said.

"She's asleep again."

"Good. Let's hope she sleeps from now until dawn."

"I'm going to try to do that myself," she said. She lay down on her side, facing the close cave wall with her back to him and her hip settled on the now empty rucksack she had brought, her head pillowed on a pile of web sling.

"I'll keep an eye on Pam," he said.

"If you think I'm not holding up . . ."

"You're holding up fine. It took guts to do what you did, coming down that snow in the dark."

She did not answer him, and soon he thought from what he could hear of her breathing that she had indeed fallen asleep. He switched off the light, tried to make himself comfortable, tried to curl up next to Myke who still slept on her back; but in spite of his exhaustion he found he could not manage anything more than a rest-less half-sleep in which he dreamed that it was not Myke but Kate whose warmth he could feel in the chilly cave; Kate who sat next to him with her dark hair and eyes and feverish cheeks; Kate who asked him in his dream:

"What time is it?"

"Four in the A.M."

"I thought you were going to say something like twenty-four hundred hours, and I'd have to ask you what it meant."

He laughed. "I'm out of the Air Force now."

"Is there really a café in Morgan that serves plank steaks?"

"Roger that."

She smiled, rested her head against his chest. He put his arms around her. "You may not think much of me for saying it," she said, "but I don't think we're going to make it to Morgan. I don't mean just Pam. I mean all of us."

"I think we will."

"I know you do. Why do you think that? There's no reason to really. You know he has the odds on his side."

"I think it because if I don't think it I'll lie down here and not bother to get up again."

"I'm not saying we won't try to survive, I'm only saying I don't think we'll succeed."

"Cut it out," he said.

She tipped her head to look at him. He thought she looked older in this light, closer to thirty than the twenty-five he had guessed; her face burnished by the wind and snow, her high cheeks lustrous, her lips chapped.

"That's crap," he said. "You know it and I know it. If you really believed it you'd still be tied to that chair back there. We always think we're going to survive, in our guts we do, if not in our brains."

"Your hands are freezing," she said. She had put her hands over his where they circled her waist.

"Myke was drying out my gloves. They're over by her somewhere."

"There's room under this flannel shirt you gave me," she said. "I'm assuming you're not the type who gets embarrassed."

"It's been a long time since I got embarrassed," he said.

He groaned in his sleep, moved his hands inside her parka, inside the shirt, let them close gently over her breasts. She winced from the cold. He closed his eyes. As the palms of his hands began to warm, her nipples swelled against them. He heard her groan softly as if by putting his hands on her he had relieved her of a fear she had had that they would not be able to know each other this way, and had at the same time created in her a tension that was more sharply defined than that created by the storm and the man with the rifle and his fat friend and all that had happened in this long day.

"It's the same thing, isn't it?" she said.

"What is?"

"Wanting to do this, to survive, here and now."

"Yes."

"I don't see how we could work it, do you? It's so crowded in here. But if this is my last night on the planet Earth . . ."

"It's not."

"It's not what?"

"Too crowded."

"Don't say that if you don't mean it. . . ."

He groaned, aroused, came reluctantly awake. Outside, he could hear the storm, the howl of its winds and the sift and swirl of its snow in the tunnel entrance of the cave. Pam was sighing in her sleep. Myke's husky snore rattled on as if she were not in this cave at all but in a barracks somewhere, as if she had gotten a pass and gone into a southern town, had gotten ginned up and was back now, sleeping it off.

No, he thought. *I don't feel sorry for Karpus or Johns.*

He imagined that he felt Kate stir in his arms. He remembered bivouacking with Marie in a similar cave in the Alps soon after they first met. They had made love. She had said she was going to be too cold, and he had said like hell she would. They had smoked a cigarette afterward, had drunk some wine and eaten some cheese; they had known they would be out safe the next day. He had been young then. They had both been young. They had talked about how many children they would have.

"I like you," he said to Kate. "I like you a lot."

She was asleep, of course, across the cave, and did not hear him say that. He closed his eyes. She had been right about the odds. They were very much against them.

"I like you," he said.

Myke stirred next to him.

5

He must have slept soundly after that, though he had no memory of dropping off. He had been listening to the storm, hoping it would spend itself, hoping Pam would wake again and show her strength, dreaming his dream of what might have been with Kate, trying not to think about the rest of it, when he himself awoke.

He found the light, switched it on, looked at his watch. It was five. The snow, still falling heavily, had all but closed the entrance to the cave. He sat up and used his ax to clear the passage. His feet and face felt numb; his hands hurt as if he had recently held them too close to a flame. One of the canteens they had brought was empty. The other, still full, had frozen in the storm, the plastic cap split and raised like the top of a frozen bottle of milk in the days he remembered when milk had been delivered in bottles and left on porches in the winter.

He scraped his finger along the crystalline wall of the cave, feeling the cold burn under his nail, scooped up a ball of snow which he put on his tongue, letting the snow melt before he swallowed it. He had been raised by Catholic nuns in an orphanage in Mitchell, South Dakota, and in all the years he had spent in that place he could only remember one morning when the milk had frozen on the porch. It had been a bitter, subzero morning in February and the sister whose responsibility it was to bring in the milk as soon as it was delivered had fallen asleep in a large upholstered chair in the front room of the Victorian house. By the time the other sisters had gotten up—which had been early, but not as early as when the milkman came—the milk had already frozen. Sister Agnes. She was one of the few sisters he had known who actually liked to sleep. He liked the memory he held of her. She had always worn a knitted shawl. She had been a good and decent woman who had kept the faith. *I wonder if she's still alive?* he thought. *I wish I'd kept in touch.*

Then suddenly Pam woke up again. Her cries broke the quiet of the cave. She seemed more fully conscious this time, more aware of what was happening, her small face clenched against the pain she felt.

"Try to take it easy," he said. "I'll give you a pill. We haven't got any water, so you'll have to take it with some snow. Can you do that all right?"

"*Please!*" she cried.

Kate woke abruptly, reached out to take the girl's hand.

"What is it? What's wrong?"

"Give her this." He handed her one of the tablets. "The water's still frozen in the canteen. . . ."

"We better start the stove, make some tea or something while she's still awake."

He was about to rouse Myke when her snoring stopped suddenly in mid-snore, as if someone had switched it off. "I can make some tea," she said sleepily, her eyes still closed.

"Good," he said. "You've got my gloves under there too, I think."

She reached under her sweatshirt, pulled them out. "They're pretty dry," she said. "I told you it was hot in there."

She got the stove going and melted a pot of snow. Soon they were sharing a cup of hot sugared tea. By the time they had finished, Pam had begun to feel the effects of the pill.

"How are you doing?" Whittaker asked her.

"I feel better."

"Can you move your arms?"

"Yes."

"How about that good leg?"

"Yes."

He reached past Myke and gently touched the girl's injured leg in the area below the knee.

"Can you feel that?"

"Yes. I really messed things up, didn't I?"

He shook his head. "You did fine," he told her. "You even picked a good place to land."

"I didn't mean to mess things up for the rest of you. . . ."

"We're just glad you're with us," Kate said.

"I didn't want my father to know what happened to me."

"He doesn't have to know," Kate said. "Not if you don't want him to."

"He'd say it was my fault. . . ."

"I know your father," Kate said. "And I know how you might feel that way about him; but he's not as bad as you think he is. If you change your mind and decide you want to tell him after all, and you think it might be easier to tell him with me there, then I'll be there, okay?"

"He'll think it was my fault," the girl said. "He'll say I'm cheap. . . ." She started to cry. Kate held one of her hands and Myke held the other while she cried quietly.

"I don't see how he could say anything like that," Myke said. "He'd have to be pretty dumb to say anything like that."

"You don't know him."

"Well, I know him," Kate said. "I've worked with him long enough. When you went out with Ruben and your father got so mad he said he was going to meet Ruben somewhere and beat him up, I was the one who talked him out of it, isn't that right?"

"I know . . ."

"So don't you worry about your father. We can handle him all right. You just get well. . . ."

"I'm sorry I did what I did. . . ."

"Geez," Myke complained. "Forget it, will you? I thought you were dead. I'm really glad you're here. I didn't think anybody could fall down something like that in the middle of the night in a storm and not be dead."

"Those are neat pills," Pam said, her voice trailing off again. "I can see why some kids like them."

"What did her father want to beat up Ruben for?" Myke asked.

"Ruben was a good boy," Kate replied. "But he had very long hair."

"Is that all?"

"Yes, Myke. That's all."

"Oh," Myke said.

Kate lay down again between Pam and the cave wall; soon Whittaker was sure she had fallen asleep. Myke lay down, but she seemed restless and before he could switch off the now feeble light, she popped up again, sitting next to him. They talked for a while about Pam and how she felt about her father. Myke said her own father was even more shy than Pam but that her mother was not. The blizzard went on and the snow fell. Whittaker let it fill the passageway again, all but a few inches near the top which he kept clear with his ax. His thirst was terrible in spite of the tea. He ate snow, which had the texture of cotton and taste of camphor, felt it burn the tissues of his throat. He kept shifting his position, trying without luck to discover some comfortable alignment between himself and the collapsed pack on which he sat to avoid the damp of the ponchos that covered the snowy floor. The walls of the cave were close, the roof low; sitting where he was he felt as helpless as he had always felt in the high-altitude chamber when he took the mandatory refresher course, bolted in and at the mercy of the machine with someone else at the controls, waiting for the sudden blast of rapid decompression. He was glad Myke was awake. He felt like talking.

"Do you smoke?" he asked, lighting another cigarette, shielding the wavering flame of the match.

"I do a little grass every once in a while," she said. "That's about all."

"You're too much."

"How come?"

"I don't know. You just are."

"What are we going to do when it stops snowing? If it ever stops that is."

"I don't know. I've been thinking about it. We're still high on the mountain; a lot higher than they are. If we're lucky we might be able to get over to the Gaddis ridge. That's a couple of miles from here going west. We'd be pretty hard to see against the ridge, I think; a lot harder than we'll be when we're crossing the snow. I think we have a good chance of getting to my truck."

"I guess we came in some other way," she said. "Some trail that was like a hundred miles long and always going up. Neil—geez, I keep saying his name like he was still around—Neil kept telling us we were almost there. We made kind of a thing out of it, Pam and I. We'd be chugging along and we'd say, 'Gee, Neil, are we there yet?' And he'd say, 'It's just over the next hill.' He was really nice. I didn't know him very well or anything like that; but he was nice, you could tell by the way he treated everybody."

"Did you do the cooking?"

"Sure. Good old Myke."

"Some guy's going to eat you up one of these days."

"I'm very available if you happen to know anybody."

He laughed.

"What happens if they do see us?" she asked after a while. "Have we like had it then?"

"That depends on where they are and where we are when it happens, if it happens. Hey, look, don't go writing us off."

"I keep telling myself not to think about it, and then I keep thinking about it anyway."

"So do I."

"I guess you're a pilot or something?"

"I was."

"Like dropping bombs and napalm and stuff like that?"

"Yes. Stuff like that."

"Wow," she said.

The wind battered the mountain, wailed in the dark night of snow that whirled outside the cave. Pam sighed in her sleep, reached out and put one gloved hand on Myke's sleeve. "Don't worry," Myke said hoarsely. "You're going to be okay. We're all going to get out of this mess somehow. . . ."

Again Whittaker switched off the light. Time seemed interminable now. He held his watch close by his eye, saw the blur of phosphorescent numbers, heard the seconds tick sharply around the measured circle. He cleared part of the entrance to the cave where the snow kept up its heavy fall. Soon the morning light would begin to reveal itself even through the storm. He wanted to sleep, but at the same time he wanted to reach some final decision and act upon it, and this kept him in a state of tension.

"It sounds like the wind's dying," Myke said after a while. Her voice was strange in the dark of the cave, chimerical, disassociated.

"It does that. Then it comes up again."

"I'm pretty cold," she said. "But I can't make up my mind whether to put my parka on or just keep sitting on it. You must be pretty cold too," she said.

"I'm all right, thanks to that sweater you gave me. Do you want it for a while?"

"No. I'm okay."

"I wish we'd brought some of Karpus's whiskey."

"Do they sell whiskey in that town you said we were going to?"

"Just beer. It's good beer, but it isn't whiskey."

"Oh," she said.

"Do you like to drink?" he asked.

"Sometimes I do. I can't drink very much; if I do I get sick."

The wind sent a mist of snow through the opening in the passageway. Whittaker brushed it off his pants and the ponchos before it could melt. "How's Pam doing?" he asked.

"Okay, I guess. She's sleeping pretty good. Kate's sleeping too, I guess. I really don't see how we're ever going to get to your truck."

"You told me you didn't see how we were going to get up the east face, didn't you?"

"Yeah, right."

"Or do the rappels."

"I know it. I've got a very negative attitude. How

come you wanted to be a pilot anyway?"

"I grew up during World War Two," he said sleepily. "I collected gum cards with pictures of fighter pilots. I never wanted to be anything else."

"I guess it was different then," Myke said.

"Yes," he said. "It was."

He sat then in the dark, moving his toes in his boots, up and down, over and over, listening to the wind whine up and down the mountain ridges and the sandy snow rasp and blow in the tunnel of the cave. His children came to him, Ben sitting by his side, Amy in his lap. Marie reached up and touched his arm. "I'd like a cigarette," she said. "All right," he said. He lit the cigarette, the cave flaring briefly into light. "What are you thinking?" she asked. "I'm thinking you're bloody outstanding in that orange dress, with your hair fixed that way." She laughed. "Okay, you kids," he said. "One kiss each, and off to bed." She laughed. "Goodnight, daddy." "Goodnight," he said. She laughed, and tipped her head to see him better. "I'll be cold," she said. "Like hell," he said.

It was different then.

6

There were other dreamers on the mountain that night. One of them was Johns. He slept on his back, zipped into a down mummy bag in a borrowed tent the sides of which rose and fell in the wind. A driven snow had whitened the north-side bark of the trees, had accumulated on the slanted ground below the trees to a depth already of fourteen inches, which meant that it covered by four inches the trip line that Karpus had rigged around the perimeter of their camp.

The tent smelled of Spam farts and kerosine. Johns, who had not eaten Spam or anything else for a long time, had not objected to either of these smells because his head had hurt too much to think about them. Karpus had always been a night-farter, and in prison Johns had often expressed his displeasure about this by going "Whew-jeez!" which until recently was as critical of Karpus as he had ever wanted to be.

He had hoped he would fall asleep, but for a long while he had not been able to. Karpus had fallen asleep at once, as he always did. There were times when Johns suspected his friend was out even before his head hit the pillow. This browned Johns off. He himself had always had trouble getting to sleep. The very prospect of sleep made him anxious for it meant he would be even more vulnerable to the legions who picked on him than he was when he was awake. They could paint his face red (as they had once in a foster home in Silver City), or they could tie a bow around his unit, or put an old dead beaver into bed with him (as they had once done in a reform school in St. George). He had a shattering snore and would wake himself with it repeatedly in the early stages of sleep when sleep finally began to come. Then, unless he suffered a wet dream, which for him was always a dry dream, he would sleep so soundly he would find it almost impossible to wake up.

Karpus was a delicately light sleeper who never snored and seldom dreamed and who could set the alarm in his head to wake himself up at any hour he chose. Earlier that night, with the tent walls heaving in and out as if they would fly apart, and a hail of freezing rain driving bulletlike from the North, and the temperature falling off, and the pressure in John's head going into the red area of his gauge, Karpus had put out the lantern and said in his husky voice, "I'll get us up at six. That should be plenty of time."

"Jesus Christ, time for *what?*" Johns had cried, but his friend had already fallen asleep.

And now at long last Johns was asleep too, dreaming he had died of an injury and gone to heaven, whereupon he had been asked to account for himself. He had not exactly gone to heaven so much as wound up there, having set off reluctantly without compass or maps on a circuitous hike and having gotten off route almost as soon as he had started and having bumped into things as he went. He carried a pack a friend of his had loaned him, and though he was not up to complaining about it, he suspected from the awful weight of this pack that his friend had secretly filled it with stones.

This hiking really sucks, he thought. Then he stumbled into heaven, or at least a place that was gauzy and up there, and the first thing he saw was that goddamn therapy guy sitting on what looked like an old barstool, and next to him the warden, who wore a cheap golf cap and asked him to account for himself. That sucked even more. What was he supposed to say? Somebody had put a beaver in his bed when he was fourteen?

He had never been able to figure it out anyway. He had gone for a walk late one night in Phoenix when he was sixteen, and a patrol car with two cops had cruised up next to him and while the one cop idled the car along at the same speed Johns was walking, the other cop rolled down the window on the passenger side and asked him what he was doing. The cop had no more gotten the question out than a drill bit had started turning at the top of Johns's skull and he had said, "What the fuck does it *look* like I'm doing? I'm taking a walk for Chrissake!"

Things had not gone well after that. The patrol car stopped and both of the officers got out and one of them told Johns to put his hands on the roof of the car and the other searched him for weapons. When Johns asked what was going on, the officers told him they would ask the questions. "What questions?" Johns asked. And they replied by asking him what his name was and why he carried no identification and did he always walk this late at night and why was the zipper down on his pants? "The what?" The zipper on his pants. "They're cheap fucking pants for Chrissake," he said, and the officers told him to take it easy with his language and how long had he been out on the street like this, this late at night?

He could not remember how long he had been out. He often had trouble sleeping and would walk aimlessly through the city, sticking to the better neighborhoods in hopes no one there would beat him up. The two officers took him down to the stationhouse where a jowly woman in an evening dress said, yes, here was the one who had called to her in a menacing way from behind a bush near her front porch as she had been coming back from a party after the symphony ball and who had then stepped out and exposed himself to her.

Could there be any mistake?

She thought not.

Johns had made a lunge for her and would have pulled her tits off if one of the officers had not stopped him. At that point in his life he had never willingly exposed himself to anybody except some whores in his dreams.

The therapy guy made tweeky noises in the stem of his unlit pipe, and the warden took off his golf cap and inspected its label as if in a place like heaven a man should be able to buy better hats.

"About this man Karpus . . ." he started to say.

"I'd take him to *ten* of you, you fucking tit," Johns said, and he shouldered his pack, which was much too heavy, and walked on out of his dream.

The down mummy bag had been aptly named: It encased him as if he had in fact died. It was narrow at his feet, snug at the hips, and tapered up to his shoulders, allowing him practically no room to move. Before putting the lantern out Karpus had zipped the bag up for him, had carefully gotten the hood snugged up around his broken head, had told him he would soon be feeling much better. But Johns had not felt better at all, had continued to feel terrible for a long time, until at last he too had fallen into the arms of Morpheus.

Now, as he began to wake very slowly from his dream, he felt an extended moment of terror. He could not remember where he was, or what this dark, flapping, batlike thing was just above his head, or why he could not freely move either his arms or legs, or why his nose was so cold. Then he felt the sleeping form of Karpus close by his right side and felt himself begin to relax in a way he had not been able to relax since his furlough had begun.

Sharing a cell with Karpus had been one of the few pleasures Johns had experienced in his life. But traveling with Karpus had been a nightmare; things had happened much too fast for him, as if all the action reels had been speeded up the way they used to be in the old movies: people chasing after each other in triple time, knocking one another over with extension ladders and falling into buckets of paint. For him, things had lost perspective even before the two of them got out of Salt Lake. He had

been juiced up and pilled out and every time he had tried
to get his head together a little bit Karpus had seemed
to sense it and had done something spectacular like
shooting a couple of hippy kids or running the truck over
a deer. He had never seen anybody walk like Karpus; half
the time he had to run to catch up. And then this crap
with these climbers and his head split in two; well, it had
all been too much.

But now at long last the camera had throttled down
to a reasonable speed, the tent was apparently going to
withstand the punishment of the storm, the down
mummy bag was warm, his friend Karpus lay at his side.
This, really, was all he had looked forward to when Karpus had told him they were going to do a little camping
in a place he knew about in Colorado in the San Juan
Range. It was not difficult for him to imagine just now
that he and his old cellmate were back in their old cell
with the barred door locked and the tier lights dimmed
and the distant sounds of the guards talking, and men
snoring, and the generators humming, and a toilet flush-
ing somewhere a long, long way away, and all the metallic sounds that never seemed to stop inside the block, as
if tin cups were being struck lightly with the tines of
forks, sounds he had never quite been able to identify as
he lay on his back on his bunk and tried to deal with his
insomnia, sounds that had become familiar and, since
Karpus had entered his life, no longer menacing.

"I feel better," he said. "You know that? My fucking
nose is cold, but my head isn't hurting like it was. I figure
if I take it easy tomorrow, maybe I can get my ass out of
here the next day, know what I mean? Maybe even tomorrow night if tomorrow goes good. We can get a motel somewhere and you can just screw around for a few
days and I can take it easy until my ears stop bleeding.

Does that sound okay to you? I mean I don't want to fuck you up or anything, but I've got to be careful I don't really hurt myself, know what I mean? Maybe you could find a doctor someplace and bring him to the motel. He could check me out, be sure that fucking pilot didn't mess me up inside."

Karpus did not reply; he was, apparently, asleep. Johns lay awake for a while, on his back in the down mummy bag, looking up at the dark tent wall that flapped like a bat just over his head. He wondered if the sleet had stopped or turned to snow because he could no longer hear it ticking away out there. He wondered how many of the climbers Karpus had killed, but only wondered this for the briefest of moments, for to think closely about what Karpus had done made him vaguely uneasy. He wondered if the police would finally catch up with them, but where this possibility had worried him a lot before he had begun to suffer so much, he found that he did not worry much about it now. His one hope was that if and when they were caught they would be caught together and returned to their old cell where on a night like this he might lie awake and listen to those unceasing metallic sounds. Karpus had said yesterday—or had it been the day before?—that if they went to prison again they might get themselves on television. That had made no sense at all to Johns who could imagine few places he would less like to be than on television.

"I feel pretty good right now except for my fucking nose," he said. "You know what I mean? I've got less pressure in my head. I wouldn't mind taking a whiz, but I can't stand the idea of getting out of this bag. I'd probably just go out there and fall on my ass. What did you do, tie up some kind of *wire* out there?"

Karpus, still sleeping, did not reply.

"Yeah, well," Johns sighed. "I'd just trip myself up." He closed his eyes, and sooner and more easily than he would have believed possible, he fell asleep again and had no further dreams. The snow continued to fall around the orange tent, the north wind to blow, the sides of the tent to luff and heave. Johns, asleep, was aware of none of these things, nor that he had begun to bleed again from his ears.

7

When Matt Whittaker woke again he knew even before he was fully awake that the wind had died and the storm had passed. Stiffly, he managed to get onto his numb hands and knees and began to clear the passageway where a liquid cold met the exposed skin of his face. He could not imagine that he would ever be warm again. A perpetual shudder ran through his chest, his legs ached, his joints felt dry and brittle as if drained of all fluid, or as if whatever fluid was left had thickened in the cold. Through the short tunnel he could see fields of new snow shrouded in mist, just visible in the soft lumines-cence of postdawn light which crept now into the cave. Pam was awake, exhausted but more coherent than she had been since her fall. Myke and Kate sat on either side of her.

"How does it look outside?" Myke asked. She had at some point gotten into her parka. Sprouts of her hair stuck out around the raised hood. She looked like a sol-emn bear.

"Good," he said. "I think we should move out."

"All of us?"

"Yes. It's pretty foggy out there right now; I don't think there's any problem about them seeing us, not for a while at least."

"Are we going to be able to see where we're going?"

"We'll see well enough. We know we're going west to the ridge and then south to the pass. We can use my compass. How do you feel this morning?" he asked Pam.

"All right," she said. "I'm all right." Her voice did not sound strong, but she smiled at him as if she accepted him now as someone she could trust; and he found that he wished Kate would do that too. She had not spoken to him as yet.

He put his hand on the boot of the injured leg. "Can you feel that?"

The girl nodded.

"Can you move your toes?"

She made an effort and cried out.

"Gosh," Myke croaked.

"I'm okay," Pam said.

"You don't sound okay."

"I am. Really. I feel better. I wouldn't mind eating something," she said shyly. "If there was something to eat I mean."

"I could start the stove," Myke offered.

"Let's hold up on that," Whittaker said. "We can cook something later, once we're out of the woods on this."

Kate, continuing her silence, gave Pam half a sandwich, then sorted out for each of them a handful of chocolate bits and raisins and small wedges of cheese. The water in the canteen had melted a little and Whittaker helped the girl drink from it, giving her two of the tablets.

"Let me know as soon as they start to work," he said.

"They really are nice," she told him.

"We'll get you some more when we get out of here."

"Are we going to?"

"You bet we are."

She looked at him and although she smiled again she also shook her head and he knew she had not been persuaded.

"We'll make it," he said.

Myke hugged herself, shivering. "I don't know," she put in. "Maybe somebody could like go for help. I mean I don't see how we can carry Pam down or anything. I'm already pooped and we haven't d-done anything yet. . . ."

"We'll rig something up," he replied. "We can manage it. That's the least of our worries."

"Maybe Myke is right," Kate said. She said it suddenly, as if she had wanted to say it for some time but for reasons of her own had not. "One of us could try and get out and bring help."

"I think the sooner we all get out of here the better," he said. "When they get through looking for us on the south slope, they may start snooping up here along this ridge. If one of us has a chance to get out, we all do. We've stuck together so far. As far as I'm concerned we should keep on doing that."

"I guess that's right," Myke replied. "We'd be out of food by tonight anyway no matter what happens. And I'd have a *stroke* if those men suddenly looked in here; and Pam like needs to get to a doctor. . . ."

"What do you say?" he asked, putting his hand on the injured girl's shoulder.

"I wish I were home."

He smiled.

"I told my father I'd take a lot of pictures so he could see what our trip was like," she said.

"You took a ton when we came in," Myke reminded her.

"I know. But I left my camera . . ."

"She's got a Polaroid. She took a neat picture of the twins. . . ." Myke started to say.

It was quiet for a moment. Finally Kate said, "Let's get things ready then," and she began sorting out what was left of the food. There were some tea bags and sugar, three candy bars, two sandwiches, half a bar of cheddar cheese, half a sack of chocolate bits and raisins. She packed these things into the outside pockets of Whittaker's pack, along with the first-aid kit and the flashlight.

"Better forget the flashlight," he said. "Let's keep it as light as we can."

"What about the ponchos?"

"Leave them here."

"Pitons and carabiners?"

"No. We're through climbing rock. We'll take the ropes and the ice ax, leave the rest of it."

"I think we should take the stove," she said.

He shook his head.

"We're going out today," he said. "Let's forget it."

"We can't count on that; I think we should take some of this. Maybe not the climbing iron, but the stove and flashlight. I'll carry them. I'd rather have them than not."

"It would be pretty nice to have the stove for tea and stuff," Myke added.

"Fill the tank then," he said, impatient to be off. "Come *on* now, let's move it."

He told Myke to help him, and together they raised Pam gently and he removed the climbing ropes from under her and coiled them. When he had finished, he pushed the coiled ropes, the two packs and his ice ax through the tunnel to the outside of the cave.

"Pills working?" he asked.

Pam nodded slowly.

"We're going to turn you around now," he said. "I'm going to pull you through the tunnel. Myke and Kate are going to help with your legs. We'll be as careful as we can."

She nodded.

She was still on the sleeping bag, and they turned her, and Whittaker backed out of the short tunnel and reached in, gripping the bag at either side of her shoulders, and pulled her through. She groaned as if she were uncomfortable but not in severe pain. Myke came through the tunnel next, a small locomotive, on her hands and knees. Kate followed, her long black hair combed and tied behind her now.

"Pam can have my parka again," Myke said. "I'll probably be too hot anyway once we get started walking. I've still got your thermal thing on."

"Okay," the pilot said. "If you do get cold we can use the sleeping bag. . . ."

"I'm pretty sure I won't get cold," she said. "It feels like it's going to warm up. It's not supposed to be cold like this in June. It's not supposed to *snow* either. I mean not like this."

She hauled the parka up over her head and she and Kate managed to get Pam into it. It was green, the same color as Neil Markham's had been. Then, while Kate rolled the sleeping bag up and put it into Whittaker's Kelty pack, he cut two slits in the bottom of the rucksack she had brought, then pulled it up the girl's legs like a pair of short pants, securing the drawstring around her waist. Then he tied her arms together loosely at the wrists with a short length of rope. As he worked, he was aware of Myke gazing across the fields of fresh snow that sloped away from the entrance to the cave. She was standing motionless, her hands hanging limply at her sides, her breath joining the heavy vapor that lay close to the ground. She looked very tired but not defeated, her brows knit in concentration as if she were estimating obstacles and conducting an inventory of what was left of her treasure.

"That looks nifty," she observed, glancing at what he had done.

"It should work fine. Give me a hand, will you?"

He had tramped a platform into the snow, moved Pam onto her side and into this area. Now he lay down so that she faced his back and he got her arms around his neck and he struggled into the straps of the pack. Myke and Kate helped him as he drew up his knees and rolled to his left until he was kneeling with the girl on his back; then he rose slowly, and by the time he was standing again, her feet were above the level of the snow. "How is she?" he asked the others.

"She's sacked out right now," Myke replied.

"Is she riding all right?"

"Yes," Kate said. "It's going to be rough going through this snow."

"If you and Myke could go first . . ."

"We can."

"You can take turns breaking trail. Pam's not heavy; I think we'll be fine."

He repeated the route he wanted them to take, a sloping diagonal that would move them down and, at the same time, closer to the Gaddis ridge, now hidden in mist. "I don't think we'll get any avalanches until things warm up," he said to Myke. "If we do, try to swim to the surface of the snow while it's still moving, the way you would do if you were caught under fast water."

She nodded, but did not reply. He felt her apprehension join his own. Kate picked up the red Kelty pack. Myke shouldered the two coiled ropes. "I'm kind of beat," she said. "I ache all over."

"We'll loosen up," he told her.

"I never spent a night in an igloo before."

"It wasn't all bad, was it?"

She shook her head. "I slept pretty good. I wasn't as cold as I thought I was going to be, but I was still pretty cold. . . ."

"Look," Kate said, helping him adjust one of the shoulder straps that had already begun to bite, "maybe we're wrong about this. Maybe just one of us should go. I'd be willing if you'd tell me how to get to your truck. I think I could make it all right."

He shook his head. "As far as I'm concerned we're going together. All the way."

For the first time, he thought she looked at him uncritically, as if to say she was glad he felt the way he did, that in spite of her reservations she agreed; and this gratified him. He hoped only that his plan was a good one and that his strength would last.

"We've got good cover in this fog," he told her. "You two can switch off breaking trail. Pam and I will be right behind you."

"I feel creepy," Myke said hoarsely. "I feel like they're right around here someplace, listening to us talk."

"They're not around here," he said. "Let's move out. We've got a good three miles to go, maybe four."

He could feel Pam's breath against the back of his ear.

"We're going now," he said to her. She did not reply. They started down through the new snow. Kate led the way at first. Myke went second. Whittaker followed in their tracks. Myke's movements seemed stiff and were, he thought, sometimes ineffective. She would look back at him as if to be sure he was still there, then look away again. He breathed deeply, used his ice ax to help balance the weight on his back. Sometimes the mist would obscure his view of the other two and he would follow the tracks blindly until the mist broke and he would see ahead of him the blue of the parka and windpants Kate wore, the red of the pack she carried and the solid gray of Myke's shirt crossed by the two coiled ropes.

He counted his steps. When he reached a hundred, he started at one again, and did this many times. The snow was knee-deep in the places where the wind had kept it from piling up, and thigh-deep in the drifted places; if it had not been dry and loose, he knew they could not have moved through it. He wiggled his toes as he walked, hoping to keep them from freezing. He felt a great and growing hunger. Sometimes he walked with his arms at his sides, but more often with his thumbs hooked under the straps of the rucksack, the ax dangling by its leather loop from his wrist. However he walked, he could feel Pam's warm breath against the back of his ear, and this sustained him. After a time, the tightness began to work out of his legs, and the muscles across his shoulders and back began to accustom themselves to her weight. Sometimes, particularly if his stride faltered, she would sigh and begin to struggle in an effort to change her position, but soon she would fall against him and drift into a deeper sleep.

He thought, *I can do this for as long as it takes.* And told himself this, and counted his steps, and knew with each step that he was using up something in himself, something that was finite and that sooner or later would be gone.

At the end of an hour, Myke and Kate stopped. When he finally caught up to them, they were still breathing heavily.

"How is Pam doing?" Kate asked.

"She's doing fine. She sleeps most of the time. Do you think we should rest?"

Myke said yes, she thought they should. He looked uneasily in the direction from which the avalanches would come. He wished they were closer to the Gaddis ridge. "Okay," he said. "Give me a hand."

They helped him set Pam down on the snow. The relief for him was intense. He raised and lowered his shoulders and rubbed his neck. Kate got out the chocolate bits and raisins and gave each of them a handful. The water in the canteen had frozen again. He ate snow. His tongue was swollen and he felt nauseated; he swallowed repeatedly, closed his eyes.

"I'll take her for a while," Kate told him.

"That's all right."

"Don't be silly about it. I'm not helpless, neither is Myke. We'll make better time if we take turns."

"She does seem to get heavier. . . ."

"Geez," Myke said. "What if it was me?"

Whittaker groaned.

"My *boobs* weigh as much as Pam," she said.

"Come on," Kate said. "Let's not waste any time. Help me, will you?"

When she stood finally with Pam's weight on her back her legs trembled, but Whittaker could see she was going to make it, at least for a while. He shouldered the Kelty pack. It felt absurdly light by comparison, as if it were filled with foam.

"Well, come on," Kate said firmly. "Please don't just stand around. . . ."

They set out from the first resting place at 7:30 by Whittaker's watch, and they rested each half-hour after that, alternating the jobs of carrying the injured girl and breaking trail through the new snow. At 11:30, with Whittaker carrying, Myke said she thought she was too beat to go on. She lay down on her back, put one arm across her forehead, the other across her stomach, as if she had been shot and had fallen there. Kate sat next to her, half propped by the frame of Whittaker's red pack.

"God," she said, "it's like wading through cement."

"I know. . . ."

"I started to feel pretty good for a while," Myke croaked. "But I really feel terrible now."

"We're doing all right," he replied, knowing it was as much to persuade himself as her. "We can take a little time."

"I'll help you with Pam," she told him. But she did not get up, and it was with Kate's assist that he managed to set the girl down.

For a few minutes he stood, winded, gazing into the mist, trying to breathe, trying to orient himself, trying to step up what had become the sluggish pace of his thoughts. He was convinced they should already have reached the Gaddis ridge. He had kept track of their direction with his compass, and they had moved west-southwest from the snow cave and surely by now should have intersected the ridge. He guessed they were moving more slowly than he had thought, and he decided to go directly west from here until the ridge was in sight. He felt weak. Small flecks of light danced through his field of vision. He was about to sit down for a moment when, in the distance above him, somewhere high on the slopes of Gaddis, he heard the low rumble of falling snow. It lasted a long time. Then it died away, and the only sound was that of a light breeze which had stirred all morning, and the breeze seemed colder now.

"What was *that?*" Myke croaked. She looked up at him.

"Avalanche," he said, still breathing much harder than he should have been, still swallowing against a rising in his throat. "We're going to have to move out now."

She groaned.

"We'll take a good long rest when we get to the ridge," he assured her. She sat in the snow, with beads of snow melting on the sleeves of her green parka, looking up at him. "We'll start the stove," he said, "and brew up some tea. We can't stay here, Myke. . . ." But now he himself made no move to leave, as if he had reached the end of his own resources and was not sure as he stood on his rubbery legs and tried to breathe normally again that he would be able to resist the need he felt to simply lie down next to her and go to sleep in the snow.

Then Pam began to groan again, and Kate went and knelt beside her. "How many pills do we have?" she asked Whittaker. She had been watching him.

"Not very many," he admitted. "We could try half a tablet. . . ."

She prepared the pill, gave it to Pam, then gave Myke a candy bar which Myke ate, tearing the paper away and shoving the bar into her mouth.

"It's my turn to lug Pam," Myke said, but her eyes were closed and still she did not get up. Kate looked at her, then at Whittaker who stood stooped over his ice ax in an attitude of desolation. His gaunt cheeks burned where they showed above the blond rake of his beard. His eyes were half closed.

"I'll take Pam for a while," she said. "I feel all right."

He shook his head.

"You break trail," she said. "I'll take Pam."

Again Whittaker shook his head, but she knew he could not carry Pam any longer, not for a while, and it was as if his inability to do so added substantially to her own strength.

"Myke, get up," she said. The chunky girl looked at her as though waiting for Whittaker's approval. "Get *up*, Myke," she said. "Help me with Pam."

When Myke stood up, she stood up slowly, boots slipping in the snow. Her nose dripped. She pawed at it with her glove. Kate took one of the coiled ropes from her, uncoiled it and tied one end around Myke's thick waist.

"What's that for?" she asked sleepily.

"We'll want to keep some distance between us now. So if there's an avalanche we won't all be in one place. He's going to go first for a while. I'll take Pam and go second. You bring up the rear. Try to keep a full rope's length between us, all right?"

Myke nodded helplessly. "I'm sorry, Matt," she croaked. "I'm sorry, Kate. I'm really pooped."

"You'll get stronger," Kate said. "I did."

"We can't be far from that ridge," Whittaker said hoarsely.

"Have you got your compass?"

"Yes. We've been heading west-southwest. I think we better go due west from here."

"I guess they'll be looking for us now, won't they?" Myke asked.

Whittaker shook his head. "They'll be on the south slope, or checking the creek trail. . . ."

"How long will it take them to do that?"

"I don't know. A couple of hours at least. Maybe more."

"I don't see why they had to do what they did," she said. "To Neil and like that."

"I don't either, Myke. But they did. We can't change any of it now."

"I wish they'd just leave us alone."

"We've been lucky so far," Kate said, glancing in the direction from which they might come. "There's still no visibility. Once we get to the ridge there'll be places to hide if we have to. The important thing now is to be quiet and careful, to keep our eyes and ears open and keep moving." Whittaker was looking at her. *I know,* she thought. *Now I'm sounding like you.*

"Are you sure about carrying Pam?" he asked finally.

"Yes," she said. "If you two will stop talking and help me get her up."

Now they both looked at her.

"Well, dammit," she said, "will you please?"

8

Kate let Whittaker go out a hundred yards ahead of her and then she started following the trail he left, moving through the new snow, pushing one of her legs forward and then the other. He had given her his ice ax; she used it as a cane in her right hand. When the rope pulled against her left hand, she waited a moment and then moved forward and the rope came with her. She counted slowly to fifty, rested a moment, then started in counting to fifty again. The pilot had his compass and he stayed out in front of her, breaking trail toward the ridge. When there were rifts in the mist she could see his orange parka and red pack when she looked for them, and when there were no rifts she plodded stubbornly along in his tracks. Twice she heard the distant rumble of snow falling somewhere above her, and in spite of the burden she now carried, she did not rest anymore unless she felt the rope pull and knew Myke had stopped; then she would rest a short time and begin again.

Pam woke up briefly once. "Please put me down," she said.

"Honey, we can't stop here," Kate told her. She tried to speak reassuringly but knew her own tensions were clear in the uncertain tone of her voice. "We haven't gotten to the ridge yet," she said. "If we stop here we'll chance getting caught in an avalanche."

"*Please* put me down," the girl said again, as if she had not heard, or, if she had heard, did not care.

"Pam honey, I can't put you down now. Try to sleep a little while longer. Try to think about going home. . . ."

"I don't care about going home."

"Yes you do, of course you do. We all care about that."

"Please put me down," she said. Then she began to cry, and after she had cried for a while she became silent again and Kate felt her breath against her ear and knew she had gone to sleep. She herself was quite cold. She shook from it even as she walked, even with the effort it took to carry Pam on her back, which was more weight than she had ever tried to carry though she had carried heavy packs before. There was a period of time when she was not sure she had the strength or the will to go on.

That's crap, he would have told her. *You know it is. Pam knows it too.*

She had felt sorry for him back there when he had looked so terribly tired and sad, as if he knew perfectly well they were not going to make it, had known it from the start. And if he had been cruel to her, as she thought sometimes he had, he had also been kind to Pam and to Myke too, and this made her wonder about the enigmatic nature of his character which seemed to combine qualities of brutality and gentleness in almost equal measure. It was incredible to her to think that the same hands that had worked with the care of a surgeon over Pam after her fall had also held the club that would have killed the fat man Johns and had dropped bombs in a senseless war.

For a while she had feared him, and then had resented him, for she had thought he would blame her for what had happened to the twins and surely for what had now happened to Pam. But last night in that dreadful cold cave where they had all been squeezed so tightly together and the air had gotten stale and full of smoke and she had felt a deep depression take her, though he had been brusque and presumptuous with his questions he had not seemed to blame her, had not implied his way would have been better, had admitted, in fact, he had been no more sure than she. She wished he had not seen her the way he had on the cot in the shack, wished what had been for her an ultimate effort of will and sacrifice of pride had never taken place. She could not help thinking that, having seen it, he had her at a disadvantage, whether he chose to exploit it or not.

I don't know what I'm going to do, she thought, trying to shift the increasing burden of Pam's weight, trying to keep her own legs from trembling, trying to breathe in an orderly way, trying to see into the mists ahead, trying

to remember that the rope in her left hand led back to
Myke, that the ice ax in her right hand belonged to the
pilot who was somewhere out ahead of her, breaking the
trail she now followed through the new snow toward the
ridge that led from Gaddis to Peak 18, toward a place
unknown to her where the pilot assured them he had left
his truck.

*I don't know what I'm going to do if anything happens to
Pam. I don't know what I'm going to do, if we do get back, about
the twins and Neil.* She had written to the parents of the
twins, a polite but warm letter of invitation, informing
them that the annual spring outing which their daughters
had participated in before and wanted to participate in
again would be conducted with all the proprieties con-
cerning which, each year, these apparently conservative
people had insisted on being reassured. There would be
no liquor, no boys. The safety of the girls would be
paramount. She felt her throat begin to clench, her eyes
pool with tears. What was she supposed to do? Write
them another letter now? *Oh, Jesus,* she thought, and for
a moment she felt as helpless as this child she carried on
her back, thought of her own mother, thought, *Oh, God.
Oh, Jesus. What am I going to do? I wish you were here, mom.
I wish dad and Paul were here. Not really I don't, but I wish you
were.*

Then, at last, she caught a glimpse of the ridge
through the mist that swirled over the basin, and this
cheered her a little. She moved steadily toward it, following Whittaker's good trail, trying to keep control over
her terrible discomfort and whatever there might have
been in her psyche that could have accepted defeat.
Once, she and a friend from the club had brought an
injured man down from the summit of Teewinot to the
climbers' camp at Jenny Lake in the midst of a Grand

Teton winter. That too had been an ordeal. She remembered it, and remembering it helped her now. She thought of the warmth of a room that the pilot had promised in this place Morgan. She thought of the smell of fried food, the gorgeous feel of a tub of hot water drawn steaming full right up to the tip of her chin. She thought of the feel and give of a pillow and mattress and springs, and later the sight of her apartment with everything in place. And she thought of Paul whom she still saw from time to time and who would tell her how he had always told her that something like this might happen, but who would be decent about it too, who would drape his rough arm over her shoulders and say something like, *Katherine, I'm damned glad you made it, you know? I wish you'd give up this climbing stuff.* He had added to her life, really, in a way he had, though she knew it had been important to leave him before she succumbed to his mastering need to use her in the conventional ways. She thought of these things, and of other things, but not of the twins or of Neil or of the two men who had killed them or of what the pilot might hold forever about her in his mind, and for a while she felt better. And then the avalanche came.

She heard the roar of it above her and stood in her tracks for what seemed only seconds with a cry of warning building in her throat, when suddenly the rope jerked out of her hand and she was spun sideways and knocked down in a flood of snow, and then she was under the snow with Pam's cries and the roar of the slide engulfing her, and she flailed helplessly with her arms and felt a wrenching at her back and skittered for what seemed only a few feet and then stopped.

The roar died away like the passing of a train. She felt cold enter her as if through her veins.

After the first stunning moments when she was unable to move, she tried and found that she could move her hands. She pushed them up and pushed the snow away from her face until she could breathe freely. She was not at all sure where she was and called Pam's name in a frightened voice and heard a childlike groan close by although the girl's weight was no longer on her back, nor her arms around her neck, nor her own arms through the straps of the rucksack. She managed to stand, stumbling up from the lightly compacted snow at the edge of the slide, and as she did she saw that Pam had been carried only a short distance from her and lay now on her back, her hands still tied together in front of her, the rucksack still secured at her waist. Quickly, she made her way to the girl who tried to struggle up, to sit, but could not.

"Pam, don't," she said, kneeling beside her, holding her, brushing the snow from her green parka, holding her tight. "Oh, God, Pam, is your leg all right? Did it hurt you? Is it worse than before?"

"No. . . ."

"Can you just stay here and not try to sit up or move? Just stay here while I try and find the others. . . ."

"Please . . ."

She heard Whittaker call her name from what seemed a great distance, in the direction of the ridge beyond the track of the avalanche, and she thought he sounded all right, but when she in turn called to Myke, who had been well into the track behind her, there was no answer. She searched for and found the pilot's ax.

"Pam," she said, trying to keep the rush of panic she felt from showing in her voice, trying to sound like the leader of a trip, "Pam, I'm going to get Myke. It may take a little while. You'll be fine here. You just lie here and wait for me to come back, all right? If you hear me call, or if you hear him call, you call back as loudly as you can so we'll be able to find you in this fog, all right?"

Pam begged her not to leave.

"I have to, honey, I have to get Myke. She could be caught under the snow, and if she is she won't be able to breathe for very long. I'll be back. You know I will. I won't leave you here."

She had to leave abruptly then, had to turn away from the girl who struggled again in an attempt to sit, to reach out. She had to go away from this one who needed her and out onto the slide itself in search of the other one who needed her. *"Myke!"* she called, her voice echoing from the ridge. But no answer came. She thought Whittaker should be here by now to help her. She thought everything was over now, and as she struggled toward the center of the slide, her ankles twisting in the rough roiled snow, she felt her sense of urgency begin to leave her, replaced by a sense of resignation. *"Myke!"* she cried. *"Answer me!"* And she thought Karpus and his friend would hear her if they were close, and maybe even if they were not close, and if there was more snow above this snow she knew any vibration of sound might send it all hurtling down this same track; but she could not think of anything else to do but call the girl's name and hope she would be able to respond somehow, cry out, call out, lead her to wherever she was.

A mist of snow was falling through the ragged vapor of cloud that lay close over the turbulent path of the avalanche. The frost of her own breath obscured what was left of her view. *Oh, God, please let her live,* she thought. *Don't let this be another one.*

"Myke!" she called, and there was no reply, and she moved in a fading aspect of hope amidst the dying, muted echoes of her cries.

9

High on the south slope of Wolf Mountain, one of the climbers' packs on his back, the Weatherby rifle in hand, Karpus had started several small avalanches of his own. He had left the orange tent at first light, had forced his way through the fresh deep snow, driving his knees against it, pulling himself ahead whenever he could by reaching for the trunks of small trees on the upslope, feeling the snow break away under his boots, hearing it slide away from him, himself falling and sliding with it sometimes, rolling back, losing ground, waiting then patiently until he had regained his wind, reoriented himself, then moving up again, unintimidated by what he knew was a deadly weight of snow poised on the fog-shrouded slope above, or by the distant sounds of avalanche in the western reaches of the basin.

He had heard the first of these in the late morning, then two more in the early afternoon. Just now, at what he guessed to be mid-afternoon, he had heard another, this one longer in duration and more distinct than the first three had been, and so he paused to rest and listen, his face drenched and, in its expression, as blank as the mist around it.

He had awakened that morning before dawn to find the storm still thrashing the sides of the orange tent, the snow still deepening outside. He had lit the lantern, fired the stove, started some water to boil. Johns, already awake, had only watched, his round, bloody face gazing silently up from the down bag as if he had vowed that from here on he was going to keep his grief to himself.

It was winter-cold in the tent, but the fat man was per-
spiring, drops of sweat glistening on his pale forehead
and lip under the frosty puff of his breath.

"How you feel this morning?" Karpus asked him,
once the breakfast was going.

"Beat."

"You sleep all right?"

"All right. Once I knocked off. You were farting," he
said softly.

Karpus nodded. Johns's voice had come in an unfamiliar monotone that made the tall man uncomfortable. "You going to be able to move out in an hour?" he
asked after a while.

Johns shook his head.

"Too weak?"

"Yeah."

"I could get you rigged up and you could head
straight for the truck. I could meet you there later."

"I'd never make it."

"It's only a few miles, all flat as your hand except for
the pass. You could wait for me. Warm yourself up with
the heater, take her easy. I could rig you up with a real
light pack. You could take the pistol just in case."

Again Johns shook his head. The bright orange
walls of the tent luffed gently as if the wind had died.

"You know," Karpus went on, fixing some pow-
dered eggs, smoking a cigarette, the stove hissing mer-
rily now, "we could run north out of Morgan, pick us up
one of those big fancy motorized homes, the kind you
drive, with bunks and a toilet and shower. Shoot for
Alaska, maybe, tie in with one of the oil companies up
there, make ourselves a bundle. . . . What's wrong?" he
asked. Johns's eyes had suddenly filled with tears.

"Why the fuck do you want me around?" the fat man

croaked. "I'm not good for anything."

"Sooner or later they're going to put that big pipe-line in up there," said Karpus, who had looked away. "We could get in on that, maybe change our looks a little first, just to be on the safe side. You could maybe start a mustache, wear a head of hair; I could bleach mine out, pick up some spectacles. . . ."

"I don't feel good," Johns blurted, sounding more like himself.

"What's wrong?"

"I've got to take an awful whiz. I feel like I'm going to bust."

"You too weak even to get up and go outside?"

"Yes."

Karpus rubbed his face with the back of his hand, glanced at the door of the tent.

"Jesus," Johns said, "I can hardly move my fucking arms."

"These eggs are near done. You'll feel a lot better once you eat. We didn't get much supper."

"I can't hold it that long, it's killing me."

Karpus nodded.

"I feel like I'm going to piss my pants," Johns said.

"Okay," Karpus said. "I'll zip your bag open and you can use one of these pots. Then I can dump it outside."

"Make it a big pot, okay?"

"Sure," Karpus said. "I've got one right here. You'll set some kind of record if you need more than this."

"I feel like I've got a gallon of it."

"You'll be okay."

By lantern light he helped Johns get ready. "There," he said finally. "Can you work it all right?"

"I'm going to mess myself up. . . ."

"Okay, I'll hold it steady for you. You just let her go."

Johns, who had reddened, closed his eyes. Sweating profusely now, he smelled like an onion. Karpus held his friend's limp penis in one hand, the large aluminum pot in the other. When Johns said he was too embarrassed to relieve himself this way, Karpus said, "You just relax. Let her come. Nobody's going to know about it 'cept you and me."

"Jesus," Johns whispered. His eyes were still shut and for almost a minute nothing happened. Then he began to go, fitfully at first, then steadily. By the time he had finished, tears of relief were trickling down his face.

Karpus set the pot carefully on the floor of the tent, zipped up Johns's pants, then rezipped the down bag. "You didn't spill a drop," he said. The fat man was sobbing quietly. Blood had begun to run from his ears. Karpus looked away. The wind had let up for a moment and the walls of the tent drooped, no longer drum-tight as they had been when he set the tent up. He wanted to tell Johns that he just liked having him around and things would be better soon, but found in this moment he could not say anything though it troubled him to hear his friend cry.

"When we get our rig," he said finally, without looking down, "I'll do all the driving and you can just stretch out on one of the bunks, okay?"

Johns did not answer. His breathing had become shallow. Mucus spilled from his nose. Karpus picked up the pot of warm piss, already beginning to cool, and crawled out of the tent to empty it. He guessed about two feet of snow had fallen, maybe more. The storm seemed to be subsiding; soon there would be enough light for him to move out. He raised the collar of his mackinaw and stood with his back to the weather, smoking one cigarette, then another. An image came to him of the pilot and the pilot's wife, together in the home with the green lawn and trees.

"Hey, Johns," he said when he finally came back into the tent. "I figure they're still on the mountain someplace. On this side or up top—" Then he saw how much blood there was, and he looked just once into Johns's wide and sightless eyes.

Now, many hours later and well up the south slope of Wolf Mountain, having heard the distant rumble of an avalanche die away, he squinted into the mists, west-southwest, and cupped his numb hands behind his ears.

10

Kate tried desperately to guess where the avalanche might have carried Myke. She crossed and recrossed the slide, looking for the girl or some trace of her equipment. She probed gently with Whittaker's ice ax. Again and again she called Myke's name. The only response was rumblings on the slopes above and she knew she should have carried Pam out of the track and checked the pilot's condition. But there had not been time, not if Myke was under the snow.

She chose grids and covered them and chose new grids. There was no sound or sign. *"Myke!"* she called. The sound of her voice sounded shockingly loud. She hoped it would carry across the slide and no further than that, but she was not at all sure. A frightening vision had come to her of the tall man with the rifle, a mile or so

distant, moving through the new snow, looking for some
sign of them and then hearing something high on the
slopes between Wolf Mountain and Gaddis. His ears
would tense like those of a predatory beast. He would lift
his head, try to locate the sound, isolate it from its
echoes, reduce it to its center. The first time it would not
be clear, but after he had heard it more than once he
would know what had created it and at least approxi-
mately where it was and he would be on a blood scent,
moving from wherever he was now on through this heavy
roiled and drifted snow, closing the distance between
himself and her and the others he had almost surely
pledged himself to find. He would pick up their trail,
then lose it in the avalanche track, then pick it up again.
The fat one would help him. And once the tall man with
the rifle had picked up their trail, she was certain he
would move quickly.

Her heart tripped. The muscles in her chest hurt.
"Myke!" she called. *"Myke, can you hear me!"* She heard
the slight sound of the breeze, the squeak of the newly
compacted snow under her boots, the echoes of her own
voice coming back to her from the ridge, not as the
gunfire had on the east face in that terrible night, sharp
and rising, but muted, truncated, as if she had called into
a large steel drum.

"Myke! Can you hear me! Can you answer me!"

And the echoes came, *Answer me! Answer me!* and she
saw from the corner of her eye a piece of the Perlon rope,
not more than a yard of it, poking above the surface of
the snow. She plunged toward it, falling, grabbing it with
both of her hands, freeing it, following it until it dipped
down and she could not free it. She got on her knees and
began to scoop away the compacted snow, following the
rope down until she saw Myke's frazzled head and found

the area around her face and heard her cough. *"Oh, Myke,"* she said. *"Oh, damn you, Myke. . . ."* And she went on digging furiously until she had freed all the area around the girl's chest and ample stomach.

"Can you breathe?" she asked, almost afraid to ask. The girl nodded, still buried in snow to her hips.

"Can you talk?"

The girl nodded again.

"Well, say something to me, will you please?"

Myke cleared her throat. "Wow," she said quietly.

"Oh, you," Kate said. She rubbed her own face with her wet gloves. "You bum, you really had me worried, don't you know that?"

"Is it like over yet?"

"Yes. It's over. At least this one is. . . ."

Then Whittaker was there, falling to his knees beside her, blowing like a whale. "How in Christ's name did you find her?" he said, already digging with his gloved hands.

"She had your rope tied on. . . ."

"You better go look after Pam. She's all right, but she's pretty shaken up; she's afraid we're going to leave her, or not be able to find her. Look, I'll take care of Myke. We made a hell of a lot of noise. . . ."

"There wasn't anything else to do."

"I know it. Christ," he said, "you were smart as hell getting this far into the slide and down. I was looking much closer to where Pam was."

She put her hand on his shoulder as she got to her feet. He looked up at her, shook his head. "We must have been close to the ridge," he said. "A few hundred yards, I'll bet. Fifteen or twenty minutes more and this sonofabitch would have missed us."

She smiled tiredly at him, but not without warmth,

and he thought if they could know each other a while longer they might wind up being friends. She untied and shook out her hair, brushed it back from her windburned cheeks; then she turned away from him and made her way into the mist across the track toward the place where Pam lay waiting.

"Where are your gloves?" he said to Myke.

"I don't know." Her hands were free now; she held them up. "I guess they came off."

"Let's get you out of there. Can you help me dig?"

"Sure. . . ."

"Pam's all right," he said. "We were lucky, we were damn lucky Kate knew what she was doing. How about the other rope? Did that come off too?"

"I guess so. Jeez," she said quietly, "I've never been in anything like this before. I was upside down a lot of the time. I couldn't remember what you told me to do."

Once she was free and standing again, he untied the rope at her waist and coiled it. Then he gave her his gloves.

"I'll be okay," she said, but her hands were abraded and looked very red as if they had been boiled.

"Put them on," he insisted.

"I'm always taking your stuff," she said.

He put his arms around her and, although he had not expected to, he cried for a moment, and she was very still in his arms.

"Hey, look, sorry," he said finally. He had never liked crying.

"Gosh," she said, "you shouldn't be sorry about that. I bawled like a cow about ten times when we were climbing. . . ."

"I wish you were my kid," he said. "I'd like to have somebody like you. If you ever need adopting, let me know, will you?"

"I'm kind of a pain," she told him. "Once you get to know me. My mother says I am."

He shook his head. *Try it, you'll like it* her sweatshirt said. On the surface of the slide, going away from them into the mist in the direction of the ridge, he could see the cleat marks Kate's Kletterschuhs had left. *We were damn lucky,* he thought.

"What are we going to do if we get to that place Morgan after the restaurant is closed?" Myke asked.

"We're going to kick down the door," he replied. She laughed. He did not tell her he had remembered not an hour ago that Karpus had taken all of his credit cards and cash. Maybe the local police would have a reserve fund for contingencies such as this. He hoped so. He hoped they were going to make it.

He and Myke were crossing the track of the slide, following Kate's shallow tracks over the hard snow, moving in the direction of the ridge and the place where the others were waiting when he heard the first shot. It was a distant, muffled sound not unlike that of a bottle exploding in the fire of a remote town dump. The first shot was followed by a second.

"I guess that's them, right?" Myke said, as if she had been expecting the shots.

"Yes."

"Do they know we're here?"

"I don't know, Myke."

"It sounded like they're pretty far away," she said. "Do you think they are?"

He didn't know. "Yes," he said. "I think so." *We'll have to be lucky now,* he thought. *We'll have to be quiet and move as quickly as we can. He's telling us he knows. I'm sure of that. Just the way he told us when he found his friend tied up and gagged on that cot.*

"I hate them," Myke said almost matter-of-factly. "I

really do. I don't usually feel like that about anybody—I don't think I've ever felt that way about anybody as far as I can remember—but I feel that way about them."

"So do I," Whittaker said, "We'll have to be quiet now."

11

It was three o'clock when they started again. Pam groaned softly, but the pilot did not want to give her the last of the pills, not yet. She had apparently not been aware of the shots and he was glad for that. Kate had heard them though. She seemed distant again, as if she had withdrawn herself from what they might signify. She had carried Pam for a long time and looked very tired, but she offered to break trail if he wanted her to, or to try carrying Pam again whenever he needed a rest. He said he thought he was all right now, that the long break had given him the rest he had needed and she should go last for a while, which she agreed to do. She shouldered his pack and then tied herself in to one end of the Perlon rope. He tied Myke into the middle of the rope and then wrapped the free end around his left hand. Then he moved out again, cautiously, expecting to hear the shots closer this time, whenever they came, whenever Karpus decided to let them know he was on his way.

When he reached the base of the ridge, he turned south and began following it down. Twice more, avalanches swept by to the left of him, and he waited, drenched in sheets of falling snow, until the roar died away and the mountains were silent again. Then he could hear the breeze moan in the hollow places of the ridge and feel the mists thicken and the temperature drop.

He kept the rope wrapped around his left hand and held the ice ax with his right and moved forward under the impulse of his will. He knew exhaustion, and frost that entered his face and hands and feet, and a pain that beat steadily in his upper right leg. His trapezius had cramped from the weight of the rucksack; he could not move his head easily. His throat was sore; when he tried to breathe through his mouth he gagged.

By four o'clock the mists had closed in until he could see no more than a few feet in any direction. He kept close to the ridge, trusting it to be his guide. There were times when he reached out and touched it with the numb tips of his fingers. The wind died, but the temperature continued to drop. He found now that when he tried to change his grip on the ice ax his hand did not respond and he had to work it loose with his other hand, which was also clumsy and stiff. Then he began to lose track of the ridge; it seemed broken up now, more a series of high scattered boulders than a solid wall; and sometimes he thought the ground under him was beginning to rise, although he could not understand why this should be so. His mind no longer functioned well. He had no idea how far they had managed to descend. From the snow cave to the truck should not have been more than four miles; it felt to him now as if they had already gone forty. To take a single step forward required all of his strength, and when he stopped and tried to orient himself, he felt hopelessly confused. He tried not to betray this confusion, to continue on as if sure of a destination, but soon Pam was asking him how much further they would have to go. Her voice was hoarse, barely audible, close by his right ear. He said it would not be very much further.

Soon she asked him again. He thought of the things that mattered, of these three good people who mattered, and he kept on going beyond that point when, had he been alone, he knew he would have stopped. There had been no more shots, at least he had heard none. He became grateful for the avalanches which had covered at least part of the trail they had left from the snow cave to the Gaddis ridge.

When he sensed the day was ending and the dusk was coming on, he began to look for shelter, anything to get them out of the cold. But there was nothing, and he kept moving forward, due south, and continued to feel uneasily that the ground beneath his boots was rising instead of falling. He stayed close to what he could find of the ridge. The surface of the snow had begun to harden, but it would not support him and the burden he carried; his ice-rimmed boots broke through the surface and he sank with each step, sometimes to his shins, sometimes to his knees. When he raised his hand to touch his face, he felt nothing.

He no longer rested at intervals, but after each step. He would take one step forward and then stop and rest, breathing heavily, and would try to shift the weight on his back. He would look into the mist that swirled around him and try to orient himself. He would eat snow, scooping it up on the back of his balled hand and pressing it against his mouth. Pam begged him to stop. Myke responded sluggishly to the rope; there were times when he had to exert pressure to bring her forward.

We've had it, he thought. *Negative. No. Put me down. Please put me down. You'll be cold. You'll be cold. Like hell. Negative. No.*

At six o'clock he realized where they were, the knowledge so unacceptable he pressed his eyes shut, locked his jaws, refused at first to believe it.

"*Please,*" he heard her say. "I can't . . ."

"All right," he replied.

"Please put me down. . . ."

"All right. You'll have to try and help me. Can you help me?"

"Yes. . . ."

He got stiffly to his knees, rolled slowly onto his side, freed himself from the straps of the rucksack. She helped him with her good leg, crying out, resting finally on her back, looking up, her small face and closely cropped red hair wet from the mist.

He shook his head, unable to speak to her.

"Is he here?" she said.

"No."

"Is Kate here?"

"I'll have to get her."

"Is she very far?"

"No. She's not very far. Myke isn't either. Can you wait?"

She nodded drowsily as if now that she was lying down nothing else was important to her. He followed the rope and his own tracks for sixty weary feet until he found Myke, standing hunched over, her eyes closed, her gloved hands hanging slothlike at her sides. Kate stood several feet behind; she carried the red Kelty pack and had gathered her half of the slack rope into coils. She waited for him to speak, seemed prepared for the kind of news he would bring.

"We're off route," he said. His lips stung; he tasted blood. "We're way off route."

Myke nodded.

"Where are we then?" Kate asked. "Do you know?"

"I think so."

"Well?" she said when he did not continue.

"This ridge flattens out on the east face of a mountain called Peak 18. Have you heard of it?"

"Yes."

"Have you climbed it?"

"No I haven't."

He took a breath then let it escape through his compressed lips. "There's a long shelf that diagonals up the face like a road," he said finally. "They call it the Ramp."

"Is that where we are?"

"Yes. It's wide as a turnpike at first, then it begins to narrow down. We've been on it a long time." He shook his head.

"Whoosh," Myke breathed. Kate untied the rope from the heavy girl's waist, finished coiling it.

"Well," she said, "what are we going to do?"

"There are a couple of rock caves," he told her. "Up ahead of us, maybe half a mile if we're where I think we are. There's no sense trying to go back, not now, not this late; we're way out of our way. Jesus," he said flatly, "if I hadn't screwed this up we'd have been out of here."

Myke nodded as if beyond feeling or caring. She lifted one hand, then let it drop. "Boy," she said.

"I knew we were going up," he said. "I could feel it, I knew it, but it didn't make sense. I was tired. . . ." He closed his eyes without finishing. *I really screwed it up*, he thought. *We could have been out.*

"How's Pam?" Kate asked him.

"She's all right."

"Is it a half-mile to these caves? Or is it more than that?"

"It could be less. I'm pretty sure I know where we are; I've been here before."

"Are the caves like any good for sleeping and stuff?" Myke asked him.

"Yes. They're pretty good-sized."

"I've got my own TV set at home," Myke said. He looked at her. The skin of her face was cracked and split like the skin of a roasted apple; the rims of her eyes were circled in red. She stood with her arms at her sides with the mist around her. "It's in my room," she said. "My father got it for me last year. It's color, really nice. I usually come home after school and get some graham crackers and milk and just watch the thing until supper. I usually don't have anything else to do."

He looked down at his frozen feet.

"We'll manage," Kate said. "I don't think any of us could have gone much further today, even if we had stayed on route."

"What about tomorrow?" Myke said. "Have we had it?"

Whittaker shook his head. He could not think of what to say.

"I know," she said. "I mean, it looks pretty bad I guess, because of his like shooting his gun. . . ."

"I think we should get started," Kate put in. "There's not going to be much daylight left. We better use it while we can."

"If we get some snow or wind," Whittaker said without conviction, "our tracks will fill in. They may not look for us up here. They'll have to find a place to hole up soon. . . ."

"I think we should go," Kate said again. "I don't think we should talk about them."

12

There was not much snow on the last half-mile of the Ramp, but it rose steadily. Whittaker went first. Kate carried Pam. Myke brought up the rear, carrying the coiled rope and the red Kelty pack. They finished the distance in less than an hour.

The Ramp ended where high cliffs formed a cul-de-sac. In the walls of these cliffs there were two caves, one larger than the other but both large enough to accommodate men sitting down. The floor of each cave was covered with old hemlock and fir boughs brought up from the lower slopes by climbers to soften the uneven rock surfaces. When Whittaker tried to remember which of the two caves he had stayed in before, he could not: Like many things in this basin, the caves were familiar and not familiar at the same time. All of his strength had left him. He felt bitter in the face of his failure to lead the others safely to his truck. In this place of no privacy he wanted very much to be left alone.

"It's going to be like pretty tight, all of us in here," Myke said after poking her head into the larger cave.

"It will do for now," Kate said. "Until we get ourselves straightened out."

"I can sleep in the little cave," Myke offered. She seemed very relieved they had finally reached a destination. "You guys can have this one if you want."

"We'll decide that later," Kate told her. "Right now, let's get as dry and warm as we can."

In what was left of the half-light of that day, they

brought Pam into the larger cave and settled her in a
place where the branches were thick and not too brittle.
Kate offered Myke her parka again, which Myke grate-
fully put on. Then Kate got the sleeping bag out of the
Kelty pack and unrolled it and together they helped get
Pam into it, zipping it up around her until only her face
showed.

"I'm just glad we're here," she said.

"You're not the only one," Myke replied. "How do
you feel? Do you feel okay or what?"

"I'm okay. My leg hurts and my bottom is sore from
sitting in that rucksack so long. . . ."

"We have one pill left," Kate said. "Should we give
it to you now?"

"I guess I better wait."

"Good. We'll eat what we have, then you can take it
and get some sleep. You did wonderfully, Pam. We all
did well, if you ask me."

"What a day *that* was," Myke said.

"At least we got through it," Kate replied, sitting
down between Pam and Whittaker. "At least we're all
here. There were times when I didn't think we would
be."

"What about tomorrow though? I mean, I guess
they know where we are, now. They'd have to know,
wouldn't they?"

"No," Whittaker said. He wanted to smoke, tried to
work the cigarettes out of his shirt pocket with his club-
like hands, but gave up finally, leaning back against the
rough cave wall, his hands pushed up under his crossed
arms. "They may not know where we are."

"I guess we shouldn't start a fire or anything," Myke
said wistfully, as if she had had her mind on a fire for a
long time.

"We could start up the stove," Kate replied.

"We wouldn't have the stove if I'd had my way," Whittaker said.

"But we do," she replied. She was shivering badly now; he could feel her shake where she sat next to him. "We can make some tea. As long as we're careful about the flame, I don't see why we have to worry."

"It's really something," Myke said wistfully. "I mean it's really a trip, isn't it? I looked forward to coming here all spring; I used to mark off the days on my calendar. My parents thought I was crazy to want to go mountain-climbing, but I wanted to try and make some friends, and then I just turned on to the whole idea, at least for a while I did. I practiced a lot with Neil and Pam and the twins. . . . Geez," she said, "I mean like every week-end in May we'd all pile into Neil's car and go up to Estes Park and he'd show us how to do things.

"I mean, isn't it really something? I thought just getting to this place was the worst thing I ever had to do in my life, and then all this. . . . Geez, 'Star Trek' is probably on right now. If I hadn't come here I'd be in my room eating about twelve pounds of graham crackers and drinking milk and watching Mr. Spock. He's the one with big ears. Do you guys ever watch 'Star Trek'? Or 'Kung Fu'? Or 'The Avengers'? Boy. Emma Peel just wrecks me. She's really beautiful, and very independent and smart too. She looks like Kate; I think she does. I get these like super fantasies where *I'm* Emma Peel—can you dig that?—and these big guys come after me and I put them down with a karate chop. Steed's kind of a drag, but Emma is really cool. Have you guys ever watched it? A lot of people get killed in the show, but Emma and Steed, they always win in the end. . . ."

She went on that way in a monologue of indignation

and puzzlement, as if by talking continuously and in a certain mode she might keep her fear at bay. She placed the stove inside a circle of stones that had been arranged by other climbers just inside the cave. When she primed and started it up, its steady hiss and slight but detectable warmth lent substance to the atmosphere of dusky haven here that was reduced but not extinguished by the fact of the men who hunted them.

Whittaker felt the beginnings of relief, although he knew the feeling would be temporary and did not take into account what lay ahead. Kate, as if to assure him he was not to blame for anything and as if he were an older brother and without making much of it at all, had put her arm around his waist. Nothing had felt better to him in a long while. Once Myke had the stove going and a pot of snow melting, she excused herself, saying cheerfully that she had to pee.

"Be careful out there," Kate advised her. "Stay close to the wall. It's getting cold and dark; things will be icing over. You don't have to go far."

"I always wished I could pee through my finger," Myke said. "Didn't you? I mean boys have *some* advantage, know what I mean?"

She crawled out of the cave on her hands and knees, careful not to bump into Pam who slept soundly now between her and Kate. Bits of twig and brush clung to her pants. Whittaker watched her, then tried to get his cigarettes again but still could not manage it.

"What's the matter?" Kate asked him.

"My hands are still numb. I thought I might have a smoke."

"I'll get them," she said. "Are your hands going to be all right?"

"I don't know."

"You should have your gloves. I'll get them from Myke when she comes back. She'll be all right without them for a while. The tea should help too."

She lit the cigarette, shielding the match with care. Then she put the cigarette between his lips, looking at him as if to be sure he was not misconstruing the act or the nature of her recent warmth toward him.

"Thanks," he said. He took a deep drag, exhaling it slowly, then moving the cigarette to one corner of his mouth, keeping his hands under his arms. "I guess I should loosen the laces on my boots," he said. She looked at him, her face lovely, he thought, framed by her long hair. "My feet or my hands," he said, shrugging, "I don't know which is worse. How are yours?"

"They're all right." She began to work on his boots.

"Boy, I really screwed this up," he said suddenly.

"You wouldn't let me talk that way last night," she replied. "You told me to cut it the fuck out."

It surprised him to hear her say that and he tried to smile and the cuts opened on his lips. She finished unlacing one boot and began working on the other.

"Feels better already," he said.

"I'm afraid we don't have any more dry socks. Would it be that chancy to light a fire? We've got plenty of brush here to burn. It could make the difference."

"I wouldn't risk it. I don't know where those two are, but they could be closer than we think," he said, squinting against the smoke that had begun to settle around him under the low rock roof of the cave. "I think if we get out of this thing," he said, "I'm going to take about four weeks in the Bahamas. A good hotel, some white sand and green water, palm trees, a beach where I won't need a suit—the whole nine yards."

She brushed her hair back from her face, and for a

moment he thought she might say, *Yes, I'd like that too, I'd like to go with you.*

"If I did something like that," she said, "I'd like a hotel where I could dress in the evenings. I'm sick of the way we all look nowadays, the affectation of slovenliness, whatever it is. I'd want to find a place with a terrace bar between the casino and the beach so I could drink expensively and listen to the ocean on one side and the roulette wheels on the other. . . ."

"You should do it then. They've got places like that."

"You said 'if.' "

"Did I?"

"Yes. You don't think we're going to get out anymore, do you?"

He did not reply. When she had unlaced his other boot, she took the cigarette from him and took a drag, then placed it between his lips again. They sat with their backs against the rear wall of the cave, facing out where the mists swirled along the ledge and the light was dying.

"You don't, do you?" she repeated.

"I want to," he replied after a while.

"I stopped thinking we were going to make it after what happened to Dianne and Dietz, after Pam fell. You got me hoping again last night. I was doing all right until I heard those shots today, until I knew they were still coming after us."

"I'm down right now, Kate," he said. "I'll come back after I eat something."

She put her arm around his waist again, and he thought whatever it was that had caused her to be wary of him had at least been reduced by circumstance, and he was glad. When Myke appeared in front of the cave she was holding two number-ten cans, both charred black, one empty, she informed them, the other containing a half-empty juice tin, a small sack of coffee, a tin of meat and a packet of onion soup.

"They were like in the other cave!" she exclaimed.

Kate told her not to raise her voice and asked her to give Whittaker his gloves, which she did. She was very excited. The snow she had put on the stove had melted and she opened the packet of soup and dumped it in. She opened the tin of meat, sliced it, put it into one of the stove's nesting pots along with some slices of cheese. Soon the cave filled with a tangy odor that made Whittaker's stomach ache. When Pam woke, they helped her eat some of the meat and cheese. Myke melted more snow, scoured her pots, adjusted the flame of the small stove, raising it for this, lowering it for that. She seemed pleased to have these chores, as if not quite sure she had contributed her fair share so far this day and, with these familiar duties of the kitchen, intended to balance her account.

By the time they had finished eating, the cave was dark and cold. Pam took the last of the pills and soon fell asleep. Whittaker and Kate sat together, sharing a cigarette, careful to shield it behind their cupped hands. Myke put away her utensils quietly, then sat down on the other side of Pam and sighed a sigh that seemed to mingle apprehension and relief.

"I can't say I'm exactly filled up," she admitted, "but I'm probably not starving anymore. Do people just leave food around like that?"

"Yes," Kate replied. "They have some left over and don't want to carry it higher on the mountain so they leave it for others."

"It's like a really great idea," Myke said. "I wish they'd left a little more." She looked down at the sleeping girl. "Pam seems pretty good. Don't you think she does?"

"Yes. I wish we had some more codeine. That's been a godsend up until now."

"We've got aspirin and some sort of nonprescription sleeping pills. They'll help," Whittaker said.

"Won't those guys like see us tomorrow? When we try to leave here?" Myke wanted to know.

"Not if we get as much fog as we did today," he said.

"What if we don't get fog? I mean, it could be a nifty day or something."

"We'll have to wait and see, Myke."

"If things keep icing up like this," Kate said, gazing toward the mouth of the cave, "we'll have a miserable time trying to go back down that Ramp or whatever it is you call it. We haven't got any crampons."

"We can rappel off this ledge."

"We've got one carabiner and one seat sling. I checked."

"That's all we need."

"With Pam?" Myke said.

"We can work that too if we have to."

"Holy cow," Myke said.

"If the Ramp really does ice up, this place is going to be about as safe as any place around," he said. "One of us can rope down and go for my truck. The rest can stay here."

"They'll have figured out where we're heading by then, don't you think?" Kate asked.

"Probably. I don't know," he replied.

They did not talk for a while after that. Outside the cave a wind had begun to rise. Whittaker could hear the ticking sound of sleet against the ledge. He hoped their tracks had filled by now with drifting snow. If they had not, he knew this sleet would preserve them a long time.

"I was really scared under the snow like that," Myke said finally. "It was packed so tight around me I could hardly breathe. I could just move my chest a little, and there was like a hollow place where I'd kept my hands in front of my face, a sort of air pocket. I guess it wouldn't have lasted very long if you hadn't found me, right Kate?"

"I'm just glad I found you," Kate said.

"Have you ever known anybody who like . . . got caught like that and didn't make it?"

"Yes. In the Tetons once."

"It must be terrible to die like that."

"It can be very quick," Kate said. "It depends on what position you're in when the snow stops moving, whether you have an air pocket or not, and how big it is."

"How come you guys do this climbing stuff anyway?" Myke wanted to know.

"I do it because I like it, Myke," Whittaker said. "I roomed with a guy at Williams Air Force Base when I was going through pilot training. He was the one who got me going on it. He lived in Durango. He showed me this place, this basin I mean. We'd come in here whenever we could and climb everything in sight. He liked these caves; he always slept in the little one, I remember that now. He liked the view from here that you can get on a clear day."

"How come he didn't come with you this time?"

Whittaker shrugged his shoulders against the increasing cold. "He's dead," he replied.

"Oh, I'm sorry," she said.

"We were in the same squadron in Thailand. He got shot up one night over Laos and tried to get the airplane back but he didn't make it. At dawn some of us were standing around waiting for him to come in and he did finally, trailing two miles of black smoke, and he got it down and then it blew up on the runway."

"Gee," she said quietly.

"Myke," Kate put in, "give me the stove will you? And one of the pots? I'm going to heat some water and wash some of the grime off my face and then try to sleep. You should do that too," she said to Whittaker. "You sound very tired."

He did not reply.

"Come on," she said.

"His name was Ike," he said, as if he had not heard her. "He liked to fly and climb and hunt and fish. You would have liked him, I think. He heard about a river in Laos called the Disappearing River. He kept telling me we were going to fish it some day once the war was over; somebody told him there was great fishing there. I saw it later. After he'd augered the plane. . . ."

"Come on," she said. "Don't talk about that. You need to get some sleep. We all do. Myke, why don't you stay here with the rest of us. We can manage all right; and the more there are the warmer it will be."

"Okay, here's the stove and stuff," Myke said, passing them over the form of the sleeping girl. She yawned conspicuously, as if she were a little relieved not to have to sleep alone now that it was dark and sleeting out. "Goodnight," she said. "I'll probably be snoring in about two minutes. My mother can't stand my snoring. She used to say it was awful to have to listen to. She even taped it once so I would know how awful it was, can you believe that? Geez, I'm tired," she said. "When I get back home I'm going to bag it for about ten days. I guess I should say *if* I get back."

"Goodnight, Myke," the pilot said.

"They're not going to come walking up here, are

they?" she croaked. "I mean, I just couldn't handle that at all."

"No. They're not going to come walking up here. Not with the Ramp iced up."

He heard her sigh as if this at least was something to be grateful for. Then he crawled out of the cave and went down the Ramp a little way to urinate. The rocky ledge was slippery under his unlaced boots and his feet were numb. The sleet was coming from the North. He kept his back to it.

The river in Laos had been the color of cocoa. It had carried the corpses of men and animals; it had held rusting trucks and flare cannisters and unexploded bombs. The perimeters around its fords were pocked with moonlike craters which filled with rain in the monsoon, and all the villages and hamlets along the river were deserted and had been deserted since the time when the trucks had first come down from the North.

I wonder where they are? he thought. *Karpus and his friend. I wonder where they're holed up?*

Ike had been one of the ones with whom, in spite of his efforts not to, he had become too close.

13

Just before dark of that same day, in the steep snow below the west ridge of Wolf Mountain, Karpus discovered a cave which he assumed the climbers had dug the night before to shelter themselves from the storm. The area in front of the cave was well tramped; tracks led away southwest in the general direction of the pass.

Earlier that afternoon he had heard the remote thunder of avalanches rumbling in the western reach of the basin; had heard voices calling. At the time, he had been up on the south slope of Wolf Mountain, looking for some sign of the climbers, and in a moment of frustration he had fired his rifle twice in the direction the voices had come from. It had been difficult to move through the new snow; visibility had been cut by fog. He had had to descend most of the south slope before he could make his way up again toward the west ridge. He had lost his way a number of times, and once he had located the base of the ridge he had stuck to it until he came upon the cave.

He was not inclined at first to spend the night in the snow cave, for he had had no prior experience with such a shelter and assumed it would be much too cold. He had brought with him one of the climbers' rucksacks and one of their orange tents and was prepared to spend the night in the tent, until he got on his hands and knees and crawled through the entrance tunnel into the cave itself and saw how roomy it was and how quickly it would set up. There were already two ponchos covering the floor, and over these he spread the orange fabric of the tent and over part of this a two-by-four-foot polyurethane pad and over the pad a down mummy sleeping bag. Then he brought the rucksack, his lantern and the Weatherby rifle into the cave.

By the time he had cooked and eaten a supper of corned-beef hash with hot sugared coffee and a candy bar for dessert, the roof of the snow cave above the lantern had begun to develop a sheen and the air inside felt comfortably warm. When he lit a cigarette, a small venting hole that had been poked through the snow to the outside took the worst of the smoke.

The bottle of whiskey he had brought was a little less than half full. He sipped from it, and while he did he examined with some care a camera he had found among the climbers' gear. It was a Polaroid weighing, he guessed, about a pound and a half and measuring in its closed position about an inch by four inches by seven. A strip of embossing tape glued across its grained leather surface identified it as belonging to Pamela Harrington, 126 East Vista Drive, Boulder, Colorado. Slowly he peeled the strip of tape off and pushed it into the hard snow wall behind him.

He put in a fresh film pack and flashbar, then focused on the burning lantern not two feet from where he sat and pressed the shutter button. There was a blinding flash of light and almost at once a card of film ejected from the front of the camera. On it the image of the lantern began to develop as he watched, blinking. The picture was grainy and indistinct at first, but soon precise and colorful.

He tried to set the camera up in such a way that he might take his own picture, and after a half-dozen unsuccessful tries he finally managed by propping it on the rucksack several feet away and touching the shutter button lightly with the muzzle of the rifle. While his portrait was developing, he took the pilot's billfold from the breast pocket of his blue and black checked mackinaw and removed from it the snapshot of the pilot in his sleek plane and the newspaper article which he scanned again briefly:

U.S. PILOT HELPS A.R.V.N. IN AMBUSH
112 VC DEAD COUNTED

His own picture, once developed, did not suit him. It was poorly focused, off center, and reminded him once

again that he needed a shave. He began forthwith to melt
a pot of snow on the stove and prepared the razor and
soap and brush he had found among the climbers' gear.
On the fabric of the orange tent he put his picture and
the pilot's picture side by side. His own picture did not
suit him at all. The pilot looked like his older brother.

For one week each year for four years, from the time
he had been nine to the time he had been twelve, his
father had taken his brother hunting in the San Juan
Mountains of Colorado. They had always gone to the
same place, driving from Morenci to Morgan in his father's pickup, going up the old logging road, hiking
across the basin to the blind canyon in its northeast
section where they would stay for a week in the abandoned prospector's shack, playing draw poker and getting drunk together and shooting mountain goats and
deer. His brother had told him all about it each time, had
shown him maps and pictures and trophies in what had
proved a futile attempt to elicit from young Karpus some
sign of anguish or envy.

His father was an immigrant who believed the only
child of importance was the first-born son. During the
times when his father and brother were away, his mother,
who always drank, would drink more than usual and
would bring men home from the smelter and would let
them undress her and do things to her in his presence.
It had never occurred to him, as she must have known,
to tell anyone about this. One of the men she used to
bring home was another shop foreman named Cable.
Cable used to make his mother bend over the sink in the
kitchen as if she were washing the dishes; then he would
come up behind her and hike up her skirt and run his
equipment, of which he was proud, as far up her as he
could, and while he fucked her he would explain drunk-
enly to the boy that no matter what a woman might say,

this was the way they really liked to get it. His father and Cable got into a fight once, and to Karpus's surprise at the time, Cable won.

He left home when he was sixteen, and the following summer he outfitted himself with some army-surplus gear and went into the San Juans and stayed in the prospector's shack alone for thirty days, which was two days more than the total number of days spent there by his father and brother over the course of four years.

Now, here in the cave, he shaved by touch, taking his time, rinsing his face with snow once he had finished: A man of few requirements, he had never liked being unshaven.

He did not think in any sequential way of the past. An image would come to him of his father and brother getting into his father's truck on the street in front of the house in Morenci and driving away, and that would be all: Like a piece of film clipped from a reel. Shortly after that an image might come of Duane Jegalian holding his hand over a candle flame. Then an image of the climbers falling from the cliff. Then one of his mother, whom he had never liked, crying in pain at the kitchen sink.

Nor, as a rule, did he think sequentially of the future. He knew that early tomorrow morning he would get up and continue his search for the pilot. But he had laid no more detailed plans than that. Tomorrow would come; he assumed his search would be successful. The pilot had not impressed him as being particularly smart. There were not many places he and the others could go, and wherever they went they would be burdened by each other and he would have the advantage. Because it was one step beyond the finding of them, he had not spent much time thinking about what he would do when he did find them. He was quite willing to take things as they came, and as far as he was concerned the situation did not call for any intricate planning.

"Hey, Johns . . ." he started to say.

Shadows moved on the cave walls which were yellow-white in the lantern light, and the orange of the tent fabric was bright on the floor. Water had begun to drip from the snow roof above the lantern and when he finished shaving he moved his pot so it would catch the drip. The water went *plink* into the pot at intervals of about five seconds. The sound did not bother him. He lit a cigarette and sipped from the whiskey and looked down at his unsatisfactory picture where it lay next to the picture of the pilot in his plane.

Duane Jegalian had a block of wood shaped like a doorknob bolted to one of the bars of his cell; he used it to keep the calluses tough on the palms of his hands. Whenever a new inmate arrived, and as soon after he arrived as possible, Jegalian and two or three of the men who were always close to him would set up a rite of initiation which consisted simply of two lighted candles above which Jegalian and the new inmate would equidistantly hold their hands palm down until the pain became unbearable for the new inmate and he withdrew. The ritual was so well known in the prison that it was often carried out in the presence of the guards. Because the calluses on Jegalian's palms were about half an inch thick and his pain threshold was high, the outcome of the contest was never in doubt. But a man could earn for himself a certain useful status if he could endure the heat of the flame for one minute or more, something most men could not do. Jegalian was good-natured about this rite of initiation for his new inmates and never insisted that a man go on beyond the limit of the pain he could endure, unless by some chance he had been guilty of an act for which he had to be punished.

When Johns's turn had come to be formally admitted to Jegalian's cellblock, he had whimpered and whined, and when finally he stuck his soft puffy hand over the flame, he had cried *"Ouch!"* almost at once and withdrawn, much to the glee of the guards and inmates who had gathered to watch.

Karpus had not withdrawn his hand. He had held it steadily over the flame and had looked at Jegalian in a relaxed way as if his hand, its skin and bone and nerve and blood, were no longer a part of him. After the first minute and a half, Jegalian, who also held his hand steadily over the flame, looked at those who had gathered to watch and said here was a good man.

"I'd appreciate your doing me a favor," Karpus had replied pleasantly.

"Like what?" Jegalian said. Two minutes had passed and a wisp of smoke had risen from Karpus's palm. In the anteroom to the shop, where the ceremony was taking place, there was now the smell of burning flesh and one or two men had gone away.

"I'd like us all to get off the back of my cellmate, Johns here."

"Sure," Jegalian said. He spoke pleasantly too, and had not moved his hand, but he had begun to perspire as if he were feeling some of the pain that Karpus should have been feeling. Two and a half minutes had passed, and a number of men who had not been present at the start had now arrived.

"I'd like to sort of look after Johns here," Karpus said, "and help him rehabilitate himself, and he can't very well do that if we're all on his back all the time. If it's all right with you and the rest of the men."

"Sure, why not?" Jegalian said. "Nobody bothers him from now on. Maybe I'll need a favor from you someday."

"Thanks," Karpus replied. "I appreciate it." And he had snatched his blistering hand away from the flame so that Jegalian would not be humiliated, for to humiliate Jegalian would serve no useful purpose as far as Karpus could see.

After that—and only to Johns—he had referred to the boss of their cellblock as the Candle Man. Johns had said if Karpus really could talk the other inmates out of ragging his ass, he could probably also talk the birds out of the trees, but Jegalian was a good man and from that night on there had been no problem.

It was sleeting now outside the cave. He crawled through the passageway and relieved himself in the dark, urinating at length into the trampled snow. The passageway slanted down to the outside and its circle of light would not, he thought, be visible from any great distance. He decided to set the alarm in his head for 4:00 A.M. and not waste any time once he got up. That early there would be no avalanches and the surface of the snow would be crusty enough to take his weight. He would go light this time—take the rifle, stick something to eat into the pockets of his mackinaw; that way he would make good time.

He crawled back into the cave and looked at his picture again. It really was not very good. He touched a match to it finally and let it burn. He put the newspaper article and the pilot's picture back into the billfold, and the billfold back into his pocket, and he tidied up his gear. Then he blew the lantern out and got into the down mummy bag.

He had never had much trouble persuading people

to do things, almost never had to raise his voice or become threatening in any obvious way. Over a period of years he had shared a cell with a good many different men, some young, some old, and with all of them (except for Johns) there had come a time one night, usually at the end of a quiet conversation, when he would look at whomever it was he had been talking to and ask him to lower his pants and lie belly-down on his bunk. There had never been any trouble. One or two of them had started to protest, had looked at him again as if to see how serious he was and after they looked at him they had lain down as he had told them to do. Sometimes they would struggle in a halfhearted way before he penetrated them, but once he had done that they would usually lie still or even sometimes go along. In the years before he had gone to prison it had been the same way with the women he had known; there had never been any real trouble.

"Hey, Johns," he said.

Usually he had no difficulty falling asleep, but tonight he was having trouble and he sat up finally and lit a cigarette, the dark cave flaring briefly to light, revealing the orange fabric of the climbers' tent that covered the floor. The other tent stood just where it had on the preceding night, contained by a trip line, surrounded by snow next to the rock ledge that blindsided the trail. He had not wanted to change anything there except the one thing he could not change.

"Hey, Johns," he said huskily.

It was cold and dark in the cave except for the small coal of his cigarette, and no reply came back except the *plink* of the water that dripped into his shaving pot, at longer intervals now. Every night for the last two years the fat man had slept near him, had been there in the morning when he woke up.

"Hey, Johns," he said again, as if by saying it often enough he might resurrect his friend.

The pilot would not know that Johns had died zipped up in a down mummy bag that had taken his blood like a wick.

14

Whittaker could not bring himself finally to return to the cave where the others were, and crawled instead into the smaller cave where Myke had found the food and where Ike had always liked to sleep. There were not as many boughs here, and those that were were dry and brittle and crackled like cellophane under him as he curled up on his side and closed his eyes, his still numb hands flat together between his legs, his parka hood up around his head. He could not stop shaking from the cold which seemed to have retreated from his extremities to center now in his chest and gut and groin, as if his body had begun a process of surrendering to the cold what was not essential to sustain its life.

Just outside the shallow cave the sleet swept along the ledge with the sound of dry rice tossed against a windowpane. He had carried rice in his pocket in the days when he first courted Marie, had tossed it against her window those summer nights that she might know he was there in the courtyard of the embassy and come to him secretly so her father, who had not approved of enlisted men, would not know she was seeing this one.

In those days he had been young and gallant and sure of himself, had loved his country, had known what he wanted to do with his life, whom he would marry, how many children he would have, the kind of home, exactly how his career would go: from rank to rank, from training to combat to the academy finally, with a rank of full colonel, where he would pass on to the young recruits the legacy of his experience and belief. He would climb mountains, teach his children to climb. He would dress well and eat well and live in such a way that people would regard him as a man who had done things right: had accepted the fact that his parents had left him a foundling, had not pitied himself, had worked hard, competed, been useful in battle, defended his country, believed in God, worshipped and prayed.

And, sometimes with a terrible tenacity, and long after the youthful dreams of other men had died, he had kept his dream intact, had kept it nearly whole until he had gone to war, where it had crumbled and turned to dry ash and dust and had left him with nothing but a sense of rage and bitterness and a deep sense of grief.

All those years he had thought he knew what he was, what his country was, and his God, *had* known, had been sure, had spoken of it many times with Marie who had admired him then and loved him then. But finally he had gone to war, and when he came home the first time she had said in a fury, "You *like* it. That's why you want to go back, why you insist on going back even though they haven't insisted on sending you." He had been stunned when she said that, had wanted to take her by the throat. *No,* he had wanted to shout, he was going back because his country was at war and he was a pilot who had been trained to help fight his country's wars and he believed that his country was right as it always had been right. But by then it was too late to say such things, for instead of one country there were two halves of a country, and one half believed as he believed, and the other half would have indicted him for crimes.

And when had he himself stopped believing? When had he changed, or begun to change? And what had he become? A gaunt, morose man whose marriage had failed, whose career had ended far short of its goals, whose children looked upon him with fear as if he were an alien who descended upon them infrequently from far and unwholesome places; a man who had once stuck with a shot-up plane long after his backseater had punched out, long after he himself should have punched out, not because he wanted to bring it home the way Ike had wanted to, but because he wanted to end a life that no longer held promise or significance or joy.

For just a little while after the twins had been killed, in those moments of terror and loss, he had felt something of himself come back, a sureness that what he was doing was inevitable and right and that he was doing it well. Then he had made the mistake that brought the others here, that all but ended whatever chance they might have had to survive, and he no longer felt anything except the cold and a terrible loneliness and a terrible need to be alone.

She found him that way only a few minutes later, thinking at first he had slipped or fallen on the ledge or gotten lost, calling his name, alarmed, afraid, taking the dim flashlight he had told her not to bring but which she had brought anyway, checking the smaller cave at last and finding him there, curled up near its rear wall, his hands folded between his legs like a child.

She had seen Paul that way once after he had lost a contract for which he had worked very hard and on which an early promotion had depended; had found the ever-confident, invincible young man she married curled up one afternoon in his blue business suit and smart black shoes on the embroidered spread that covered their king-size bed. There had been tears in his eyes, although he had not allowed himself to cry. She had held his head in her lap while he told her what had happened to bring him down, a complex and finally unsuccessful series of corporate maneuvers in which, except as they bore upon him, she had no interest. During most of the time that he had talked and talked, she had tried and failed to imagine her father with tears in his eyes and his head cradled in her mother's lap.

"You didn't tell me you weren't coming back," she said.

He did not reply, although she sensed he was awake.

"I've got some hot tea going on the stove," she said. "It's weak, but it does help."

Then, as if irritated at her finding him here, he sat up suddenly, putting his hands under his crossed arms, trembling with cold. By the indirect weak yellow beam of the flashlight she could see his matted beard and cadaverous features framed by the oval hood of his parka, his eyes gazing past her, beyond the ledge where the sleet played, beyond anything she had known. *It was you who was going to kill him,* she thought. She was on her hands and knees facing him, close enough to reach out and touch his shoulder; but she did not reach out.

"Pam and Myke are asleep," she said. "I think you should come back and be with us. I don't think you should stay here alone."

For a long moment she thought he would not respond at all, but then he moved to follow her into the larger cave where, silently, he took the place he had occupied before, between her and one of the cave's walls, sitting and facing out. She kept the stove going for the slight light and warmth it provided, helped him drink a cup of tea, and, when he had finished that, she lit a cigarette and placed it between his lips, no longer bothering to shield it or the dancing flame of the match.

"There are only a couple left," she told him.

"I'll be sorry when they're gone," he said.

"I think we were warmer last night, don't you?"

"Yes."

"How far do you think we came?"

"Three or four miles."

"My God."

"I know."

"How far is your truck from here?"

"Mile and a half, two miles."

"Up and down?"

"Yes."

"And they know where the place is?"

"Yes. They've got a truck there too."

"We came in Neil's station wagon," she said, shivering. Whittaker could see the cloud of her breath as she talked, could see the light from the flame of the stove reflect from the mist and sleet that blew along the ledge, the soft flickering shadows it sent across the rough rock surface of the cave's interior. "We left it at the depot in Durango and took the narrow-gauge train as far as Needleton. Then we hiked up the creek trail."

"Kids like the train?"

"Yes, they loved it. Have you ever come in that way?"

He nodded. "Did you and Neil . . . ?" He paused.

"Have anything going?"

"Yes."

"I didn't know him that well. I'd see him around the club, went climbing with him a couple of times. He was a nice guy, very polite. I can't imagine him ever hurting anyone's feelings or getting angry. We were sharing a tent on this trip, but I still didn't know him very well, not really. He . . ." She stopped to take a last long drag from the cigarette before putting it out.

"He what?" Whittaker asked idly.

"He asked me on that last night if I wanted to sleep with him. We'd been having a good time, the trip was going pretty well, and I guess he thought it was worth bringing up although I don't think I had encouraged him to. He just said 'Would you like to make love before we turn in?' as he might have said 'Would you like some more tea?' I've been approached a few times, but never quite like that. If I had known . . ."

"You might have done it," he finished for her.

"Yes. I might have, would have probably."

"Then Neil would have been lucky."

"Why do you say that?" she wanted to know, and he thought she had become defensive again.

"Usual reasons I guess; you're good-looking. . . ."

"That, even if true, wouldn't mean I'm a wizard in bed."

He managed to laugh, his hands still tucked under his arms.

"Well, would it?" she said, as if by laughing he had accused her of something.

"No."

"I had very Victorian parents," she said. "As far as I know they were born wearing clothes. If we hadn't had adjoining rooms I might have grown up thinking they had slept with each other once, conceived me, then given it up. Look," she said, hugging herself against the cold, "I don't know why the hell I'm talking about all this to you, but I'd like you to know I am not a cheap floozy, or dumb broad, or somebody who cries in her beer all the time."

"Hey, I never said—"

"As far as you're concerned, I would like to like you," she continued. "I want to. I even started to a little bit today. But you make it goddamned hard, do you know that? Saying some of the things you do? Looking murderous half the time?" She looked at him. "Do you think it was easy for me to go behind that blanket in that shack and do what I did there?"

"Christ, no!"

"Don't wake the girls," she said. "They don't need to hear this. I just want it straight with you. I don't want you carrying around some asinine picture of me, which I think you do. You're very cozy with Myke, which is fine, but Myke isn't a woman yet and she hasn't been in charge of anything yet and she hasn't had that fat man's prick in her mouth or been married and divorced, and if you think I'm some Miss Goody Two Shoes or what*ever* you think, you're wrong."

He looked at her, amazed.

"You're just Irish as *hell*," he said.

"I never told you that."

"You didn't have to, your name's on your parka for Christ's sake. I think you're terrific. I got the idea *I* was the one who wasn't measuring up."

"Well, can't we just get along?" she said. "Can't we give all the rest of it up?"

"Sure," he replied. "I'd like that."

They reached toward each other, held each other.

"I don't want to die," she said after a while. "I don't want any more of us to die."

"I know."

"Were you responsible for people over there, in Viet Nam or wherever it was?"

"Yes."

"Did you lose some?"

He nodded slowly. "Half a squadron in one year," he said. "Over the trail at night."

"Was there anything you could have done?"

"I don't think so."

"Did it make you feel sick the way I feel because of what happened to Dietz and Dianne and Neil?"

"Yes."

"It's a rotten poor life isn't it?"

"Sometimes."

She looked at him. "Right now I think I could make love," she said. "If it would make any difference."

He held her in his awkward arms, could feel her shivering join his own. He closed his eyes. "I guess it wouldn't make much of a difference," he said. "But it's a nice idea. I even worked up a dream about it last night, vivid as hell."

"Was I part of it?"

"Yes."

"Was it any good?"

"I gave it four stars."

She smiled, drew back from him, pushed a strand of hair back under the hood of her parka.

"Maybe someday," she said.

"Sure," he said. "Why not."

She put away the stove and pots, checked to be sure the two sleeping girls were all right, then lay down by his side. The last things he remembered hearing were the businesslike sounds of Myke's snore and the sharp ticking of the sleet along the ledge.

15

He slept a long, fitful sleep, troubled by dreams of war. When he woke, the dawn had begun to reveal itself in a band of dark orange that lay at the far limit of the basin between the summits of the eastern range and the blue-black surfaces of the retreating night. He sat up, rubbed his eyes with the backs of his gloved hands, his hands intensely painful now. Kate continued to sleep beside him; muffled in the hood of her parka, she sighed uneasily as he moved away from her.

He crawled out of the cave and managed to stand up. His feet were numb; he found it difficult to move his toes. His legs were stiff, particularly his upper right leg. The muscles through his back and shoulders were clenched and aching. Twenty feet across the ice-rimmed ledge of the Ramp, a vertical wall dropped a hundred feet to gentle slopes. Across these at a distance of three miles he could see the area above timberline on the south slope of Wolf Mountain where Kate and the others had erected their three orange tents near the mouth of the blind canyon. He could not see the tents, which he assumed Karpus had struck, nor could he see any sign of the man himself, or the fat man, though he looked in this direction carefully for several moments.

I remember this place, he thought.

Above the area of what had been the climbers' base camp, the uptilted summit of Wolf Mountain reflected the first long shafts of light from the sun. Below and to the south, the stream meandered as a dark line etched across the newly whitened meadows of the basin floor.

Avalanche tracks scarred the visible slope of Peak 18, sweeping toward timberline and into the first of the timber itself. He could see the exploded trunks of many small firs, the green-branch rubble atop the snow. When he looked in the direction he and the others had come, trying to find some vestige of the tracks they had left, he could find no distinguishable trail across the ice-crazed crust. But he knew it was unlikely that all evidence of their having passed that way had been obliterated by the avalanches or by the sleet and snow that had fallen during the night. Karpus and his fat friend would locate them sooner or later. Perhaps they already had.

He hunched his shoulders painfully, moving from one numb foot to the other, breathing the thin cold air above the Ramp. He guessed from the look of things the day would prove to be cool and clear. The ice that covered the Ramp would not melt quickly on such a day, if it melted at all. As long as it did not melt, the Ramp would be impassable for anyone without crampons, and these caves would be a sanctuary. That, he thought, was in their favor. But the clearness of the day was not in their favor, and, aware they would have to reach a decision soon, he found it difficult to concentrate. It was as if during the long, cold and uncomfortable night he had begun to lose again the sharp edge of his will and therefore his capacity to survive.

He raised his left hand to his mouth, got the glove between his teeth and pulled it off. Below the second joint of each of his fingers the skin had grown dusky; there were gangrenous-looking patches across the back of the hand and along the thumb. The fingers were stiff, and when he tried to put the glove back on, the pain was intense. Yesterday he had thought his hands were dead or dying, but the pain reassured him somewhat. He decided not to remove the other glove, supposing the damage to both hands was similar.

His feet, which had felt like frozen stumps nailed to his legs somewhere in the vicinity of his shins, tingled now as if they were being lanced repeatedly with many small needles. He thought if he moved around enough they might begin to come back. He could not imagine himself without toes and fingers, or hands and feet. He had been checked out by some army doctors in a field hospital in Viet Nam once, had seen men there who had lost arms and legs to booby traps and mines. He could not imagine that; he thought he might rather be dead.

"Good morning," Kate said, appearing next to him, working the tangles out of her long hair with her comb. He liked that, that she would bother to comb her hair in such a place and time.

"Morning," he said.

"Any sign of them?"

"No."

"Maybe they've given up."

"Maybe they have."

"It's going to be beautiful, isn't it?" she said, looking in the direction of the rising sun. She was shivering and her voice wavered from the cold as she talked. He was shivering too.

"Yes," he said.

"Did you get any sleep?"

"Some."

"Were you as cold and miserable as I was?"

"I think I probably was."

"How are your hands?"

"They're all right. I've got some frostbite, but I don't think it's all that bad. I'm beginning to get some feeling in my feet for the first time in a while."

"Have you come up with a plan?"

"I'm working on it. Nothing definite yet."

"I hope it's not too Irish of me to say," she said, "but the girls and I are going to need a rest room. We can't be lugging Pam down the Ramp as iced up as it is, and it's probably not smart to be standing around out here anyway. I thought we could use the smaller cave."

"Good idea."

"You could stand to have your beard combed," she said, looking at him critically. "Would you hold still for a thing like that?"

"Sure, why not?" he said. "I don't want to go around looking like hell."

She smiled and reached up, working the widely spaced points of her comb through the short, bristly hair on his face.

"There," she said when she had finished. "Now you look like the Marlboro man."

"You were good last night," he said. She would know what he meant, and although she did not reply, he thought she was glad he had said it.

She went into the smaller cave and he went back into the larger cave where Myke and Pam lay close to each other in sleep. The girl's bruises where they showed around the bandages were dark and angry-looking. Myke's cheeks were blistered and red. Their expressions were gentle, possessed he thought of the innocence of children, a quality so long absent in his own makeup that he was moved to encounter it here.

He was kneeling beside them looking down when Pam, who was closest to him, woke up. She was lying on her back, zipped into his sleeping bag. The upper half of the bag trembled from her shivering. "Is he here?" she asked weakly, the frost of her breath hazing up.

"No, he's not here. I don't see any sign of him, or his friend. How do you feel?"

"I'm all right I guess. My leg hurts. Myke gave me a pill the last time I woke up. . . ."

"Do you want another one now?"

"Are there any left?"

"Yes, some aspirin and sleeping pills. They're not as strong as the others, but they should help."

He was trying to open the kit when Myke woke up, stretching, yawning, rubbing her hands together to warm them. Her green parka was covered with dust and bits of twig and sap. She shook her head vigorously, as if to rid it once and for all of the notion of sleep. "I can get that," she croaked, reaching for the kit.

"Sleep well?" he asked.

"I always sleep well," she replied. "My mother says it shows I'm not very smart. She thinks people who are smart lie awake half the night thinking up big ideas. Are we going to leave here or what? There isn't any fog anymore, I notice. That's not too cool, is it?"

"We'll have to talk about it."

"Boy," she croaked, "I really don't need those men showing up all of a sudden."

"I don't either," he agreed. "But I don't think they're as close as all that."

"What have we got for breakfast? Anything?"

"Couple of sandwiches. Some tea, maybe."

"Wow."

"I feel like eating scrambled eggs," Pam said shyly.

"*Wow!*" Myke croaked.

"Ruben used to meet me every Saturday morning at this nice restaurant he knew about, and he would always have lox and bagels and stuff like that, and I would al-

ways have scrambled eggs and a small glass of milk.
That's all I ever felt like. It used to make him mad because this restaurant had all different kinds of food from
lots of different countries, and he always told me I could
eat scrambled eggs at home."

"I guess he was pretty nice though, wasn't he?"
Myke said, as if she would settle for just about any young
man who would take her to breakfast on Saturday morn-
ings.

"Yes," Pam admitted. "I liked him a lot. Better than
anyone else I ever knew."

"Are you still like going around with him or anything?"

"No. He got tired of me after a while."

"Two aspirins," Whittaker told Myke. "And one of
those sleeping pills. That should help. If it doesn't," he
said, looking down at the girl whose anxiety was more
evident in her expression than tone of voice, "you let me
know, okay?"

"Okay."

"The only guys I get are boob freaks," Myke said.
"They've each got twenty-six pairs of very aggressive
hands, you know? I mean they can't even keep their
minds on me when I'm talking. They're always looking
down like I'd spilled ketchup on my shirt or something.
Jeez. I mean, how can you develop a relationship that
way?"

"I don't have any boobs," Pam said shyly, "so I
never had to worry about that."

Whittaker smiled. He thought she had blushed.

"Yeah, well, you're lucky," Myke croaked. "If you
ask me you are. I mean it's no picnic, believe me. I've
even thought about putting some kind of trap in my bra,
like a mousetrap, right? Then when some creep sneaks

his hand in there without asking me, *pow!*"

"Hey," Whittaker warned, half laughing, "keep it down, will you?"

"I know," Myke said. "I forget."

He was about to reply when Kate appeared suddenly in front of the cave. She wore her blue parka and windpants and held her comb in one hand. As soon as he saw her expression he knew something was wrong.

"What?" he said quietly as she ducked in beside him, sat down between him and the cave wall.

"He's coming."

"Who?"

"The tall one . . ."

"Where?"

"Along the base of the cliff . . ."

"Did he see you?"

"No, I don't think so. He's still pretty far. . . ."

"How far?"

"Half a mile . . ."

"He's not on the Ramp, is he?"

"No. God, no. It's really iced up."

"What are we going to do now?" Myke croaked.

"Sit tight," he said. "Be a hundred percent quiet. If we're lucky, he'll go right by."

"Yeah, but what if he doesn't . . . ?"

"Shhh," Kate warned. *"Don't talk."* She took Whittaker's hand, held it in her own.

They sat together in the closeness of the cave, looking out across the now reddening snow of the basin floor to the upthrust silhouette summits of the eastern range and a great sphere of rising sun. There was as yet no whisper of breeze. The loose stone that would soon begin to fall from the ridges and high rock faces was still frozen into place. There was no kitchen drip of water, no rush or gurgle, no distant boom of avalanching snow. They sat together, waiting, encapsulated in an atmosphere of silence, until at last they heard the first clear sound of Karpus's approach.

It was a remote yet distinct and brittle sound, like a man's boot in normal stride breaking through a skin of ice stretched across a shallow puddle on a late spring morning. Whittaker caught the sound and, as it repeated itself, rising in volume, advancing inexorably along the base of the cliff a hundred feet below where they sat, he felt a tightening of Kate's hand against his own, saw Myke close her eyes, felt Pam's hand reach out and touch his leg.

The sounds were clear and shattering now as they approached. It was as if Karpus were not looking for them at all, but rather moving out toward a specific destination, the high pass perhaps, from which he could command a view of both the pass itself and the distant stream along which wound the standard trail. He would have them bottled up then, could wait until they had to show themselves.

Whittaker closed his eyes. He thought the man must have kept coming through most of the night, ignoring the sleet and the cold and dark, ignoring how tired he must have been, finding his way somehow, not holing up as the pilot had been certain he would, leaving his fat friend behind to cover the basin's east side.

You sonofabitch, he thought.

Then, suddenly, the sound of Karpus's stride stopped somewhere just below the cliff. Abruptly the injured girl raised her head. Whittaker warned her with a gesture not to make a sound. She struggled to sit, still encased in the sleeping bag. Myke eased her back. There was no more noise from below the cliff. Kate held her comb in her right hand expectantly. She looked at Whittaker as if she knew there would be no time now for either of them to do the things they had said they wanted to do, to visit tropical hotels, to reach out to each other again, perhaps, as they had reached out to each other for a few minutes last night.

The sun had risen higher; its rays reached across the icy surfaces of the Ramp, almost reached into the cave itself. Whittaker thought he caught a whiff of cigarette smoke, glanced at Kate who pointed to her lips and then across the ledge. He nodded. The odor was neither persistent nor clear, but it was unmistakable and seemed to collect in the cave as if borne on the beginnings of the morning breeze. Myke's eyes were closed. She was shaking her head slowly back and forth.

Still they waited, heard the man clear his throat and hawk once into the snow, the sound as clear as if he were standing just in front of them on the ledge outside the cave instead of on the ground a hundred feet below. Had he seen something? Sensed something? Whittaker shuddered from the cold. Kate held his numb right hand. He thought he could hear his watch tick, thought Karpus might hear it too.

Then, after an interminable time, they heard him move out again, his boots plunging through the icy surfaces of the new snow, the racket dying as he went, on south toward the pass.

"*Boy!*" Myke breathed. She rubbed her bright cheeks with her fists.

"Take it easy," Whittaker said. "Let's keep it quiet."

"What now?" Kate asked.

"Wait until he's into the timber between here and the pass. We'll have a little time then when we can go out on the Ramp and he won't be able to see us."

"Then what?"

"I'm going to rope down."

"If you're going, we'll all go," she told him.

"No, Kate, that's no good. You three stay here."

"Your hands and feet are in a lot worse shape than mine," she said testily. "I can find my way to your truck if you tell me where it is. This is just as much my problem as yours. Why should you be the one to take the risk?"

"Because if it comes to it," he said, "I know I can kill him, and you're not sure."

She looked at him, her brows knit in an expression of disapproval as if, by saying this, he had reminded her of the thing about him she had for a while last night tried to forget.

"We'll all be taking a risk," he said finally. "Listen now and I'll tell you what we're going to do."

16

He sketched out for them what had become his plan. When he finished, Kate shook her head. "I don't like it," she said.

"I don't like it either. But I can't think of anything better."

"We could all wait here."

"How long?"

She nodded.

"We don't have anything to eat," Myke said, as if this by itself was reason enough to accept Whittaker's plan. "And anyway, Pam needs to get to a doctor, right?"

"If we're careful and a little bit lucky it can work,"

he said. "At least we'll have a chance."

"How can you be sure that he's not just on his way out of here?" Kate asked.

"Giving up on us you mean?"

"Yes. He could have decided we were all buried in one of those avalanches yesterday."

"I don't think so. For one thing, his friend isn't with him. And for another, he's covered too much ground. If he thought we'd all been caught he would have taken time this morning looking for proof. I think he found the cave we dug below the west ridge, or the trail we left on the other side of the slide, and he came across and picked up some sign along the Gaddis ridge and knows we're headed out this way. He may think we've gotten ahead of him somehow, but when he gets up on top of that pass and sees my truck is there, he'll dig in and wait. He'll know sooner or later we'll have to come out. He's probably got his friend covering the creek trail. He didn't strike me as someone who would walk away from something like this."

"Me either," Myke said.

But again Kate shook her head. "If he figures out what you're doing . . ." she started to say.

"Let's hope he doesn't."

"Do you think you can do the rappel? With your hands like they are?"

"Yes."

"Is there a descending ring up there?"

"Yes. It looks solid enough to hang a truck from."

"What are we supposed to do if you don't make it? I'm sorry if that sounds blunt. . . ."

"I'll make it."

"I don't just mean the rappel."

"I'll make it," he said. "You'll hear from me. If you

don't, you can try going out tonight. There's a spare key
in a magnetized case stuck to the frame below the tailgate
hinge."

"Is your truck hard to drive?"

"No. It's four-wheel drive, but you shouldn't have
any trouble with it."

"How far would I go?"

"As far as the road goes. When it ends, you're in
Morgan. When did you say you were due out of here?"

"Not for five more days," Myke said. "Nobody is
even going to think about looking for us until then,
right?"

Kate nodded.

"We can't make five more days," Whittaker said.

"I'll set up the rappel, then," Kate said, "and fix the
seat sling for you."

"Good. Let's give him a little more time though."

"Do you want a sandwich or something," Myke
croaked, "before you go?"

He nodded.

It could work, he thought. They would have to be
lucky all right, but that would be true no matter what
they did. The rappel worried him most, although he had
tried to make light of it. Without additional carabiners to
brake the speed of his descent, and with his hands like
this . . . Karpus worried him too. They would have to fool
the tall man with the rifle, and that, he knew, would not
be an easy thing to do. They would have to depend on
the possibility that the man was tired and just as eager
to finish the encounter as they were themselves; that he
would be a little less wary, a little less canny than he had
been up until now.

"Myke," he said after a while. "You rig up my pack
too. Just the way I said."

"Okay," she replied. "Jeez, I mean, if it happens like you want it to, are you going to like shoot him or something?"

"If I have to I will."

"Boy," she said softly.

"I hope you do," said Pam, who had not said anything for a long time. "I hope you do kill him."

17

The morning breeze had freshened. Kate rigged the rappel, securing one end of the rope to the heavy descending ring which had been bolted into the wall above the larger cave, dropping the coils over the edge a hundred feet down to the ground where Karpus not a half-hour ago had stopped to smoke his cigarette. She helped Whittaker get into the seat sling and into position over the rope. She worked silently, glancing now and then in the direction south of the place where the terrain began its rise toward the high mountain pass.

"Any sign of him?" Whittaker asked.

"Not yet. He's still got a way to go. Are your hands really going to be all right?"

"I think so," he said, but he was not at all sure.

Kate put her arms around him briefly. "Don't let him win this thing," she said. "If you get to your truck and you think it's best, just drive on out and try to get help. We'll be all right."

"You and Myke didn't work it that way when we were tied up in the shack. If I make it to my truck, you'll be hearing from me. You can count on that."

Myke stuck a sandwich and two chocolate bars in the pocket of his parka.

"You're not giving me everything, are you?" he said.

"No," she told him. "We've got some stuff left. Anyway, we're just going to be sitting around up here."

He smiled.

"I guess we'll see you for supper," she croaked.

"I wouldn't miss it."

"Kiss him goodbye," Kate said, as if she had guessed that was something Myke might like to do. The chunky girl tottered up to Whittaker, closed her eyes and pecked him on the cheek. "I never kissed an older man before," she admitted.

"Try it," he said. "You'll like it."

She laughed, but not for long, and began to look worried about him and ducked finally back into the cave.

"Did you say goodbye to Pam?" Kate asked.

"Yes," he said.

"Did she tell you about her and Ruben?"

"Yes," he said, and now it was hard for him to talk.

"She wanted you to know," Kate said. "She told me when I was carrying her yesterday. She thought it might make us feel better about what happened to her in that shack."

He shook his head. "She's a great kid," he said. "They're both great kids. . . ."

"Goodbye," she said. "Be careful, all right?" She kissed him lightly on the cheek, then stood by the wall as he leaned back to test the rappel. When he was satisfied that it ran properly, he backed to the edge, moving very slowly across the iced-up surface of the Ramp, paused for a moment, and then leaned back against the rope, out over the edge. Myke came out of the cave and waved solemnly to him as he started to go down. She was dragging his Kelty pack behind her.

At first things went better than he had supposed they would. His hands hurt, but by concentrating on the rappel he found he was able to keep this pain at a distance. He let the rope run slowly through his left hand which he held by his left hip, and steadied himself with his right hand which he held at about the level of his eyes. He leaned well back with the soles of his boots against the wall, knees slightly flexed, and moved down awkwardly, one foot at a time, bumping and swaying.

The melting had not yet started on the cliffs, at least he could not hear it. The breeze caught once in a crevice he passed, sounding as it might have sounded against a high, taut wire; it sounded that way too when it blew against the rope. He had started with his parka hood up, but the breeze had blown it back and was cold on his neck. For what seemed a long time he kept moving down, until at last he glanced up and saw he had descended only about twenty feet; the ground was still eighty feet below him. He decided to rest at this point, but as soon as he paused he felt his forearms begin to cramp and he began descending again, this time a little faster, and the faster he went the more severe the pain in his hands became until he jammed to a stop suddenly at a distance of sixty feet above the ground, crying out.

He gripped the rope as tightly as he could with each hand, swaying back and forth, his forearms knotted in spasms of pain. The wall had become a dark gray blur in front of him, the breeze loud in his ears. The land of level rock and snow was an impossible gray-white distance below his left hip where he glimpsed it, his vision crossed by the wind-whipped slack of rope.

Christ, he thought, *I'm going to come off.*

He wanted to let go more than he had ever wanted anything in his life, his teeth punching suddenly through his swollen tongue, his mouth starting to fill with warm salt blood which he gulped and gagged on and spit out, choking, his grip failing now, his high right hand already loose, his low left hand loosening in spite of all he did to force it tight, moving down again much too fast, crying out, then screaming out, wisps of smoke rising from all the places where the rope crossed him, the acrid smell of burning synthetics sharp in his nostrils, the gloves tugging away from him until the rope was searing across the exposed flesh of his right hand and then his left, across the flesh of his shoulder where it had melted and burned through his parka and sweater and shirt, his boots scraping and sliding down the rough stone wall, the wall hurtling by, his eyes pressed shut, his cry an unreality in the rush of wind that filled his ears, finally snatching his hands away from the melting-hot rope, falling free for less than two seconds to be knocked windless and stunned blind by a blow that slammed against his back, twisting onto his stomach, shoving on up to his hands and knees, trying to stand but falling back, the right side of his face pressed in the snow, his left eye gazing up at the place where the long rope moved slowly in the breeze against the wall and Myke and Kate peered down at him . . .

Alive.

18

His hands were bleeding. When he could, he got up and found his gloves, pulling them on, so relieved to have finished the rappel he did not mind the pain which came to him as if from a distance of miles. Kate had already hauled up the rope. He could see her at the edge a hundred feet above where he stood, tying on his pack, then lowering it and his ice ax down.

Myke had filled the pack with brush from the two caves. It also held his scope, which he fastened to his belt by means of a leather thong, and the brass fuel tank from the stove, which he stuck into one of the cargo pockets of his combat pants. He untied the loose knots which secured the pack and the ice ax to the rope, tied the seat sling and carabiner on, waved to Kate, and she took up the rope again.

Then, hooking his arm under the straps of the Kelty pack and using his ice ax for balance, he made his way along the base of the cliff, following the tracks Karpus had left, stepping into the tracks themselves, trying to hurry, trying to keep watch in many directions at once.

Karpus had followed the cliff for less than a quarter-mile and then had gone a quarter-mile down pitched snow to the place where the timber began. He was in the timber now where he would descend another half-mile; then he would begin to climb up through timber toward the high pass. When he came out onto the snow again, he would first be visible from the Ramp on Peak 18, and then, moments later, from the place where his tracks had moved away from the cliff below the Ramp and had gone down the quarter-mile of pitched snow toward the trees.

Whittaker stopped now beside the cliff just above the pitched snow. He was breathing heavily in spite of the fact that he had not come very far and had the benefit of the trail Karpus had broken. From here there was no sign as yet of the man with the rifle on the snow of the pass, but the pilot guessed it would not be long before Kate and Myke would see him. When he looked back and up in the direction of the Ramp, he could not see either girl although he knew at least one of them and perhaps both of them were lying on the ledge in front of the caves, waiting for Karpus to come into view.

Give me a little time, he thought, conscious of the beating of his heart.

He leaned the pack against the cliff, opened the brass fuel tank and placed it carefully on top of the pack in such a way that it would not spill. Then he pulled off his right-hand glove and got his matches out of his parka pocket. He tried lighting several of the matches and found the best way he could manage it was by putting the match between the thumb and second joint of his index finger and then moving it slowly across the striker until the match burst into flame. When the time came to move, he knew he was going to have to move quickly, for once Karpus had gained sufficient elevation in the pass he would almost certainly make some reconnaissance of the basin, and one of the first places he would look would be in this sector.

For what seemed a long while, as the breeze sounded along the cliff and the sun rose higher above the basin, he stood waiting by his pack, eyes riveted now on the Ramp where Kate or Myke would signal him the moment they spotted Karpus coming out onto the snow above the distant trees. He wondered still if his plan was reasonable, for he thought it was not too late to give it up. He knew it was risky and depended on many things. Most of all it depended on his own absolute certainty that Karpus would not leave this place until he was persuaded all four of them were dead, would not assume they had been buried under an avalanche of snow, or had fallen somewhere high on the mountain, or tried some improbable exit from the basin by descending the precipitous north face of Wolf Mountain and going on deeper into the range. The man with the rifle might consider any or all of these things as possibilities, probably had, but he would not assume them.

It was much more likely he would assume that what he had heard during the time of the avalanching snow yesterday was indeed the voices of the four people he sought to kill. He would assume they had heard his answering shots, that they had managed to elude him somehow, were still in the basin, somewhere in its western sector. He would go up onto the pass, would see Whittaker's green truck parked beside his own. Then he would wait, for he was, Whittaker thought, a man of patience and tenacity.

Kate came into view just then on the Ramp, a familiar blue-clad figure already a long way away. She kept one hand on the rappel rope where it came down in front of the caves, and waved to him with the other. He returned her wave, and as soon as he did, she disappeared again from his view.

He tipped the brass tank so that the gasoline would spill down over the dry brush Myke had stuffed into his pack; then he stepped back from it and struck a match, tossing it toward the red pack, missing with the first match but hitting the pack with the second, hearing the *whump* of the explosion, seeing the flame flash up, feeling a trace of its heat against his bearded, blistered face. He pulled on his glove, picked up his ice ax, began to move.

He plunged several yards down the crusty snow, departing from Karpus's tracks in such a way that his own tracks ran on a diagonal away from the cliff and toward the basin floor. When he thought he had gone far enough, he threw himself sideways onto the crusty surface of the snow, his ice ax held as tightly as he could hold it in both gloved hands, one hand just below the head of the ax, the other just above the butt, not using the pick of the ax to brake his descent at first, not wanting to leave any sign if he could help it, picking up speed down the quarter-mile of pitched snow until he was moving incredibly fast, flashing toward the first of the trees, spinning, twisting, driving the pick of the ax in now, trying to brake himself, trying to rudder himself away from the trees and onto the avalanche track, sweeping past the randomly spaced and exploded trunks of what had been stately conifers the day before, driving the pick in deeply now, rolling up onto the ax, driving his boots into the crust of the snow, feeling the green-branch rubble slash along his face and chest and legs, seeing a dazzling bright rooster tail of granular spray rise beyond the pick of the ax, then fall as he slowed down and finally came to a stop near the end of the track, well into the trees that bordered it on either side.

His tension, which had risen with the speed of his descent, now began to drain away. He felt weak. For several moments, although he knew it was essential not to lose even this much time, he lay belly down on the snow with the ax under him, trying to quiet the beating of his heart and the harsh, labored measure of his breath.

When he could, he stood up and unhooked the small scope from his belt. It had been bent slightly during his glissade, and water had condensed along its lens, but he was able to make it operational again, and when it was he adjusted it to infinity and trained it on the east face of Peak 18 in what he knew was the area of the Ramp. From this position he could not see the caves themselves, but he could see the wall above the caves and was satisfied that Kate had had time to remove the rope from the descending ring, had taken it with her into the cave. At the base of the cliff a quarter-mile from the place where the Ramp ended, he could see the column of smoke that rose conspicuously for many feet before it began to haze off in the breeze. The only way Karpus could miss it on his climb up into the pass would be if he did not turn around to look in this direction. That, Whittaker knew, was not likely.

The risk he had taken did not lie, really, in whether or not the man with the rifle would see the smoke. It lay in what he would decide to do once he had seen it.

19

Kate sat, shaking with cold, just inside the larger of the two caves, knees drawn up, back resting against the rocky wall behind her. From here she could watch, without fear of being seen, the dark, toylike figure of the man called Karpus who stood motionless over a mile away, several hundred feet beyond the last of the trees, on the great white slope of snow that led to the high pass. Ice had begun to melt from the upper face of Peak 18. Water dripped onto the ledge in front of the cave: *plop, plink, plop, plink.* She thought the sound might drive her mad.

"What's he doing?" Pam asked. She lay on her back in the sleeping bag. Myke sat shivering in one corner of the cave, her eyes red from having cried for a while after Whittaker left, the corners of her mouth turned down, her expression now half sullen, half sad.

"Standing still," Kate replied.

"Is he looking this way?"

"I can't tell. I think so."

"Is there still some smoke?"

"Yes. Myke must have done a good job stuffing that pack."

Myke did not comment.

"Can you see Mr. Whittaker?" Pam asked.

"You don't have to call him Mr. Whittaker," Myke complained. "You can call him Matt. I mean he's got a first name, right?"

"That's enough, Myke," Kate warned.

"Well I don't see why you both can't just call him Matt like I do and—"

"No, I *don't* see him," Kate interrupted, pressing her nails into the heel of her hand. Since Whittaker left, Myke had been getting to her.

"It's not that I don't like him," Pam explained. "I always call older people 'Mr.' or 'Mrs.' or something dumb like that."

"Oh, sure," Myke said.

"Well I do."

"Dammit," Kate snapped, *"I don't want to hear another word about that, do you understand?"*

Myke looked away. Pam said she was sorry. Hands trembling, Kate lit the last cigarette from what had been Neil Markham's pack. The smoke tasted stale in her mouth. She thought she should have given the cigarette to Whittaker before he left, but in their haste she had forgotten to. She knew he had almost come off his rappel, and the image of him in the agony of the final forty feet was clear in her mind, as clear as the image of Neil suddenly falling back, falling back and down, landing in the sickening way he had, bent over an outcropping of rock not a dozen feet from where she and Dianne had stood talking, the towering echo of the single shot ringing in their ears.

I should have been the one to go, she thought. *I shouldn't have listened to him. He told me his hands were all right, but they weren't all right and now they're worse. I might have had some kind of chance with that man that he won't have because he's a man too.*

"If we decide to leave here," she said, exhaling smoke, keeping her eyes fixed on the distant field of snow where the toylike figure still had not moved, trying to keep things together, keep herself together, "Myke and I will lower you; then we'll rope down, Myke first, then me."

"Do you think you *can* lower me?" Pam asked.

"I think the two of us can, yes. You'll have to untie once you're down. We can do it."

"I'm sorry," Myke said. She was rubbing her eyes with her fists.

"I am too," Kate replied, hunching her shoulders against the cold, wishing the sun were warmer than it was. "All of us are uptight. I want him to make it too, as much as you do. So does Pam."

"I know."

"You liked him as soon as you saw him, didn't you, Myke?"

"Yes."

Kate nodded. She tossed what was left of the cigarette into the sheet-thin pool of water that had collected in front of the cave. Karpus, over a mile away, still had not moved. The thread of smoke still rose above the smoldering pack.

I wonder why Myke only saw one side of him, she thought, *and I only saw the other?*

He would not have been a gentle lover, she decided, although he might have begun that way. Paul had been gentle enough, but perfunctory. He had kept track of her orgasms until she had finally been unable to reach them.

Don't let him kill you, Whittaker, she thought. *Don't let any more of us be killed.*

As if to answer her, the water dripped incessantly, *plop, plink, plop, plink, plop, plink,* on the ledge in front of the cave. It was a horrible sound and for a few seconds she closed her eyes. When she opened them again, the toylike figure had gone from the distant high slope of snow.

20

As Whittaker had conceived it, the ploy of the burning pack depended primarily on one thing: Karpus's assumption that, whatever the unarmed climbers were up to, it would do them no good; that he with his guns was going to prevail. By now he would almost certainly be tired, impatient, eager to finish them off. He would know that whoever had started the fire could not be far from the fire itself. There would be fresh tracks in the snow. Unless Whittaker had misjudged him badly, he was certain the man would not be able to resist investigating the smoke.

For fifteen minutes the pilot moved down through the timber, moving as quietly as he could, using what exposed surfaces of rock he could find, avoiding the crusty patches of snow which, since he had left the avalanche track, had become scattered and quite shallow. As he descended, the trees around him became more substantial, rising well above his head, their gnarled roots twisted into the pitched ground of slab rock and wet sandy soil from which they sustained themselves. He could hear the breeze sough in their branches, feel the warm sun along the left side of his neck whenever its beams slanted down between the trees, could smell the brisk resin smell of this place. Now and then a bird would chitter away from him, startled by his approach, and he would stop dead and listen and wonder if Karpus, who should be coming this way now, had heard the chittering sound of the bird, had guessed the cause of its alarm.

He tried to watch everything at once. The uneven and still downsloping ground at his feet. The area ahead of him and on either side. The trees he had to get through before the ground would begin to rise finally toward the high pass. How long would it take Karpus to descend from that slope of snow? What route would he take? What route had he taken when he passed this way earlier? Whittaker shook his head, rubbed his face with the back of his sleeve. Whatever the answers to these and the other questions that worried him, he knew he would have to conceal himself soon.

Ten minutes later he found the first sign: a clear line of rib-soled tracks that crossed the wet floor of a narrow wash between the downslope from Peak 18 and the upslope that rose toward the pass. The tracks led out of the gully, following the thread of a game trail that wound its way up into the trees on the opposing slope, and were quickly lost from sight. Whittaker's sense of time running out now became oppressive. So this was the way Karpus had gone. Would he return the same way? The pilot thought the odds were at least even that he would, and not wanting to take any chance of leaving signs of his own which the man might see, he began to follow the gully down toward the basin floor, not walking in the gully itself but keeping just inside the trees that lined it.

He had not gone far when he heard the sudden high-pitched cawing of a crow rising from the timber on the opposing slope. He dropped to his belly and lay flat, feeling the trip of his heart against the earth. The crow flew directly overhead; he saw the quick passing of its shadow across the damp gully floor, heard the shriek of its cawing rise in pitch above him and then fade away in the direction of the sun where it was answered by other more distant crows. Then all the other birdsong and chitter in the woods suddenly ceased, and Whittaker knew that Karpus was coming toward him.

The pilot had not taken his parka off. It was bright orange and conspicuous against the earth. He thought he should try and struggle out of it, get it under him where it would not show, but he was afraid to move, even to breathe; he lay belly-down just inside the last of the trees, looking up toward the place where Karpus would cross the gully if he crossed in the place that he had before. That place was not sixty yards distant from where he now lay; he could see clearly the slight gap in the trees on the opposing slope where the game trail opened out onto the gully.

When Karpus appeared it was as if he had always stood in that place. He was tall and lean in his faded green pants and blue and black checked mackinaw. He did not carry a pack. Below the mackinaw, Whittaker could see part of the holster he wore at the right side of his belt and could see the rifle he held in the crook of his right arm. The man looked across the gully for several moments, then up the gully and then down the gully toward the place where Whittaker lay flat just inside the trees. The sound of the crows was remote now, just audible over the sound of the breeze which passed through the needled branches of the firs around him, creating a gentle, peaceful hum that rose and fell within a narrow range. He closed his eyes. Karpus appeared to be looking directly at him; it seemed impossible he had not been discovered. Without thought or hope it might not come, he waited for the final explosive sound of the gun.

It was not until he caught a whiff of sulphur on the air that he dared to look again. The man stood in the same place and in the same attitude except that he had lit a cigarette which he held between his lips, dragging deeply from it, then exhaling the smoke where the breeze picked it up and wafted it down the gully toward the place where Whittaker lay. He thought Karpus sensed that somebody was there, that something was wrong, that something had changed since he had passed this way not an hour ago. The man seemed to be listening, to be probing with his eyes and ears, not in a way that suggested he was apprehensive but more that he was curious, that he was perhaps wondering if somehow they had managed to outflank him, or had tried to do that, or were trying it now.

Whittaker's hands throbbed with pain, his muscles ached where rocks and roots pressed against him. Karpus looked the same as he had in the prospector's shack, not tired at all, his movements efficient and quick.

When he finished the cigarette, he flipped it away, then stepped into the gully after it and turned, raising the rifle, aiming it down the gully. Whittaker winced reflexively, but the man did not shoot, or indicate in any way that he had in fact seen the pilot where he lay inside the line of trees. He kept the rifle at his shoulder and appeared to be looking through its scope in the direction of the basin floor, perhaps trying to locate his friend. Finally, he settled the rifle once more into the crook of his right arm, crossed the gully and moved up into the trees that led toward the Ramp caves on Peak 18.

"Christ," Whittaker breathed.

He waited ten minutes. Then he crossed the gully, heading up toward the pass. He knew it was a long way from being over, but for the first time since early that morning, Karpus did not occupy ground between him and the revolver he had left in the glove box of his truck. By the time the man reached the remains of the burning pack, Whittaker would be on his way up the last thousand feet of snow. Even if he was spotted there, he would be able to reach the top of the pass, glissade down its far slope and get to his truck long before Karpus could hope to catch up.

This had been his plan, as far as he had taken it, and so far it had worked.

21

Moving through the timber, halfway now between the gully and the smoke, Karpus stopped abruptly as if he had heard something behind him although he had not.

He watched, listened, squatted finally to break a crust of rotten snow from a small shadowed drift that lay across his path. He pressed the snow against his face, closed his eyes, sighed. He was tired. For a long time he had ignored the fatigue, but it was persistent, like being shackled on a long march and trying to ignore the weight of the chains.

Early that morning, when he had first seen the smoke rising in the distance on his backtrail, he had felt for the first time since he had been a child the rising within him of a sense of rage. Quiescent for years, it had welled up briefly, catching him off guard, causing him to clench his fists, to spit contemptuously between his feet.

The pilot had killed Johns, of that Karpus was now certain. Not the fat girl whom he had seen freeing her hands—he had erased her from his mind as neatly as he had erased his family long ago. This pilot. This Air-Force major who had made one mistake after another: had gotten himself caught like a fish outside the shack; had tried to take the others up that cliff; had left tracks yesterday; had let his females yowl like cats after the avalanche . . . who now was sending up this smoke for some reason of his own, probably to try and let the women make a run for the creek trail, because that was the kind he was. And because he was that kind, he had killed Johns, did not even know that he had.

These thoughts had come to Karpus in fragmented sentences and in images that were confusing, vivid and incomplete; and these too had provoked his rage. Again it welled up, and again he choked it down, for in some inarticulate way it threatened him more than anything he had experienced since he had learned to live his life without feeling.

The smoke had threaded into the morning sky, slanted off on the westerly breeze.

"You cocksucker," he had said finally.

Then he had started down from the snow, going back into the trees, back across the gully, back the way he had come.

As yet he had formed no plan. His instincts told him the pilot had created the smoke and would be somewhere near the place where it rose. Would he try an ambush? Unarmed, that would be a stupid thing to do—but then the pilot was not very smart. Karpus chewed up and swallowed what was left of his crust of snow, ignoring its sandy texture and taste. When he lit a cigarette, he inhaled slowly, taking the smoke deep into his lungs.

The last cigarette he had had was at the gully. He had almost decided to stay there, to find the right kind of cover and wait. The gully had given him a good view of the basin; he had been able to see the creek trail in sharp detail through the oval lens of the Weatherby's scope. Sooner or later the climbers would have to try for that trail, or for the pass, if they knew about the pass. Maybe the pilot would split them up and try for both.

Karpus finished his cigarette, crushed the coal between his finger and thumb. For a moment he stood expressionless, his mind empty of thought. Then he turned and went back to the gully, where, when he reached it, he saw the pilot's tracks.

22

When Whittaker moved up onto the field of snow that rose toward the pass, following the tracks Karpus had left earlier that morning, he saw no sign of the man on the opposing high slope of snow, although by now he knew Karpus should have been visible making his way up toward the remains of the burning pack.

He continued to climb slowly, using his ax for balance, moving one foot in front of the other, kicking his boot toes into the firm snow, feeling the breeze against him which was cooler at this elevation, its thrust no longer reduced by trees. When Karpus's tracks ended, halfway up the slope, he turned again and this time took out the small scope, peering through it, moving it slowly along the line formed by the bottom of the gray granite face of Peak 18 and the top of the falling slope of snow. Still no sign.

He began to feel uneasy again and sat for a moment, using the scope, sweeping all of the snow now along the route of his glissade and then along the line of tracks Karpus had left earlier that day when he had come along the cliff below the caves, had smoked his cigarette and then continued on down into the trees. Nothing. The breeze was in the west, coming down over the pass, but the sun was quite high over the basin now and he could see patches of green showing in the meadow below where the recent snow was already melting away, could see where the light of the sun glinted on the running surfaces of the stream.

He sat, raising the hood of his orange parka. He had counted on the fact that by the time he reached this exposed place he would be well beyond the range of Karpus's rifle. Now he was not sure. There had been something about the man when he paused at the gully that seemed to say he sensed something was wrong, that he had not been entirely fooled by the diversion of the burning pack. And yet, the pilot was certain the man had not seen him, even when he had turned to look through the scope of his rifle, down the gully toward the basin floor.

He had reached a decision to get to his feet again when he saw a glint of light flash from the area of the gully itself, and before he could rise he heard the whip-like rush of a bullet as it passed to his right and almost simultaneously the explosive crack of the rifle; and before the brief echoes of the first shot had died away he heard the whip of a second bullet and the second explosive crack of the gun. He tried to twist away from where he had been sitting, thinking at first to go down toward the shelter of the trees. But then, realizing the uselessness of that, he got to his feet, and dodging and weaving as best he could, he went on up the slope, heading for the top of the pass, his numb feet responding sluggishly to the command of his will, his breath choking off in his throat, his blood pounding against his temples, his progress so clumsy and slow he knew he was finished, knew even at this considerable range Karpus could not fail to hit him before he reached the top of the pass which appeared as a bright white belly of snow in front of a dark blue expanse of sky impossibly distant from the place where he now struggled toward it, feinting to the right and left, bobbing down, twisting, kicking his boots into the compacted snow, reaching with his ax, unable finally to go any higher, dropping to his knees still 200 feet below the top of the pass, winded, blowing, accepting the inevitability of a bullet which still did not come, waiting, scooping his gloved hands along the surface of the snow, pressing the cold snow against his face, trying to clear his vision which had become crossed with dizzying flecks of light, hearing the whip of a bullet again, this time to his left, wincing reflexively, hearing another whip to his right, realizing finally that Karpus was not trying to hit him but was rather deliberately missing him, tormenting him, waiting for him to reach the last hundred feet, the last fifty feet perhaps, before he would zero in and put a single high-grain bullet between his shoulder blades as he had done to the lead twin and the man called Neil.

And yet, when he could, in spite of what he took to be the inevitability of his death, he got up and began to move again toward the top of the pass, no longer trying to move deceptively, but simply putting one foot in front of the other, using the ax as a cane, thinking he would wait until just below the top of the pass, when, if he could manage it, he would try to weave and twist again and maybe receive the miracle of avoiding the final bullet from Karpus's gun. But when he did finally reach the terrain just below the white belly of the pass, he found he was not only unable to move deceptively but unable to move at all, and he stood winded, his head bowed, the cool slice of the breeze against him.

"I'm not going to make it, Kate," he said. And wished he could have seen his children again.

Then he turned and saw Karpus just emerging from the last of the trees, his rifle in one hand at his side, his faded green pants and blue and black checked mackinaw rising in sharp relief against the bright snow a thousand gradual feet below the place where Whittaker stood. For a moment the two men looked at each other. Then Whittaker turned and went across the belly of the pass, and when the snow began to slope down again toward the distant small clearing where even now he could see the sunlight glint from the windshield of his truck, he began to run as best he could, and when he had developed what he thought was enough momentum, he threw himself onto his side again and did a long and scarcely braked glissade down more than half a mile of gradual snow that ran out finally just above the clearing where, his heart hammering against him, he tried to get to his feet, fell, knew he was blacking out, and did.

When he came to—how much later he could not have said—Karpus had not yet reached the top of the pass. But Whittaker knew he would have to reach it soon, and he got unsteadily to his feet and half walked, half stumbled across the clearing, his boots sucking out of the wet earth until at last he reached his truck. Then he turned, tearing his right-hand glove away with his teeth, reaching for his keys, trying with numb fingers to remove them from the cargo pocket of his pants, watching until he saw Karpus appear at the top of the pass, a tall figure reduced by distance, a small but inexorable silhouette against a blue clarity of sky.

Birds were twittering in the brush and trees around the clearing. The keys stubbornly evaded his grip. He tried to rip the pocket away, succeeded in doing that at last, and the keys fell to the muddy ground at his feet where he had to bend in order to pick them up. When he glanced behind him now he saw that Karpus had begun his own glissade, using the butt of his rifle in place of the ax, moving down the pitched snow at what seemed an incredible rate of speed.

He fumbled the key into the lock of the door at the passenger side of the cab, jerked open the door and pulled himself into the cab, locking the door behind him. He was panicked, all but unable to think. He got the glove box open, got the Webley out of its holster and brought it with him as he slid along the seat to a position behind the wheel. When he tried to put the key into the ignition lock, his hands shook so badly he had to stop and close his eyes and breathe deeply and deliberately before he could try again. This time he got the key into the lock and managed to turn it to its start position, the starter motor responding instantly with a high-pitched stuttering sound. He pumped the gas peddle twice; the engine sprang to life.

He was forcing the gearshift into low when he heard the flat crack of the rifle, felt a thump, saw the right front hood drop several inches. He tried to pull away, but in his panic he popped the clutch and the engine stalled. Again he heard the sound of the gun, felt the rear of the truck settle this time and knew Karpus had hit that tire as well. When he bent down to look across the clearing and up toward the pass, he saw the man had already reached the last of the snow and was rising from what had been a kneeling position, the rifle in his right hand.

Frantically, Whittaker turned the key in the ignition again, and, as he did, the truck lurched forward and he realized too late he had forgotten to take it out of gear. Karpus was at the far edge of the clearing now, advancing in a normal stride, as if he thought there was no longer reason to hurry, as if he knew he had finally won.

Whittaker took the revolver in both hands, keeping it close to the seat, pulling the hammer back with the insensate thumb of his numb right hand, having to look before he could be sure the hammer was all the way back and his index finger was inside the trigger guard, pointing the muzzle of the gun then as accurately as he could, up toward the center of the window toward which the man with the rifle was coming.

He had expected Karpus to smile when he finally approached the window, but the man did not smile. His expression was livid with an anger that had apparently risen beyond his ability to contain it. As he came up to the truck he reached out with his left hand and yanked brutally at the handle of the locked door. Whittaker felt the cab begin to rock. Karpus was shouting something to him; he could hear the man's cries inarticulate behind the glass. In what was no more than a fraction of a second after the man was at last framed by the window, the pilot held his breath and squeezed off his shot. The sound of it was deafening in the enclosed cab. He felt the gun buck against his hands, caught the acrid smell of powder, saw the passenger window fracture into opacity around a jagged hole through which he could see the man backing away in a half-tilting, drunken way, his hands clutched at a point on his chest that was just below his throat.

He cocked the revolver again and took it with him when he got awkwardly out of the truck, getting out on the driver's side in order to keep the truck between himself and the man he had shot. When he saw that Karpus was on his hands and knees, facing him, in the mud just beyond the right front fender of the truck, he steadied the revolver on the hood, holding it in both hands at arm's length and keeping his feet spread for balance. The gun wavered at first, but then steadied down finally and was still, Karpus's head lined up perfectly in the sights.

The pilot was engorged with his own blood; his heart beat rapidly and painfully. His mind was empty of all thought except that he would have to remember to hold his breath and squeeze the trigger slowly if he decided to shoot again.

Karpus remained on his hands and knees in the mud a few feet beyond the fender of the truck. His rifle was lying in the mud near him, but not so near he could reach it. His breath was coming in short, bubbly gasps; when he coughed he brought up blood. Whittaker watched without compassion, thinking only of the necessity of holding his breath and squeezing the trigger slowly if he decided to shoot again.

"*You killed Johns,*" Karpus finally said.

Whittaker did not reply. When the man pulled his right hand slowly from the mud as if to reach for the automatic he carried in a holster at his right side, Whittaker shot him again, and then once more, first through the head and then through the chest. Then Karpus lay on his back in the mud, his eyes fixed on the blue sky above the clearing, small fountains of blood diminishing where they had first sprung in the places where the bullets had gone in.

Whittaker walked around the truck to look at the man he had killed. First he stood over him, raising his right boot and pushing the man's jaw slowly to one side. Then he squatted down and, awkwardly with his damaged hands, he went through the man's pockets, removing his keys and a half-empty package of cigarettes and his own wallet which, though it had been rifled, still contained some cash and his military I.D.

He took the man's weapons and threw them well into the brush at the close edge of the clearing. Then he took a canvas tarp he kept behind the seat of his truck and, after he had looked once more at Karpus's body, covered it with the tarp, rolling stones onto each corner to keep the wind from taking it.

Then he replaced the spent shells in the Webley, stuck the revolver into his belt, smoked a cigarette, and when he felt up to it, which was not for a while, he picked up his ice ax and went across the clearing and up onto the snow.

23

It was early afternoon when he finally reached the top of the pass and signaled to the others by firing the Webley in a prearranged series of shots that he was all right, that it was over; and it was late afternoon when they joined him at last, toiling up the thousand feet of snow below the place where he waited for them, too tired to help, too moved by the sight of them to call out.

Myke was the first to reach him. She came up pumping her legs and swinging her fists as if to flatten the distance between them. Kate was well behind her, carrying Pam on her back.

When the chunky girl collapsed beside him, he put his arm around her. "How you doing, old buddy?" he said.

"I'm okay," she said. "I did the rappel."

"I know. I watched you through the scope."

"We lowered Pam. . . ."

"Was the Ramp still iced up?"

"In places it was. Kate said we maybe could have gone down that way, but it would take forever and we all just wanted to get it over with."

"It didn't worry you any, did it?"

"Are you kidding?" she croaked. "I thought I was going to pee again. I mean, we didn't have a belay or anything."

"How's Pam?"

"She says she's all right. I don't know. I think she just wants to get out of here."

He smiled. He could see Kate coming up, taking a step, resting, then taking another step. Her blue-clad figure was bent well forward against the pitch of the slope and the weight of the girl. Pam's arms were around her. Her splinted leg stuck out like a fence rail. Behind them the trees fell away in a blue-green wedge to the basin floor. Across the basin the eastern chain of summits were snow-capped and brilliant under the late sun.

"We took turns carrying Pam," Myke explained. "But then I got pooped. Did you . . ." She paused for a moment, wrinkling her nose, as if she was not quite sure how to put this thing she was about to ask. "Did you—like—kill him?" she said.

"Yes."

"I guess you had to," she said, looking away.

"He wasn't much fooled by that fire we set."

"I know. We saw him when you were up here and he was coming after you. How come he didn't . . . I mean, couldn't he have just shot you then?"

"I think he wanted to talk to me first."

"Boy." She sighed. "He was really a freak, wasn't he?" And after another moment of silence she said, "Do you think we'll get to that town tonight? With the beer and all that?"

"I don't know," he said. "I bet we give it one hell of a try."

Then Kate and Pam came up and they all hugged each other a little awkwardly and Pam cried for a few minutes, saying she was sorry but she couldn't help it, and he told them just what had happened and how Karpus had said his friend Johns was dead too.

Their descent to the clearing was clumsy and took a long time, and at one point, with Myke out ahead carrying Pam, Kate took Whittaker's hand lightly and looked at him and said, "I lost the faith for a little while."

"So did I," he said.

"You should have seen Myke carry on after you left. I'm afraid she's got a terrible crush on you."

He smiled.

"I'm not much looking forward to going home," she said.

"I'll go along if it will help," he offered.

"Thanks, but I'll have to face up to it. Pam and Myke can help. We'll see you again though, won't we? We'll keep in touch?"

"Sure," he said, but he sensed already they probably would not, and he thought she was quite beautiful and he wished he were not as old as he was, or as shot-up.

"Will there be police in Morgan?" she asked.

"We can get in touch with them there."

"How do you tell anyone what it was like to go through a thing like this?"

"I don't know," he said. "I never had any luck trying to explain what it was like being in the war."

She looked at him and then away.

"Did you feel anything when you killed him?"

"Relief."

She nodded.

"He had some cigarettes in his pocket," Whittaker said. "Do you want one?" At first he thought she was going to refuse, but then she said, "Yes, please," and he gave her the pack and she lit up for them, placing his cigarette at the corner of his mouth where she had observed he liked to keep it.

"Pam's going to be glad to get out of that damn rucksack," she said, exhaling smoke, looking down the long and now shadowy slant of snow where the two girls were already far ahead of them.

"She's a nice kid," Whittaker said. "She'll get over what happened here."

24

They used Karpus's truck to go out. They put Pam on the rear seat of the crew cab, lying down, and she fell asleep. Myke drove. Whittaker sat next to the passenger window. Kate sat between them. After a while, she went to sleep too. It was a clear, cold, moonlit night. The sky when it showed through the canopy of trees above the narrow road was filled with bright twinkling stars. At first the road was difficult to negotiate, but it improved as the hours passed and a ground frost developed, firming up the potholes and bogs enough for the truck to roll through them on the long downhill run. There were more cigarettes in the glove box and Whittaker would keep one lit most of the time, holding it idly. When he saw they had reached the place where older tracks swerved unnaturally to one side of the road, he asked Myke to stop, and the two of them got out. With the engine idling and the parking lights on, they stood for a moment together, leaning against the gently vibrating cab of the truck.

"This is where it began for me," he said, explaining what had happened. "It seems a long time ago now, but it wasn't. Three days, I guess."

"Wow," Myke said. "It seems like a year to me."

He stretched, yawned, felt the tension begin to go out of him as it always had after each mission he had flown. The combat had become part of him finally, some-

time toward the end of his first tour, had become the
central fact of his life, more important in a way than his
family; and even before he had left it he had known he
would have to come back to it if the Air Force let him.
Marie had been right about that, and about the war,
though it was too late to change any of these things. *I
don't think I can change what I am either,* he thought. And
he was not even sure he should want to change, unless
the nature of life changed first.

"There's a tape deck in the truck," Myke said. "You
think it would be okay if I used it so long as I kept it
down?"

"Sure," he said. "I don't think you're going to wake
those two characters up. What have you got?"

"Johnny Cash," she said brightly.

"You like him, do you?"

"Yeah," she admitted. "I get silly whenever I hear
him."

He smiled, reached out and tousled her hair.

"Well, do it then," he said.

They stood silent for a moment, enveloped by the
sounds of the night; the singing of frogs and hooting of
owls, the soughing of the wind in the close branches of
the trees. Then she opened the door for him and he got
in, and she went around and got behind the wheel. There
was a pack of gum on the dash and she offered him a stick
which he refused, and so she took two sticks for herself.
She switched on the tape and heard Cash open with
"Wanted Man," a song that had never failed to knock her
out, and she put the truck in gear in a businesslike way
and began to follow the flare of its lights down the long
tunnel of road. Pam was asleep, stretched out on the seat
behind her, and Kate was asleep beside her, and soon
she realized that the pilot had fallen asleep too, his

gaunt, angular face pillowed by his parka hood against the passenger window, just visible in the soft glow that came up from the bank of lights on the dash.

God, he's a hunk, she thought, chewing her gum.

It was a very beautiful thing—being alive. She had never seriously considered it before. All you really needed were a few good friends and some good wheels and almost any kind of road and some gum and Johnny Cash and something at the end of the road like a steak and a Coke or a bottle of beer.

"Don't hassle me," she said when a startled coyote jumped out of the road. "This bunch is going to be in that café in time for breakfast."

They reached Morgan at dawn.

Glossary of Climbing Terms

BELAY: To pay out or take in a climber's rope from a fixed position and to secure the rope in the event the climber falls.

BIVOUAC: An unexpected, hence temporary and usually primitive, encampment.

CARABINER: A snap link used to connect a climbing rope to a piton.

CHOCK: A metal nut or wedge mounted on a short length of looped cable—functions the same as a piton but does less damage to rock surface, hence is increasingly popular with climbers.

DESCENDING RING: A circle of iron about two inches in diameter used to anchor rappel.

EXPOSED: Steep, high and hairy.

GLISSADE: An intentional slide down a steep slope of snow.

ICE AX: A picklike tool used for cutting footholds into snow or ice, braking the speed of a glissade, belaying on steep snow and other purposes.

LEAD: The distance the first man on a rope climbs above his second before establishing a belay.

PITON: An iron spike of varying shape and size designed for insertion into rock cracks.

RAPPEL: A method used by climbers to descend steep rock via a fixed but retrievable rope.

SEAT SLING: A short length of rope or webbing worn like a diaper to facilitate rappel.

SIERRA CLUB SCALE: An arbitrary but useful classification of rock climbs from 1 + (easiest) to 6 + (most difficult).

TALUS: A sloping pile of rock fragments at the foot of a cliff.

TRAVERSE: Lateral movement while ascending rock face.